TIMETABLE
FOR MURDER

OSTEND:
A gray wet dusk—a dancer meets a rich young man, who is grateful for the love money can buy.

COLOGNE:
Sloppy, drunk—a woman journalist jumps aboard the last car, after a scoop and the girl she adores.

SUBOTICA:
Trouble at the frontier—a radical leader crucified in a rat-filled barn. The girl sees him die. . . .

CONSTANTINOPLE:
The end of a whirling trip across Europe in the famous Stamboul Train—a tangle of surprise, drama, passion and adventure.

Books by Graham Greene

Novels

The Confidential Agent
The End of the Affair
England Made Me
    (Also published as
    The Shipwrecked)
The Honorary Consul
Our Man in Havana
This Gun for Hire (Original
    British title: A Gun for Sale)

Short Stories

Twenty-One Stories

Autobiography

A Sort of Life

Published by POCKET BOOKS

GRAHAM GREENE

Orient Express

PUBLISHED BY POCKET BOOKS NEW YORK

 POCKET BOOKS, a Simon & Schuster division of
GULF & WESTERN CORPORATION
1230 Avenue of the Americas, New York, N.Y. 10020

ISBN: 0-671-83257-3

First Pocket Books printing September, 1975

10 9 8 7 6 5 4 3 2

POCKET and colophon are trademarks of Simon & Schuster.

Printed in the U.S.A.

For Vivien with love

'Everything in nature is lyrical in its ideal essence;
tragic in its fate, and comic in its existence.'

George Santayana

Contents

PART ONE
Ostend

[1]

The purser took the last landing-card in his hand and
watched the passengers cross the grey wet quay, over
a wilderness of rails and points, round the corners of
abandoned trucks. They went with coat-collars turned
up and hunched shoulders; on the tables in the long
coaches lamps were lit and glowed through the rain like
a chain of blue beads. A giant crane swept and de-
scended, and the clatter of the winch drowned for a
moment the pervading sounds of water, water falling
from the overcast sky, water washing against the sides
of channel steamer and quay. It was half-past four in
the afternoon.

'A spring day, my God,' said the purser aloud, trying

to dismiss the impressions of the last few hours, the drenched deck, the smell of steam and oil and stale Bass from the bar, the shuffle of black silk, as the stewardess moved here and there carrying tin basins. He glanced up the steel shafts of the crane, to the platform and the small figure in blue dungarees turning a great wheel, and felt an unaccustomed envy. The driver up there was parted by thirty feet of mist and rain from purser, passengers, the long lit express. I can't get away from their damned faces, the purser thought, recalling the young Jew in the heavy fur coat who had complained because he had been allotted a two-birth cabin; for two God-forsaken hours, that's all.

He said to the last passenger from the second class: 'Not that way, miss. The customs-shed's over there.' His mood relaxed a little at the unfamiliarity of the young face; this one had not complained. 'Don't you want a porter for your bag, miss?'

'I'd rather not,' she said. 'I can't understand what they say. It's not heavy.' She wrinkled her mouth at him over the top of her cheap white mackintosh. 'Unless you'd like to carry it—Captain.' Her impudence delighted him. 'Ah, if I were a young man now you wouldn't be wanting a porter. I don't know what they are coming to.' He shook his head as the Jew left the customs-shed, picking his way across the rails in grey suède shoes, followed by two laden porters. 'Going far?'

'All the way,' she said gazing unhappily past the rails, the piles of luggage, the lit lamps in the restaurant-car, to the dark waiting coaches.

'Got a sleeper?'

'No.'

'You ought to 'ave a sleeper,' he said, 'going all the way like that. Three nights in a train. It's no joke.

What do you want to go to Constantinople for anyway? Getting married?'

'Not that I know of.' She laughed a little through the melancholy of departure and the fear of strangeness. 'One can't tell, can one?'

'Work?'

'Dancing. Variety.'

She said good-bye and turned from him. Her mackintosh showed the thinness of her body, which even while stumbling between the rails and sleepers retained its self-consciousness. A signal lamp turned from red to green, and a long whistle of steam blew through an exhaust. Her face, plain and piquant, her manner daring and depressed, lingered for a moment in his mind. 'Remember me,' he called after her. 'I'll see you again in a month or two.' But he knew that he would not remember her; too many faces would peer during the following weeks through the window of his office, wanting a cabin, wanting money changed, wanting a berth, for him to remember an individual, and there was nothing remarkable about her.

When he went on board, the decks were already being washed down for the return journey, and he felt happier to find the ship empty of strangers. This was how he would have liked it always to be: a few dagoes to boss in their own tongue, a stewardess with whom to drink a glass of ale. He grunted at the seamen in French and they grinned at him, singing an indecent song of a 'cocu' that made his plump family soul wither a little in envy. 'A bad crossing,' he said to the head steward in English. The man had been a waiter in London and the purser never spoke a word more French than was necessary. 'That Jew,' he said, 'did he give you a good tip?'

'What would you believe? Six francs.'

'Was he ill?'

'No. The old fellow with the moustaches—he was ill all the time. And I want ten francs. I win the bet. He was English.'

'Go on. You could cut his accent with a knife.'

'I see his passport. Richard John. Schoolteacher.'

'That's funny,' the purser said. And that's funny, he thought again, paying the ten francs reluctantly and seeing in his mind's eye the tired grey man in the mackintosh stride away from the ship's rail, as the gangway rose and the sirens blew out towards a rift in the clouds. He had asked for a newspaper, an evening newspaper. They wouldn't have been published in London as early as that, the purser told him, and when he heard the answer, he stood in a dream, fingering his long grey moustache. While the purser poured out a glass of Bass for the stewardess, before going through the accounts, he thought again of the schoolteacher, and wondered momentarily whether something dramatic had passed close by him, something weary and hunted and the stuff of stories. He too had made no complaint, and for that reason was more easily forgotten than the young Jew, the party of Cook's tourists, the sick woman in mauve who had lost a ring, the old man who had paid twice for his berth. The girl had been forgotten half an hour before. This was the first thing she shared with Richard John—below the tramp of feet, the smell of oil, the winking light of signals, worrying faces, clink of glasses, rows of numerals—a darkness in the purser's mind.

The wind dropped for ten seconds, and the smoke which had swept backwards and forwards across the quay and the metal acres in the quick gusts stayed for that time in the middle air. Like grey nomad tents the smoke seemed to Myatt, as he picked his way through the mud. He forgot that his suède shoes were ruined, that the customs officer had been impertinent over two pairs of silk pyjamas. From the man's rudeness and his contempt, the syllables 'Juif, Juif', he crept into the shade of those great tents. Here for a moment he was at home and required no longer the knowledge of his fur coat, of his suit from Savile Row, his money or his position in the firm to hearten him. But as he reached the train the wind rose, the tents of steam were struck, and he was again in the centre of a hostile world.

But he recognized with gratitude what money could buy. It could not always buy courtesy, but it had bought celerity. He was the first through the customs, and before the other passengers arrived, he could arrange with the guard for a sleeping compartment to himself. He had a hatred of undressing before another man, but the arrangement, he knew, would cost him more because he was a Jew; it would be no matter of a simple request and a tip. He passed the lit windows of the restaurant car, small mauve-shaded lamps shining on the linen laid ready for dinner. 'Ostend—Cologne—Vienne—Belgrade—Istanbul.' He passed the rows of names without a glance; the route was familiar to him; the names travelled back at the level of his eyes, like the spires of minarets, cupolas or domes of the cities themselves, offering no permanent settlement to one of his race.

The guard, as he had expected, was surly. The train was very full, he said, though Myatt knew he lied. April was too early in the year for crowded carriages, and he had seen few first-class passengers on the Channel steamer. While he argued, a bevy of tourists scrambled down the corridor, middle-aged ladies clutching shawls and rugs and sketch-books, an old clergyman complain-

ing that he had mislaid his *Wide World Magazine*—
'I always read a *Wide World* when I travel'—and in the
rear, perspiring, genial under difficulties, their conduc-
tor wearing the button of an agency. 'Voilà,' the guard
said and seemed to indicate with a gesture that his train
was bearing an unaccustomed, a cruel burden. But
Myatt knew the route too well to be deceived. The
party, he guessed from its appearance of harassed culture, belonged to the slip-coach for Athens. When he
doubled the tip, the guard gave way and pasted a re-
served notice on the window of the compartment. With
a sigh of relief Myatt found himself alone.

He watched the swim of faces separated by a safe
wall of glass. Even through his fur coat the damp chill
of the day struck him, and as he turned the heating-
wheel, a mist from his breath obscured the pane, so that
soon he could see of those who passed no more than
unrelated features, a peering angry eye, a dress of
mauve silk, a clerical collar. Only once was he tempted
to break this growing solitude and wipe the glass with
his fingers in time to catch sight of a thin girl in a white
mackintosh disappearing along the corridor towards the
second class. Once the door was opened and an elderly
man glanced in. He had a grey moustache and wore
glasses and a shabby soft hat. Myatt told him in French
that the compartment was taken.

'One seat,' the man said.

'Do you want the second class?' Myatt asked, but
the man shook his head and moved away.

Mr Opie sank with conscious luxury into his corner
and regarded with curiosity and disappointment the
small pale man opposite him. The man was extraordinarily commonplace in appearance; ill-health had
ruined his complexion. Nerves, Mr Opie thought,

watching the man's moving fingers, but they showed no other sign of acute sensibility. They were short, blunt and thick.

'I always think,' Mr Opie said, wondering whether he had been very unfortunate in his companion, 'that as long as one can get a sleeper, it is so unnecessary to travel first class. These second-class carriages are remarkably comfortable.'

'Yes—that's so—yes,' the other answered with alacrity. 'But 'ow did you know I was English?'

'I make a practice,' Mr Opie said with a smile, 'of always thinking the best of people.'

'Of course,' the pale man said, 'you as a clergy-man——'

The newsboys were calling outside the window, and Mr Opie leant out. *'Le Temps de Londres.* Qu'est que c'est que ça? Rien du tout? *Le Matin* et un *Daily Mail.* C'est bon. Merci.' His French seemed to the other full of copybook phrases, used with gusto and inaccurately. 'Combien est cela? Trois francs. Oh la-la.'

To the white-faced man he said: 'Can I interpret for you? Is there any paper you want? Don't mind me if you want *La Vie.'*

'No, nothing, nothing, thank you. I've a book.'

Mr Opie looked at his watch. 'Three minutes and we shall be away.'

She had been afraid for several minutes that he would speak, or else the tall thin woman his wife. Silence for the time being she desired more than anything else. If I could have afforded a sleeper, she wondered, would I have been alone? In this dim carriage the lights flickered on, and the plump man remarked, 'Now we shan't be long.' The air was full of dust and damp, and the flicker of light outside reminded her for a moment of familiar things: the electric signs flashing and changing over the theatre in Nottingham High Street. The stir of life, the passage of porters and paper-boys, recalled for a moment the goose market, and to the memory of the market she clung, tried to externalise it in her mind, to build the bricks and lay the stalls, until they had as much reality as the cold rain-washed quay, the changing signal lamps. Then the man spoke to her, and she was compelled to emerge from her hidden world and wear a pose of cheerfulness and courage.

'Well, miss, we've got a long journey together. Suppose we exchange names. Mine's Peters, and this is my wife Amy.'

'Mine's Coral Musker.'

'Get me a sandwich,' the thin woman implored. 'I'm so empty I can hear my stomach.'

'Would you, miss? I don't know the lingo.'

And why, she would have liked to cry at him, do you suppose I do? I've never been out of England. But she had so schooled herself to accept responsibility wherever and in whatever form it came, that she made no protest, opened the door and would have run down the slippery dusky road between the rails in search of what he wanted if she had not seen a clock. 'There's no time,' she said, 'only one minute before we go.' Turning back she caught sight at the corridor's end of a face and figure that made her catch her breath with longing: a last dab of powder on the nose, a good-night to the door-keeper, and outside in the bright glittering betrayal of the dark, the young waiting Jew, the chocolates, the car round the corner, the rapid ride and the furtive dangerous embrace. But it was no one she knew; she was back in the unwanted, dreaded adventure of a foreign land, which could not be checked by a skilful word; no carefully-measured caress would satisfy the approaching dark.

The train's late, Myatt thought, as he stepped into the corridor. He felt in his waistcoat pocket for the small box of currants he always carried there. It was divided into four sections and his fingers chose one at random. As he put it into his mouth, he judged it by the feel. The quality's going off. That's Stein and Co. They are getting small and dry. At the end of the corridor a girl in a white mackintosh turned and gazed at him. Nice figure, he thought. Do I know her? He chose another currant and without a glance placed it. One of our own. Myatt, Myatt and Page. For a moment with the currant upon his tongue he might have been one of the lords of the world, carrying destiny with him. This is mine and this is good, he thought. Doors slammed along the line of coaches, and a horn was blown.

Richard John, with his mackintosh turned up above his ears, leant from the corridor window and saw the sheds begin to move backwards towards the slow wash of the sea. It was the end, he thought, and the beginning. Faces streamed away. A man with a pickaxe on his shoulder swung a red lamp; the smoke from the engine blew round him, and obscured his light. The brakes ground, the clouds parted, and the setting sun flashed on the line, the window and his eyes. If I could sleep, he thought with longing, I could remember more clearly all the things that have to be remembered.

The fire-hole door opened and the blaze and the heat of the furnace for a moment emerged. The driver turned the regulator full open, and the footplate shook with the weight of the coaches. Presently the engine settled smoothly to its work, the driver brought the cut-off back, and the last of the sun came out as the train passed through Bruges, the regulator closed, coasting with little steam. The sunset lit up tall dripping walls, alleys with stagnant water radiant for a moment with liquid light. Somewhere within the dingy casing lay the ancient city, like a notorious jewel, too stared at, talked of, trafficked over. Then a wilderness of allotments opened through the steam, sometimes the monotony broken by tall ugly villas, facing every way, decorated with coloured tiles, which now absorbed the evening. The sparks from the express became visible, like hordes of scarlet beetles tempted into the air by night; they fell and smouldered by the track, touched leaves and twigs and cabbage-stalks and turned to soot. A girl riding a cart-horse lifted her face and laughed; on the bank beside the line a man and woman lay embraced. Then darkness fell outside, and passengers through the glass could see only the transparent reflection of their own features.

[2]

'Premier Service, Premier Service.' The voice went echoing down the corridor, but Myatt was already seated in the restaurant-car. He did not wish to run the danger of sharing a table, of being forced into polite openings, of being, not improbably, snubbed. Constantinople, for many of the passengers the end of an almost interminable journey, approached him with the speed of the flying climbing telegraph-poles. When the journey was over, there would be no time to think: a waiting car, the rush of minarets, a dingy stair, and Mr Eckman rising from behind his desk. Subtleties, figures, contracts would encoil him. Here beforehand, in the restaurant-car, in the sleeping-berth, in the corridor, he must plan every word and rehearse every inflection. He wished that his dealings were with Englishmen or Turks, but Mr Eckman, and somewhere in the background the enigmatic Stein, were men of his own race, practised in reading a meaning into a tone of voice, the grip of fingers round a cigar.

Up the aisle the waiters came carrying the soup. Myatt felt in his breast-pocket and again he nibbled a currant, one of Stein's, small and dry, but, it had to be admitted, cheap. The eternal inevitable war between quality and quantity was fought out to no issue in his mind. Of one thing he had been as nearly certain as possible while tied to a desk in London, meeting only Stein's representatives and never Stein, hearing at best Stein's voice over the long-distance telephone, a ghost of a voice from whose inflections he could tell nothing: Stein was on the rocks. But what rocks? In mid-ocean or near shore? Was he desperate or only resigned to uncomfortable economies? The affair would have been simple if Myatt and Page's agent in Constantinople, the invaluable Mr Eckman, had not been suspected of intricate hidden relations with Stein skirting the outer fringe of the law.

He dipped his spoon into the tasteless Julienne; he preferred his food rich, highly seasoned, but full of a harsh nourishment. Out in the dark nothing was visible, except for the occasional flash of lights from a small station, the rush of flame in a tunnel, and always the transparent likeness of his own face, his hand floating like a fish through which water and weeds shine. He was a little irritated by its ubiquity and was about to pull down the blind when he noticed, behind his own reflection, the image of the shabby man in the mackintosh who had looked into his compartment. His clothes, robbed of colour and texture and opacity, the ghosts of ancient tailoring, had still a forced gentility; the mackintosh thrown open showed the high stiff collar, the over-buttoned jacket. The man waited patiently for his dinner—so Myatt at first thought, allowing his mind to rest a little from the subtleties of Stein and Mr Eckman —but before the waiter could reach him, the stranger was asleep. His face for a moment disappeared from view as the lights of a station turned the walls of the coach from mirrors to windows, through which became visible a throng of country passengers waiting with children and packages and string bags for some slow cross-country train. With the darkness the face returned, nodding into sleep.

Myatt forgot him, choosing a medium Burgundy, a Chambertin of 1923, to drink with the veal, though he knew it a waste of money to buy a good wine, for no bouquet could survive the continuous tremor. All down the coach the whimper and whine of shaken glass was audible as the express drove on at full steam towards Cologne. During the first glass Myatt thought again of Stein, waiting in Constantinople for his arrival with cunning or despair. He would sell out, Myatt felt sure, for a price, but another buyer was said to be in the field. That was where Mr Eckman was suspected of playing a double part, of trying to put up the price against his own firm with a fifteen per cent commission from Stein as the probable motive. Mr Eckman had written that Moult's were offering Stein a fancy price for his stock and good-will; Myatt did not believe him. He had lunched one day with young Moult and casually introduced into their talk the name of Stein. Moult was not a Jew; he had no subtlety, no science of evasion; if he wished to lie, he would lie, but the lie would be confined to the words; he had no knowledge how the untrained hand gives the lie to the mouth. In dealing with an Englishman Myatt found one trick enough; as he introduced the important theme or asked the leading question, he would offer a cigar; if the man was lying, however prompt the answer, the hand would hesitate for the quarter of a second. Myatt knew what the Gentiles said of him: 'I don't like that Jew. He never looks you in the face.' You fools, he would triumph secretly, I know a trick worth two of that. He knew now for example that young Moult had not lied. It was Stein who was lying, or else Mr Eckman.

He poured himself out another glass. Curious, he thought, that it was he, travelling at the rate of sixty miles an hour, who was at rest, not Mr Eckman, locking up his desk, picking his hat from the rack, going downstairs, chewing, as it were, the firm's telegram between his sharp prominent teeth. 'Mr. Carleton Myatt will arrive Istanbul 14th. Arrange meeting with Stein.' In the train, however fast it travelled, the passengers were compulsorily at rest; useless between the walls of glass to feel emotion, useless to try to follow any activity except of the mind; and that activity could be followed without fear of interruption. The world was beating now on Eckman and Stein, telegrams were arriving, men were interrupting the threads of their thought with speech, women were holding dinner-parties. But in the rushing reverberating express, noise was so regular that it was the equivalent of silence, movement was so continuous that after a while the mind accepted it as stillness. Only outside the train was violence of action possible, and the train would contain him safely with his plans for three days; by the end of that time he would know qiute clearly how to deal with Stein and Mr Eckman.

The ice and the dessert over, the bill paid, he paused beside his table to light a cigar and thus faced the stranger and saw how again he had fallen into sleep between the courses; between the departure of the veal, *au Talleyrand,* and the arrival of the iced pudding he had fallen victtm to what must have been a complete exhaustion.

Under Myatt's gaze he woke suddenly. 'Well?' he asked. Myatt apologised. 'I didn't mean to wake you.' The man watched him with suspicion, and something in the sudden change from sleep to a more accustomed anxiety, something in the well-meaning clothes betrayed by the shabby mackintosh, touched Myatt to pity. He presumed on their earlier encounter. 'You've found a compartment all right?'

'Yes.'

Myatt said impulsively: 'I thought perhaps you were finding it hard to rest. I have some aspirin in my bag. Can I lend you a few tablets?' The man snapped at him, 'I have everything I want. I am a doctor.' From habit Myatt watched his hands, thin with the bones showing. He apologised again with a little of the excessive humility of the bowed head in the desert. 'I'm sorry to have troubled you. You looked ill. If there is anything I can do for you——'

'No. Nothing. Nothing.' But as Myatt went, the other turned and called after him, 'The time. What is the right time?' Mayatt said, 'Eight-forty. No, forty-two,' and saw the man's fingers adjust his watch with care for the exact minute.

As he reached the compartment the train was slowing down. The great blast furnaces of Liège rose along the line like ancient castles burning in a border raid. The train lurched and the points changed. Steel girders rose on either side, and very far below an empty street ran diagonally into the dark, and a lamp shone on a café door. The rails opened out, and unattached engines converged on the express, hooting and belching steam. The signals flashed green across the sleepers, and the arch of the station roof rose above the carriage. Newsboys shouted, and a line of stiff sedate men in black broadcoth and women in black veils waited along the platform; without interest, like a crowd of decorous strangers at a funeral, they watched the line of first-class coaches pass them, Ostend—Cologne—Vienne—Belgrade—Istanbul—the slip coach for Athens. Then with their string bags and their children they climbed into the rear coaches, bound perhaps for Pepinster or Verviers, fifteen miles down the line.

Myatt was tired. He had sat up till one o'clock the night before discussing with his father, Jacob Myatt, the affairs of Stein, and he had become aware as never before, watching the jerk of the white beard, of how affairs were slipping away from the old ringed fingers clasped round the glass of warm milk. 'They never pick off the skin,' Jacob Myatt complained, allowing his son to take the spoon and skim the surface clear. There were many things he now allowed his son to do, and Page counted for nothing; his directorship was a mere decoration awarded for twenty years' faithful service as head clerk. I am Myatt, Myatt and Page, he thought without a tremor at the idea of responsibility; he was the first born and it was the law of nature that the father should resign to the son.

They had disagreed last night over Eckman. Jacob

Myatt believed that Stein had deceived the agent, and his son that the agent was in league with Stein. 'You'll see,' he promised, confident in his own cunning, but Jacob Myatt only said, 'Eckman's clever. We need a clever man there.'

It was no use, Myatt knew, settling down to sleep before the frontier at Herbesthal. He took out the figures that Eckman proposed as a basis for negotiation with Stein, the value of the stock in hand, the value of the goodwill, the amount which he believed Stein had been offered by another purchaser. It was true that Eckman had not named Moult in so many words; he had only hinted at the name and he could deny the hint. Moult's had never previously shown interest in currants; the nearest they had come to it was a brief flirtation with the date market. Myatt thought: I can't believe these figures. Stein's business is worth that to us, even if we dumped his stock into the Bosphorus, because we should gain a monopoly; but for any other firm it would be the purchase of a rocky business beaten by our competition.

The figures began to swim before his eyes in a mist of sleep. Ones, sevens, nines became Mr Eckman's small sharp teeth; sixes, fives, threes reformed themselves as in a trick film into Mr Eckman's dark polished eyes. Commissions in the form of coloured balloons floated across the carriage, growing in size, and he sought a pin to prick them one by one. He was brought back to full wakefulness by the sound of footsteps passing and re-passing along the corridor. Poor devil, he thought, seeing a brown mackintosh disappear past the window and two hands clasped.

But he felt no pity for Mr Eckman, following him back in fancy from his office to his very modern flat, into the shining lavatory, the silver-and-gilt bathroom, the bright cushioned drawing-room where his wife sat and sewed and sewed, making vests and pants and bonnets and socks for the Anglican Mission: Mr Eckman was a Christian. All along the line the blast furnaces flared.

The heat did not penetrate the wall of glass. It was bitterly cold, an April night like an old-fashioned Christmas card glittering with frost. Myatt took his fur coat from a peg and went into the corridor. At Cologne there was a wait of nearly forty-five minutes; time enough to get a cup of hot coffee or a glass of brandy. Until then he could walk, up and down, like the man in the mackintosh.

While there was nothing worth his notice in the outside air he knew who would be walking with him in spirit the length of the corridor, in and out of lavatories, Mr Eckman and Stein. Mr Eckman he thought, trying to coax some hot water into a gritty basin, kept a chained Bible by his lavatory seat. So at least he had been told. Large and shabby and very 'family' amongst the silver-and-gilt taps and plugs, it advertised to every man and woman who dined in his flat Mr Eckman's Christianity. There was no need of covert allusions to Church-goings, to the Embassy chaplain, merely a 'Would you like a wash, dear?' from his wife, his own hearty questions to the men after the coffee and the brandy. But of Stein, Myatt knew nothing.

'What a pity you are not getting out at Buda, as you are so interested in cricket. I'm trying—oh, so hard—to get up two elevens at the embassy.' A man with face as bleak and white and impersonal as his clerical collar was speaking to a little rat of a man who crouched opposite him, nodding and becking. The voice, robbed of it characteristic inflections by closed glass, floated out into the corridor as Myatt passed. It was the ghost of a voice and reminded Myatt again of Stein speaking over two thousand miles of cable, hoping that he would one day soon have the honour of entertaining Mr Carleton Myatt in Constantinople, agreeable, hospitable and anonymous.

He was passing the non-sleeping compartments in the second class; men with their waistcoats off sprawled along seats, blue about the chin; women with hair in dusty nets, like the string bags on the racks, tucked their skirts tightly round them and fell in odd shapes over the seats, large breasts and small thighs, small breasts and large thighs hopelessly confused. A tall thin woman woke for a moment to complain, 'That beer you got me. Shocking it was. I can't keep my stomach quiet.' On the seat opposite, the husband sat and smiled; he rubbed one hand over his rough chin, squinting sideways at the girl in the white mackintosh, who lay along the seat, her feet against his other hand. Myatt paused and lit a cigarette. He liked the girl's thin figure and her face, the lips tinted enough to lend her plainness an appeal. Nor was she altogether plain; the smallness of her features, of her skull, her nose and ears, gave her a spurious refinement, a kind of bright prettiness, like the window of a country shop at Chrismas full of small lights and tinsel and coloured common gifts. Myatt remembered how she had gazed at him down the length of the corridor and wondered a little of whom he had reminded her. He was grateful that she had shown no distaste, no knowledge of his uneasiness in the best clothes that money could buy.

The man who shared her seat put his hand cautiously on her ankle and moved it very slowly up towards her knee. All the time he watched his wife. The girl woke and opened her eyes. 'How cold it is,' Myatt heard her say and knew from her elaborate and defensive friendliness that she was aware of the hand withdrawn. Then she looked up and saw him watching her. She was tactful, she was patient, but to Myatt she had little subtlety; he knew that his qualities, the possibilities of annoyance which he offered, were being weighed against her companion's. She wasn't looking for trouble: that was the expression she would use; and he found her courage, quickness and decision admirable. 'I think I'll have a cigarette outside,' she said, fumbling in her bag for a packet; then she was beside him.

'A match?'

'Thanks.' And moving out of view of her compartment they started together into the murmuring darkness.

'I don't like your companion,' Myatt said.

'One can't pick and choose. He's not too bad. His name's Peters.'

Myatt for a moment hesitated. 'Mine's Myatt.'

'Mine's Coral—Coral Musker.'

'Dancing?'

'Sure.'

'American?'

'No. Why did you think so?'

'Something you said. You've got a bit of the accent. Ever been there?'

'Ever been there? Of course I have. Six nights a week and two afternoons. The Garden of the Country Club, Long Island; Palm Beach: A Bachelor's Apartment on Riverside Drive. Why, if you can't talk American you don't stand a chance in an English musical comedy.'

'You're clever,' said Myatt gravely, releasing Eckman and Stein from his consideration.

'Let's move,' the girl said, 'I'm cold.'

'Can't you sleep?'

'Not after that crossing. It's too cold, and that fellow's fingering my legs the whole time.'

'Why don't you smack his face?'

'Before we've reached Cologne? I'm not making trouble. We've got to live together to Buda-Pesth.'

'Is that where you are going?'

'Where he is. I'm going all the way.'

'So am I,' said Myatt, 'on business.'

'Well, we are neither of us going for pleasure, are we?' she said with a touch of gloom. 'I saw you when the train started. I thought you were someone I knew."

'Who?'

'How do I know? I don't trouble to remember what a boy calls himself. It's not the name the post-office knows him by.' There seemed to Myatt something patient and courageous in her quiet acceptance of deceit. She flattened against the window a face a little blue with cold; she might have been a boy avidly examining the contents of a shop, the clasp-knives, the practical jokes, plate lifters, bombs that smell, buns that squeak, but all that was offered her was darkness and their own features. 'Do you think it will get any warmer,' she asked, 'as we go south?' as though she thought herself bound for a tropical climate. 'We don't go far enough for it to make much difference,' he said. 'I've known snow in Constantinople in April. You get the winds down the Bosphorus from the Black Sea. They cut round the corners. The city's all corners.'

'I hope the dressing-rooms are warm,' she said. 'You don't wear enough on the stage to keep the chill out. How I'd like something hot to drink.' She leant with blue face and bent knees against the window. 'Are we near Cologne? What's the German for coffee?' Her expression alarmed him. He ran down the corridor and closed the only open window. 'Are you feeling all right?'

She said slowly with half-closed eyes, 'That's better. You've made it quite stuffy. I'm warm enough now. Feel me.' She lifted her hand; he put it against his cheek and was startled by the heat. 'Look here,' he said. 'Go back to your carriage and I'll try and find some brandy for you. You are ill.' 'It's only that I can't keep warm,' she explained. 'I was hot and now it's cold again. I don't want to go back. I'll stay here.'

'You must have my coat,' he began reluctantly, but before he had time to limit his unwilling offer with 'for a while' or 'until you are warm', she slid to the floor. He took her hands and chafed them, watching her face with helpless anxiety. It seemed to him suddenly of vital necessity that he should aid her. Watching her dance upon the stage, or stand in a lit street outside a stage-door, he would have regarded her only as game for the senses, but helpless and sick under the dim unsteady lamp of the corridor, her body shaken by the speed of the train, she woke a painful pity. She had not complained of the cold; she had commented on it as a kind of necessary evil, and in a flash of insight he became aware of the innumerable necessary evils of which life for her was made up. He heard the monotonous tread of the man whom he had seen pass and re-pass his compartment and went to meet him. 'You are a doctor? There's a girl fainted.' The man stopped and asked reluctantly, 'Where is she?' Then he saw her past Myatt's shoulder. His hesitation angered the Jew. 'She looks really ill,' he urged him. The doctor sighed. 'All right, I'm coming.' He might have been nerving himself to an ordeal.

But the fear seemed to leave him as he knelt by the girl. He was tender towards her with the impersonal experienced tenderness of a doctor. He felt her heart and then lifted her lids. The girl came back to a confusing consciousness; she thought that it was she who was bending over a stranger with a long shabby moustache. She felt pity for the experience which had caused his great anxiety, and her solicitude went out to the friendliness she imagined in his eyes. She put her hands down to his face. He's ill, she thought, and for a moment shut out the puzzling shadows which fell the wrong way, the globe of light shining from the ground. 'Who are you?' she asked, trying to remember how it was that she had come to his help. Never, she thought, had she seen a man who needed help more.

'A doctor.'

She opened her eyes in astonishment and the world cleared. It was she who was lying in the corridor and the stranger who bent over her. 'Did I faint?' she asked. 'It was very cold.' She was aware of the heavy slow movement of the train. Lights streamed through the window across the doctor's face and on to the young Jew behind. Myatt, My'at. She laughed to herself in sudden contentment. It was as though, for the moment, she had passed to another all responsibility. The train lurched to a standstill, and the Jew was thrown against the wall. The doctor had not stirred. If he had swayed it was with the movement of the train and not against it. His eyes were on her face, his finger on her pulse; he watched her with a passion which was trembling on the edge of speech, but she knew that it was not passion for her or any attribute of her. She phrased it to herself: If I'd got Mistinguett's legs, he wouldn't notice. She asked him, 'What is it?' and lost all his answer in the voices crying down the platform and the entrance of blue uniformed men but 'my proper work.'

'Passports and luggage ready,' a foreign voice called to them, and Myatt spoke to her, asking for her bag: 'I'll see to your things.' She gave him her bag and helped by the doctor sat up against the wall.

'Passport?'

The doctor said slowly, and she became aware for the first time of his accent: 'My bags are in the first class. I can't leave this lady. I am a doctor.'

'English passport?'

'Yes.'

'All right.' Another man came up to them. 'Luggage?'

'Nothing to declare.' The man went on.

Coral Musker smiled. 'Is this really the frontier? Why, one could smuggle anything in. They don't look at the bags at all.'

'Anything,' the doctor said, 'with an English passport.' He watched the man out of sight and said nothing more until Myatt returned. 'I could go back to my carriage now,' she said.

'Have you a sleeper?'

'No.'

'Are you getting out at Cologne?'

'I'm going all the way.'

He gave her the same advice as the purser had done. 'You should have had a sleeper.' The uselessness of it irritated her and made her for a moment forget her pity for his age and anxiety. 'How could I have a sleeper? I'm in the chorus.' He flashed back at her with astonishing bitterness, 'No, you have not the money.'

'What shall I do?' she asked him. 'Am I ill?'

'How can I advise you?' he protested. 'If you were rich, I should say: Take six months' holiday. Go to North Africa. You fainted because of the crossing, because of the cold. Oh yes, I can tell you all that,

33

but that's nothing. Your heart's bad. You've been overstraining it for years.'

She implored him, a little frightened, 'But what shall I do?' He opened his hands: 'Nothing. Carry on. Take what rest you can. Keep warm. You wear too little.'

A whistle blew, and the train trembled into movement. The station lamps sailed by them into darkness, and the doctor turned to leave her. 'If you want me again, I'm three coaches farther up. My name is John. Dr John.' She said with intimidated politeness, 'Mine's Coral Musker.' He gave her a little formal foreign bow and walked away. She saw in his eyes other thoughts falling like rain. Never before had she the sensation of being so instantly forgotten. 'A girl that men forget,' she hummed to keep up her courage.

But the doctor had not passed out of hearing before he was stopped. Treading softly and carefully along the shaking train, a hand clinging to the corridor rail, came a small pale man. She heard him speak to the doctor, 'Is anything the matter? Can I help?' He was a foot shorter and she laughed aloud at the sight of his avid face peering upwards. 'You mustn't think me inquisitive,' he said, one hand on the other's sleeve. 'A clergyman in my compartment thought someone was ill.' He added with eagerness, 'I said I'd find out.'

Up and down, up and down the corridor she had seen the doctor walking, clinging to its emptiness in preference to a compartment shared. Now, through no mistake on his part, he found himself in a crowd, questions and appeals sticking to his mind like burrs. She expected an outbreak, some damning critical remark which would send the fellow quivering down the corridor.

The softness of his reply surprised her. 'Did you say a priest?'

'Oh no,' the man apologised, 'I don't know yet what sect, what creed. Why? Is somebody dying?'

Dr John seemed to become aware of her fear and called down the corridor a reassurance before he brushed by the detaining hand. The little man remained for a moment in happy possession of a situation. When he had tasted it to the full, he approached. 'What's it all about?'

She took no notice, appealing to the only friendly presence she was left with. 'I'm not sick like that, am I?'

'What intrigues me,' the stranger said, 'is his accent. You'd say he was a foreigner, but he gave an English name. I think I'll follow him and talk.'

Her mind had worked clearly since she fainted; the sight of a world reversed, in which it had been the doctor who lay beneath her needing pity and care, had made the old images of the world sharp with unfamiliarity; but words lagged behind intuition, and when she appealed, 'Don't bother him,' the stranger was already out of hearing.

'What do you think?' Myatt asked. 'Is he right? Is there a mystery?'

'We've all got some secrets,' she said.

'He might be escaping from the police.'

She said with absolute conviction, 'He's good.' He accepted the phrase; it dismissed the doctor from his thoughts. 'You must lie down,' he said, 'and try to sleep,' but it did not need her evasive reply, 'How can I sleep with that woman and her stomach?' to remind him of Mr Peters lurking in his corner for her return and the renewal of his cheap easy harmless satisfactions. 'You must have my sleeper.'

'What? In the first class?' Her disbelief and her longing decided him. He determined to be princely on an Oriental scale, granting costly gifts and not requiring, not wanting, any return. Parsimony was the traditional reproach against his race, and he would show one Christian how undeserved it was. Forty years in the wilderness, away from the flesh pots of Egypt, had entailed harsh habits, the counted date and the hoarded water; nor had a thousand years in the wilderness of a Christian world, where only the secret treasure was safe, encouraged display; but the world was altering, the desert was flowering; in stray corners here and there, in western Europe, the Jew could show that other quality he shared with the Arab, the quality of the princely host, who would wash the feet of beggars and feed them from his own dish; sometimes he could cease to be the enemy of the rich to become the friend of any poor man who sought a roof in the name of God. The roar of the train faded from his consciousness, the light went out in his eyes, while he built for his own pride the tent in the oasis, the well in the desert. He spread his hands before her. 'Yes, you must sleep there. I'll arrange with the guard. And my coat—you must take that. It will keep you warm. At Cologne I'll find you coffee, but it will be better for you to sleep.'

'But I can't. Where will you sleep?'

'I shall find somewhere. The train's not full.' For the second time she experienced an impersonal tenderness, but it was not frightening as the first had been; it was a warm wave into which she let herself down, not too far, if she felt afraid, for her feet to be aware of the sand, but only far enough to float her without effort on her own part where she wanted to go—to a bed and a pillow and a covering and sleep. She had

an impression of how grace came back to him with
confidence, as he ceased to apologise or to assert and
became only a ministering shadow.

Myatt did not go to find the guard but wedged himself between the walls of corridor and compartment,
folded his arms and prepared to sleep. But without
his coat it was very cold. Although all the windows of
the corridor were shut, a draught blew past the swing
door and over the footboard joining coach to coach.
Nor were the noises of the train regular enough now
to be indistinguishable from silence. There were many
tunnels between Herbesthal and Cologne, and in each
the roar of the express was magnified. Myatt slept
uneasily, and the rush of the loosed steam and the
draught on his cheek contributed to his dream. The
corridor became the long straight Spaniards Road with
the heath on either side. He was being driven slowly
by Isaacs in his Bentley, and they watched the girls'
faces as they walked in pairs along the lamp-lit eastern
side, shopgirls offering themselves dangerously for a
drink at the inn, a fast ride, and the fun of the thing;
on the other side of the road, in the dark, on a few
seats, the prostitutes sat, shapeless and shabby and
old, with their backs to the sandy slopes and the
thorn bushes, waiting for a man old and dumb and
blind enough to offer them ten shillings. Isaacs drew
up the Bentley under a lamp and they let the anonymous young beautiful animal faces stream by. Isaacs
wanted someone fair and plump and Myatt someone
thin and dark, but it was not easy to pick and choose,
for all along the eastern side were lined the cars of
their competitors, girls leaning across the open doors
laughing and smoking; on the other side of the road a
single two-seater kept patient watch. Myatt was irritated by Isaacs' uncompromising taste; it was cold in

the Bentley with a draught on the cheek, and presently when he saw Coral Musker walking by, he jumped from the car and offered her a cigarette and after that a drink and after that a ride. That was one advantage with these girls, Myatt thought; they all knew what a ride meant, and if they didn't care for the look of you, they just said that they had to be going home now. But Coral Musker wanted a ride; she would take him for her companion in the dark of the car, with the lamps and the inns and the houses left behind and trees springing up like paper silhouettes in the green light of the head-lamps, and then the bushes with the scent of wet leaves holding the morning's rain and a short barbarous enjoyment in the stubble. As for Isaacs, he must just put up with his companion, although she was dark and broad and lightly clothed, with a great nose and prominent pointed teeth. But when she was seated next Isaacs in the front of the car she turned and gave him a long smile, saying, 'I've come out without a card, but my name's Stein.' And then in the teeth of the wind he was climbing a great stair with silver and gilt handrails, and she stood at the top wearing a small moustache, pointing to a woman who sat sewing, sewing, sewing, and called out to him, 'Meet Mrs Eckman.'

Coral Musker flung her hand away from the blankets in protest, as she danced and danced and danced in the glare of the spot-light, and the producer struck at her bare legs with a cane, telling her she was no good, that she was a month late, that she'd broken her contract. And all the time she danced and danced and danced, taking no notice of him while he beat at her legs with the cane.

Mrs Peters turned on her face and said to her husband, 'That beer. My stomach won't be quiet. It makes so much noise, I can't sleep.'

Mr Opie dreamed that in his surplice with cricket bat under his arm and batting-glove dangling from his wrist he mounted a great broad flight of marble steps towards the altar of God.

Dr. John asleep at last with a bitter tablet dissolving on his tongue spoke once in German. He had no sleeper and sat bolt upright in the corner of his compartment, hearing outside the slow singing start, 'Köln, Köln. Köln.'

PART TWO
Cologne

[1]

'But of course, dear, I don't mind your being drunk,' said Janet Pardoe. The clock above Cologne station struck one, and a waiter began to turn out the lights on the terrace of the Excelsior. 'Look, dear, let me put your tie straight.' She leant across the table and adjusted Mabel Warren's tie.

'We've lived together for three years,' Miss Warren began to say in a deep melancholy voice, 'and I have never yet spoken to you harshly.'

Janet Pardoe put a little scent behind her ears. 'For heaven's sake, darling, look at the time. The train leaves in half an hour, and I've got to get my bags, and you've got to get your interview. Do drink up your gin and come along.'

Mabel Warren took her glass and drank. Then she rose and her square form swayed a little; she wore a tie and a stiff collar and a tweed 'sporting' suit. Her eyebrows were heavy, and her eyes were dark and determined and red with weeping.

'You know why I drink,' she protested.

'Nonsense, dear,' said Janet Pardoe, making certain in her compact mirror of the last niceties of appearance, 'you drank long before you ever met me. Have a little sense of proportion. I shall only be away a week.'

'These men,' said Miss Warren darkly, and then as Janet Pardoe rose to cross the square, she gripped her arm with extraordinary force. 'Promise me you'll be careful. If only I could come with you.' Almost on the threshold of the station she stumbled in a puddle. 'Oh, see what I've done now. What a great clumsy thing I am. To splash your beautiful new suit.' With a large rough hand, a signet ring on the small finger, she began to brush at Janet Pardoe's skirt.

'Oh, for God's sake, come on, Mabel,' Janet said.

Miss Warren's mood changed. She straightened herself and barred the way. 'You say I'm drunk. I am drunk. But I'm going to be drunker.'

'Oh, come on.'

"You are going to have one more drink with me or I shan't let you on the platform.'

Janet Pardoe gave way. 'One. Only one, mind.' She guided Mabel Warren across a vast black shining hall into a room where a few tired men and women were snatching cups of coffee. 'Another gin,' said Miss Warren, and Janet ordered it.

In a mirror on the opposite wall Miss Warren saw her own image, red, tousled, very shoddy, sitting beside another and far more familiar image, slim, dark,

41

and beautiful. What do I matter? she thought, with the melancholy of drink. I've made her, I'm responsible for her, and with bitterness, I've paid for her. There's nothing she's wearing that I haven't paid for, sweated for, she thought (although the bitter cold defied the radiators in the restaurant), getting up at all hours, interviewing brothel-keepers in their cells, the mothers of murdered children, 'covering' this and 'covering' that. She knew with a certain pride what they said in the London office: 'When you want sob-stuff, send Dizzy Mabel.' All the way down the Rhine was her province; there wasn't a town of any size between Cologne and Mainz where she hadn't sought out human interest, forcing dramatic phrases onto the lips of sullen men, pathos into the mouths of women too overcome with grief to speak at all. There wasn't a suicide, a murdered woman, a raped child who had stirred her to the smallest emotion; she was an artist to examine critically, to watch, to listen; the tears were for paper. But now she sat and wept with ugly grunts because Janet Pardoe was leaving her for a week.

'Who is it you are interviewing?' Janet Pardoe asked. She was not at all interested, but she wanted to distract Mabel Warren from thoughts of separation; her tears were too conspicuous. 'You ought to comb your hair,' she added. Miss Warren wore no hat and her black hair, cut short like a man's, was hopelessly dishevelled.

'Savory,' said Miss Warren.

'Who's he?'

'Sold a hundred thousand copies. *The Great Gay Round*. Half a million words. Two hundred characters. The Cockney Genius. Drops his aitches when he can remember to.'

'What's he doing on the train?'

'Going East to collect material. It's not my job, but as I was seeing you off, I took it on. They've asked me for a quarter of a column, but they'll cut it down to a couple of sticks in London. He's chosen the wrong time. In the silly season he'd have got half a column among the mermaids and sea-horses.' The flare of professional interest guttered as she looked again at Janet Pardoe: no more of a morning would she see Janet in pyjamas pouring out coffee, no more of an evening come in to the flat and find Janet in pyjamas mixing a cocktail. She said huskily, 'Darling, which pair will you be wearing tonight?' The feminine question sounded oddly in Miss Warren's deep masculine voice.

'What do you mean?'

'Pyjamas, darling. I want to think of you tonight just as you are.'

'I don't suppose I shall even undress. Look, it's a quarter past one. We must go. You'll never get your interview.'

Miss Warren's professional pride was touched. 'You don't think I need to ask him questions?' she said. 'Just a look at him and I'll put the right words in his mouth. And he won't complain either. It's publicity.'

'But I must find the porter with my bags.' Everyone was leaving the restaurant. As the door opened and closed the cries of porters, the whistle of steam, came faintly down to where they sat. Janet Pardoe appealed again to Miss Warren. 'We must go. If you want any more gin I shall leave you to it.' But Miss Warren said nothing, Miss Warren ignored her; Janet Pardoe found herself attending one of the regular rites of Mabel Warren's journalistic career, the visible shedding of her drunkenness. First a hand put the hair into order, then a powdered handkerchief, her compromise with femininity, disguised the redness of her cheeks and lids. All the while she was focusing her eyes, using whatever lay before her, cups, waiter, glasses and so to the distant mirrors and her own image, as a kind of optician's alphabetic scroll. On this occasion the first letter of the alphabet, the great black A, was an elderly man in a mackintosh, who was standing beside a table brushing away his crumbs before leaving to catch the train.

'My God,' said Miss Warren, covering her eyes with her hand, 'I'm drunk. I can't see properly. Who's that there?'

'The man with the moustache?'

'Yes.'

'I've never seen him before.'

'I have,' said Miss Warren, 'I have. But where?' Something had diverted her effectually from the thought of separation; her nose was on a scent and leaving half a finger of gin in the bottom of her glass, she strode in the man's wake to the door. He was out and walking quickly across the black shining hall to a flight of stairs before Miss Warren could extricate herself from the swing door. She crashed into a porter and fell on her knees, swaying her head, trying to free it from the benevolence, the melancholy, the vagueness of drink. He stopped to help her and she seized his arm and stayed him until she could control her tongue. 'What train leaves platform five?' she asked. 'Vienna,' the man said.

'Belgrade?' 'Yes.'

It had been pure chance that she had said Belgrade and not Constantinople, but the sound of her own voice brought her light. She called out to Janet Pardoe: 'Take two seats. I'm coming with you as far as Vienna.'

'Your ticket?'

'I've got my reporter's pass.' It was she who was

now impatient. 'Hurry. Platform five. It's twenty-eight past. Only five minutes.' She still kept the porter to her side with a muscular grip. 'Listen. I want you to take a message for me. Kaiser Wilhelmstrasse 33.'

'I can't leave the station,' he told her.

'What time do you come off duty?'

'Six.'

'That's no good. You must slip out. You can do that, can't you? No one will notice.'

'I'd get the sack.'

'Risk it,' said Miss Warren. 'Twenty marks.'

The man shook his head. 'The foreman would notice.'

'I'll give you another twenty for him.'

The foreman wouldn't do it, he said; there was too much to lose; the head foreman might find out. Miss Warren opened her bag and began to count her money. Above her head a clock struck the half-hour. The train left in three minutes, but not for a moment did she allow her desperation to show; any emotion would frighten the man. 'Eighty marks,' she said, 'and give the foreman what you like. You'll only be away ten minutes.'

'It's a big risk,' the porter said, but he allowed her to press the notes into his hand. 'Listen carefully. Go to Kaiser Wilhelmstrasse 33. You'll find the offices of the London *Clarion*. Somebody's sure to be there. Tell him that Miss Warren has taken the Orient Express for Vienna. She won't be letting him have the interview tonight; she'll telephone it from Vienna tomorrow. Tell him she's on to a bill page lead. Now repeat that.' While he stumbled slowly through the message she kept an eye on the clock. One-thirty. One-thirty-one and a half. 'Right. Off with it. If you don't get it to them by one-fifty I'll report you for taking bribes.' She grinned at him with malicious playfulness, showing great square teeth, and then ran for the stairs. One-thirty-two. She thought that she heard a whistle blown and took the last three steps in one stride. The train was moving, a ticket-collector tried to block her way but she knocked him to one side and roared 'Pass' at him over her shoulder. The last third-class coaches were slipping by with increasing speed. My God, she thought, I'll give up drink. She got her hand on the bar of the last coach, while a porter shouted and ran at her. For a long ten seconds, with pain shooting up her arm, she thought that she would be dragged off the platform against the wheels of the guard's van. The high step daunted her. I can't make it. Another moment and her shoulder would give. Better drop on the platform and risk concussion than break both legs. But what a story to lose, she thought with bitterness, and jumped. She landed on her knees on the step just in time as the edge of the platform fell away. The last lamp vanished, the door under the pressure of her body opened inwards, and she fell on her back into the corridor. She propped herself up against the wall with care for her aching shoulder and thought with a wry triumph, Dizzy Mabel comes on board.

Morning light came through the slit in the blind and touched the opposite seat. When Coral Musker woke it was the seat and a leather suitcase that she first saw. She felt listless and apprehensive, thinking of the train which had to be caught at Victoria, the dry egg and the slices of the day before yesterday's loaf awaiting her downstairs. I wish I'd never taken the job, she thought, preferring now when the moment of departure was upon her the queue on the stairs of Shaftesbury Avenue, the forced cheerfulness of long waits outside the agent's door. She lifted the blind and was for a moment astonished by a telegraph-pole flashing past, a green river running by, touched with orange by the early sun, and wooded hills. Then she remembered.

It was still early, for the sun was low, only just emerging above the hills. A village on the opposite bank glittered with little lights; a few thin streams of smoke lay in the windless air above the small wooden houses, where early fires were being lit, breakfasts for labourers prepared. The village was so far from the line that it remained still, to be stared at, while the trees and cottages on the near bank, the tethered boats, fled backwards. She raised the other blind and in the corridor saw Myatt sleeping with his back against the wall. Her first instinct was to wake him; her second to let him sleep and lie back herself in the luxury of another's sacrifice. She felt tender towards him, as though he had given her new hope of a life which was not a continuous struggle for one's own hand; perhaps the world, she thought, was not so hard. She remembered how the purser had spoken to her kindly and called to her, 'Remember me'; it seemed not unlikely now, with the young man sleeping outside the door, ready to suffer some hours' discomfort for a stranger, that the purser might still remember her. She thought for the first time, with happiness: Perhaps I have a life in people's minds when I am not there to be seen or talked to. She looked out of the window again, but the village was gone, and the particular green hills she had stared at; only the river was the same. She fell asleep.

Miss Warren staggered down the train. She could not bear to hold the rail with her right hand, for her shoulder pained her still, although she had sat for nearly two hours in the third-class corridor. She felt battered, faint and drunk, and with difficulty arranged her thoughts, but her nose held yet the genuine aroma of the hunt. Never before in ten years of reporting, ten years of women's rights, rapes and murders, had she come so close to an exclusive bill page story, not a story which only the penny papers would trouble to print, but a story which *The Times* correspondent himself would give a year of life to know. It was not everyone, she thought with pride, who would have been capable of seizing the moment as she had done when drunk. As she lurched along the line of first-class compartments triumph sat oddly on her brow like a tip-tilted crown.

Luck favoured her. A man came out of a compartment and made his way towards the lavatory and, as she leant back against a window to let him by, she saw the man in the mackintosh dozing in a corner, for the moment alone. He looked up to see Miss Warren swaying a little forward and back in the doorway. 'Can I come in?' she asked. 'I got on the train at Cologne, and I can't find a seat.' Her voice was low, almost tender; she might have been urging a loved dog towards a lethal chamber.

'The seat's taken.'

'Only for a moment,' said Miss Warren. 'Just to rest my legs. I am so glad that you speak English. I am always so afraid of travelling on a train with nothing but a lot of foreigners. One might want anything almost in the night, mightn't one?' She grinned at him playfully. 'I believe that you are a doctor.'

'I was once a doctor,' the man admitted.

'And you are travelling out to Belgrade?' He looked at her sharply with a sense of uneasiness, and he caught her unawares, the square tweeded form leaning a little forward, the flash of the signet ring, the flushed hungry face. 'No,' he said, 'no. Not so far.'

'I am only going to Vienna,' said Miss Warren.

He said slowly, 'What made you think—?' wondering whether he did right to question her; he was unused to danger in the form of an English spinster a little drunk with gin; he could smell her all across the carriage. The risks he had faced before required only the ducked head, the quick finger, the plain lie. Miss Warren also hesitated, and her hesitation was like a breath of flame to an imprisoned man. She said, 'I thought I had seen you in Belgrade.'

'I have never been there.'

She came roughly into the open, tossing subterfuge aside. 'I was at Belgrade,' she said, 'for my paper at the Kamnetz trial.' But she had given him all the warning he needed and he faced her with a complete lack of interest.

'The Kamnetz trial?'

'When General Kamnetz was charged with rape. Czinner was the chief evidence for the prosecution. But of course, the general was acquitted. The jury was packed. The Government would never have allowed a conviction. It was sheer stupidity on Czinner's part to give evidence.'

'Stupidity?' His polite interest angered her. 'Of course you've heard of Czinner. They had tried to shoot him a week before while he sat in a café. He was the head of the Social Democrats. He played into their hands by giving evidence against Kamnetz; they had a warrant out for his arrest for perjury twelve hours before the trial ended. They simply sat and waited for the acquittal.'

'How long ago was all this?'

'Five years.' He watched her narrowly, judging what reply would most irritate her. 'An old story now then. Is Czinner out of prison?'

'He got away from them. I'd give a lot to know how. It would make a wonderful story. He simply disappeared. Everyone assumed he'd been murdered.'

'And hadn't he?'

'No,' said Mabel Warren, 'he got away.'

'A clever man.'

'I don't believe it,' she said furiously. 'A clever man man would never have given evidence. What did Kamnetz or the child matter to him? He was a quixotic fool.' A cold breath of air blew through the open door and set the doctor shivering. 'It's been a bitter night,' he said. She brushed the remark on one side with a square worn hand. 'To think,' she said with awe, 'that he never died. While the jury were away he walked out of the court before the eyes of the police. They sat there unable to do anything till the jury came back. Why, I swear that I saw the warrant sticking out of Hartep's breast pocket. He disappeared; he might never have existed; everything went on exactly as before. Even Kamnetz.'

He could not disguise a bitter interest. 'So? Even Kamnetz?' She seized her advantage, speaking huskily with unexpected imagination. 'Yes, if he went back now, he would find everything the same; the clock might have been put back. Hartep taking the same bribes; Kamnetz with his eye for a child; the same slums; the same cafés with the same concerts at six and eleven. Carl's gone from the Moscowa, that's all, the new waiter's a Frenchman. There's a new cinema, too, near the Park. Oh yes, there's one change. They've built over Kruger's beer garden. Flats for civil servants.' He remained silent, quite unable to meet this new move of his opponent. So Kruger's was gone with its fairy lights and brightly-coloured umbrellas and the gipsies playing softly from table to table in the dusk. And Carl had gone too. For a moment he would have bartered with the woman all his safety, and the safety of his friends, to know the news of Carl; had he gathered up his tips and retired to a new flat near the Park, folding up the napkins for his own table, drawing the cork for his own glass? He knew that he ought to interrupt the drunken dangerous woman opposite him, but he could not say a word, while she gave him news of Belgrade, the kind of news which his friends in their weekly coded letters never sent him.

There were other things, too, he would have liked to ask her. She had said the slums were the same, and he could feel under his feet the steep steps down into the narrow gorges; he bent under the bright rags stretched across the way, put his handkerchief across his mouth to shut out the smell of dogs, of children, of bad meat and human ordure. He wanted to know whether Dr Czinner was remembered there. He had known every inhabitant with an intimacy which they would have thought dangerous if they had not so implicitly trusted him, if he had not been by birth one of themselves. As it was, he had been robbed, confided in, welcomed, attacked and loved. Five years was a long time; he might already be forgotten.

Mabel Warren drew in her breath sharply. 'To come to facts. I want an exclusive interview for my paper. "How I escaped?" or "Why I am returning home?" '

'An interview?' His repetitions annoyed her; she had a splitting headache and felt 'wicked'. It was the term she used herself; it meant a hatred of men, of all the shifts and evasions they made necessary, of the way they spoiled beauty and stalked abroad in their own ugliness. They boasted of the women they had enjoyed; even the faded middle-aged face before her had in his time seen beauty naked, the hands which clasped his knee had felt and pried and enjoyed. And at Vienna she was losing Janet Pardoe, who was going alone into a world where men ruled. They would flatter her and give her bright cheap objects, as though she were a native to be cheated with Woolworth mirrors and glass beads. But it was not their enjoyment she most feared, it was Janet's. Not loving her at all, or only for the hour, the day, the year, they could make her weak with pleasure, cry aloud in her enjoyment. While she, Mabel Warren, who had saved her from a governess's buried life and fed her and clothed her, who could love her with the same passion until death, without satiety, had no means save her lips to express her love, was faced always by the fact that she gave no enjoyment and gained herself no more than an embittered sense of insufficiency. Now with her head aching, the smell of gin in her nostrils, the knowledge of her flushed ugliness, she hated men with a wicked intensity and their bright spurious graces.

'You are Doctor Czinner.' She noted with an increase of her anger that he did not trouble to deny his identity, proffering her carelessly the name he travelled under, 'My name is John.'

'Doctor Czinner,' she growled at him, closing her great teeth on her lower lip in an effort at self-control.

'Richard John, a schoolmaster, on holiday.'

'To Belgrade.'

'No.' He hesitated a moment. 'I am stopping at Vienna.' She did not believe him, but she won back her amiability with an effort. 'I'm getting out at Vienna, too. Perhaps you'll let me show you some of the sights.' A man stood in the doorway and she rose. 'I'm so sorry. This is your seat.' She grinned across the compartment, lurched sideways as the train clattered across a point, and failed to hold a belch which filled the compartment for a few seconds with the smell of gin and shaken motes of cheap powder. 'I'll see you again before Vienna,' she said, and moving down the corridor leant her red face against the cold smutty glass in a spasm of pain at her own drunkenness and squalor. 'I'll get him yet,' she thought, blushing at her belch as though she were a young girl at a dinner-party. 'I'll get him somehow. God damn his soul.'

A tender light flooded the compartments. It would have been possible for a moment to believe that the sun was the expression of something that loved and suffered for men. Human beings floated like fish in golden water, free from the urge of gravity, flying without wings, transparent, in a glass acquarium. Ugly faces and misshapen bodies were transmuted, if not into beauty, at least into grotesque forms fashioned by a mocking affection. On that golden tide they rose and fell, murmured and dreamed. They were not imprisoned, for they were not during the hour of dawn aware of their imprisonment.

Coral Musker woke for the second time. She stood up at once and went to the door; the man dozed wearily, his eyes jerking open to the rhythm of the train. Her mind was still curiously clear; it was as if the golden light had a quality of penetration, so that she could understand motives which were generally hidden, movements which as a rule had for her no importance or significance. Now as she watched him and he be-

came aware of her, she saw his hands go out in a gesture which stayed half-way; she knew that it was a
trick of his race which he was consciously repressing.
She said softly, 'I'm a pig. You've been out there all
night.' He shrugged his shoulders deprecatingly; he
might have been a pawnbroker undervaluing a watch
or vase. 'Why not? I didn't want you to be disturbed.
I had to see the guard. Can I come in?'

'Of course. It's your compartment.'

He smiled and was unable to resist a spread of the
hands, a slight bow from the hips. 'Pardon *me*. It's
yours.' He took a handkerchief from his sleeve, rolled
up his cuffs, made passes in the air. 'Look. See. A
first-class ticket.' A ticket fell from his handkerchief
and rolled on the floor between them.

'Yours.'

'No, yours.' He began to laugh with pleasure at her
consternation.

'What do you mean? I couldn't take it. Why, it
must have cost pounds.'

'Ten,' he said boastfully. 'Ten pounds.' He straightened his tie and said airily, 'That's nothing to me.'

But his confidence, his boastful eyes, alienated her.
She said with a deep suspicion, 'What are you getting
at? What do you think I am?' The ticket lay between
them; nothing would induce her to pick it up. She
stamped her foot as the gold faded and became no
more than a yellow stain upon the glass and cushions.
'I'm going back to my seat.'

He said defiantly, 'I don't think about you. I've got
other things to think about. If you don't want the
ticket you can throw it away.' She saw him watching
her, his shoulders raised again boastfully, carelessly,
and she began to cry quietly to herself, turning to the
window and the river and a bridge that fled by and a

bare beech pricked with early buds. This is my gratitude for a calm long sleepy night; this is the way I
take a present; and she thought with shame and disappointment of early dreams of courtesans accepting
gifts from princes. And I snap at him like a tired
waitress.

She heard him move behind her and knew that he
was stooping for the ticket; she wanted to turn to
him and express her gratitude, say: 'It would be like
heaven to sit on these deep cushions all the journey,
sleep in the berth, forget that I'm on the way to a
job, think myself rich. No one has ever been so good
to me as you are,' but her earlier words, the vulgarity
of her suspicion, lay like a barrier of class between
them. 'Lend me your bag,' he said. She held it out
behind her, and she felt his fingers open the clasp.
'There,' he said, 'I've put it inside. You needn't use
it. Just sit here when you want to. And sleep here
when you are tired.' I am tired, she thought. I could
sleep here for hours. She said in a voice strained to
disguise her tears, 'But how can I?'

'Oh,' he said, 'I'll find another compartment. I only
slept outside last night because I was anxious about
you. You might have needed something.' She began to
cry again, leaning the top of her head against the window, half shutting her eyes, so that her lashes made a
curtain between herself and the hard admonishments
of old dry women of experience: 'There's only one
thing a man wants.' 'Don't take presents from a
stranger.' It was the size of the present she had been
always told that made the danger. Chocolates and a
ride, even in the dark, after a theatre, entailed no more
than kisses on the mouth and neck, a little tearing of
a dress. A girl was expected to repay, that was the point
of all advice; one never got anything for nothing. Novel-

ists like Ruby M. Ayres might say that chastity was worth more than rubies, but the truth was it was priced at a fur coat or thereabouts. One couldn't accept a fur coat without sleeping with a man. If you did, all the older women would tell you the man had a grievance. And the Jew had paid ten pounds.

He put his hand on her arm. 'What's the matter? Tell me. Do you feel ill?' She remembered the hand that shook the pillow, the whisper of his feet moving away. She said again, 'How can I?' but this time it was an appeal for him to speak and to deny the accumulated experience of poverty. 'Look,' he said, 'sit down and let me show you things. That's the Rhine.' She found herself laughing. 'I guessed that.' 'Did you see the rock we passed jutting out into the stream? That's the Lorelei rock. Heine.'

'What do you mean, Heine?' He said with pleasure, 'A Jew.' She began to forget the decision she was forced to make and watched him with interest, trying to find a stranger behind the too familiar features, the small eyes, the large nose, the black oiled hair. She had seen this man too often, like a waiter in a dinner-jacket sitting in the front row at provincial theatres, behind a desk at agents' offices, in the wings at rehearsal, outside the stage door at midnight; the world of the theatre vibrated with his soft humble imperative voice; he was mean with a commonplace habitual meanness, generous in fits and starts, never to be trusted. Soft praise at a rehearsal meant nothing, in the office afterwards he would be saying over a glass of whisky, 'That little girl in the front row, she's not worth her keep.' He was never angered or abusive, never spoke worse of anyone than as 'that little girl', and dismissal came in the shape of a typewritten note left in a pigeon-hole. She said gently, partly because none of these qualities prevented her liking Jews for their very quietness, partly because it was a girl's duty to be amiable, 'Jews are artistic, aren't they? Why, almost the whole orchestra at *Atta Girl* were Jewish boys.'

'Yes,' he said with a bitterness which she did not understand.

'Do you like music?'

'I can play the violin,' he said, 'not well.' For a moment it was as if behind the familiar eyes a strange life moved.

'I always wanted to cry at "Sonny Boy",' she said. She was aware of the space which divided her understanding from her expression; she was sensible of much and could say little, and what she said was too often the wrong thing. Now she saw the strange life die.

'Look,' he said sharply. 'No more river. We've left the Rhine. Not long before breakfast.'

She was a little pained by a sense of unfairness, but she was not given to argument. 'I'll have to fetch my bags,' she said, 'I've got sandwiches in it.'

He stared at her. 'Don't tell me you've brought provisions for three days.'

'Oh, no. Just supper last night and breakfast this morning. It saves about eight shillings.'

'Are you Scotch? Listen to me. You'll have breakfast with me.'

'What more do you expect me to have with you?'

He grinned. 'I'll tell you. Lunch, tea, dinner. And tomorrow——' She interrupted him with a sigh. 'I guess you're a bit rocky. You haven't escaped from anywhere, have you?' His face fell and he asked her with sudden humility, 'You couldn't put up with me? You'd be bored?'

'No,' she said, 'I shouldn't be bored. But why do you do all this for me? I'm not pretty. I guess I'm

57

not clever.' She waited with longing for a denial. 'You are lovely, brilliant, witty,' the incredible words which would relieve her of any need to repay him or refuse his gifts; loveliness and wit were priced higher than any gift he offered, while if a girl were loved, even old women of hard experience would admit her right to take and never give. But he denied nothing. His explanation was almost insulting in its simplicity. 'I can talk so easily to you. I feel I know you.' She knew what that meant.'Yes,' she said with the dry trivial grief of disappointment, 'I seem to know you too,' and what she meant were the long stairs, the agent's door, and the young friendly Jew, explaining gently and without interest that he had nothing to offer her, nothing to offer her at all.

Yes, she thought, they knew each other; they had both admitted the fact, and it had left them beggared of words. The world shifted and changed and passed them by. Trees and buildings rose and fell against a pale-blue clouded sky, beech changed to elm, and elm to fir, and fir to stone; a world, like lead upon a hot fire, bubbled into varying shapes now like a flame, now like a leaf of clover. Their thoughts remained the same and there was nothing to speak about, because there was nothing to discover.

'You don't really want me to have breakfast with you,' she said, trying to be sensible and break the embarrassment of their silence. But he would have nothing to do with her solution. 'I do,' he said, but there was a weakness in his voice which showed her that she had only to be masterful, to get up and leave him and go to her carriage, and he would make no resistance. But in her bag there were stale sandwiches and some of yesterday's milk in a wine bottle, while down the corridor came the smell of boiling coffee and fresh white loaves.

Mabel Warren poured out her coffee, black and strong with no sugar. 'It's the best story I've ever been after,' she said. 'I saw him five years ago walk out of court, while Hartep watched with the warrant in his pocket. Campbell, of the *News,* was after him at once, but he missed him in the street. He never went home, and no more was heard of him from that day to this. Everyone thought he had been murdered, but I never understood why, if they meant to murder him, they took out a warrant for his arrest.'

'Suppose,' said Janet Pardoe, without much interest, 'that he won't speak.'

Miss Warren broke a roll. 'I've never failet yet.'

'You'll invent something?'

'No, that's good enough for Savory, but not for him.' She said viciously, 'I'll make him speak. Somehow. Between here and Vienna. I've got nearly twelve hours. I'll think of a way.' She added thoughtfully, 'He says he's a schoolteacher. It may be true. That would be a good story. And where is he going? He says that he's getting out at Vienna. If he does I'll follow him. I'll follow him to Constantinople if necessary. But I don't believe it. He's going home.'

'To prison?'

'To trial. He's trusting the people perhaps. He was always popular in the slums. But he's a fool if he thinks they'll remember him. Five years. No one's ever remembered for so long.'

'Darling, how morbid you are.'

Mabel Warren came back with difficulty to her immediate surroundings, the coffee swaying in her cup, the gently-rocking table, and Janet Pardoe. Janet Pardoe had pouted and protested and grieved, but now she was squinting sideways at a Jew who shared a table with a girl, common to Miss Warren's eyes, but with a bright attraction. As for the man, his only merits were youth and money, but they were enough, Mabel Warren thought with bitter knowledge, to catch Janet's eye. 'You know it's true,' she said with useless anger. She tore at another roll with her square worn hand, while her emotion grew, how grotesquely she was aware. 'You'll have forgotten me in a week.'

'But of course I shan't, darling. Why, I owe you everything.' The words did not satisfy Mabel Warren. When I love, she thought, I do not think of what I owe. The world to her was divided into those who thought and those who felt. The first considered the dresses which had been bought them, the bills which had been paid, but presently the dresses went out of fashion and the wind caught the receipt from the desk and blew it away, and in any case the debt had been paid with a kiss or another kindness, and those who thought forgot; but those who felt remembered; they did not owe and they did not lend, they gave hatred or love. I am one of those, thought Miss Warren, her eyes filling with tears and the bread drying in her throat, I am one of those who love and remember always, who keep faith with the past in black dresses or black bands, I don't forget, and her eyes dwelt for a moment on the Jew's girl, as a tired motorist might eye with longing the common inn, the scarlet curtains and the watered ale, before continuing his drive toward the best hotel, with its music and its palms. She thought: "I'll speak to her. She has a pretty figure.' For after all one could not live always with a low voice like music, with a tall figure like a palm. Faithfulness was not the same as remembrance; one could forget and be faithful and one could remember and be faithless.

She loved Janet Pardoe, she would always love Janet Pardoe, she protested inwardly; Janet had been a reve-

lation to her of what love could mean ever since the
first evening of their meeting in a cinema in Kaiser
Wilhelmstrasse, and yet, and yet . . . They had come
together in a mutual disgust of the chief actor; at least
Mabel Warren had said aloud in English to relieve her
feelings in the strained hush of the dark theatre, 'I
can't bear these oiled men,' and had heard a low
musical agreement. Yet even then Janet Pardoe had
wished to stay till the end, till the last embrace, the final
veiled leachery. Mabel Warren urged her to come and
have a drink, but Janet Pardoe said that she wanted to
see the news and they both stayed. That first evening
seemed now to have revealed all of Janet's character
that there was to reveal, the inevitable agreement which
made no difference to what she did. Sharp words or
disagreements had never ruffled her expressionless
mood until the evening before, when she had thought
herself rid of Mabel Warren. Miss Warren said viciously, not troubling to lower her voice at all, 'I don't
like Jews,' and Janet Pardoe, turning her large luminous eyes back to Mabel Warren's, agreed, 'Nor do I,
darling.'

Mabel Warren implored her with sudden desperation, 'Janet, when I've gone, you'll remember our love
for each other? You wouldn't let a man touch you?'
She would have welcomed dissent, the opporounity to
argue, to give reasons, to fix some kind of seal upon
that fluid mind, but again all she got was an absent-
minded agreement. 'But of course not, darling. How
could I?' If she had faced a mirror she would have received more sense of an alien mind from the image
there, but not, Miss Warren thought, the satisfaction
of something beautiful. It was no good thinking of herself, her coarse hair, red lids, and obstinately masculine
and discordant voice; there was no one, even the young

Jew, who was not her physical rival. When she was gone, Janet Pardoe would remain for a little while a beautiful vacancy, hardly existing at all, save for the need of sleep, the need of food, the need of admiration. But soon she would be sitting back crumbling toast, saying, 'But of course I agree. I've always felt that.' The cup shook in Mabel Warren's hand, and the coffee trickled over the brim and drops fell to her skirt, already stained with grease and beer. What does it matter, she asked herself, what Janet does so long as I don't know? What does it matter to me if she lets a man take her to bed as long as she comes back? But the last qualification made her wince with mental pain, for would Janet, she wondered, ever return to an ageing plain infatuated woman? She'll tell him about me, Mabel Warren thought, of the two years she had lived with me, of the times when we have been happy, of the scenes I've made, even of the poems I've written her, and he'll laugh and she'll laugh and they'll go to bed laughing. I had better make up my mind that this is the end, that she will never come back from this holiday. I don't even know whether it's really her uncle she's visiting. There are as many fish in the sea as ever came out of it, Miss Warren thought, crumbling a roll, desperately aware of her uncared-for hands, the girl with the Jew, for instance. She was as poor as Janet was that evening in the cinema; she was not lovely as Janet was, so that it was happiness to sit for an hour and watch every motion of Janet's body, Janet doing her hair, Janet changing her dress, Janet pulling on her stockings, Janet mixing a drink, but she probably had twice the mind, common and shrewd though it might be.

'Darling,' Janet Pardoe asked with amusement, 'are you getting a pash for that little thing?' The train rocked and roared into a tunnel and out again, eliminating Mabel Warren's answer, taking it, as an angry hand might take a letter, tearing it across and scattering the pieces, only one phrase falling face upwards and in view: 'For ever,' so that no one but Mabel Warren could have said what her protest had been, whether she had sworn to remember always or had declared that one could not be faithful for ever to one person. When the train came out again into the sunlight, coffee-pots glimmering and white linen laid between an open pasture, where a few cows grazed, and a deep wood of firs, Miss Warren had forgotten what she had wished to say, for she recognised in a man who entered the restaurant-car Czinner's companion. At the same moment the girl rose. She and the young man had spoken so seldom Miss Warren could not decide whether they were acquainted; she hoped that they were strange to each other, for she was forming a plan which would not only give her speech with the girl but would help her to nail Czinner once and for all to the bill page of the paper, an exclusive crucifixion.

'Good-bye,' the girl said. Mabel Warren, watching them with the trained observer's eye, noted the Jew's raised shoulder, as of the ashamed habitual thief who leaning forward from the dock protests softly, more from habit than any real sense of injustice, that he has not had a fair trial. The casual observer might have read in their faces the result of a lover's quarrel; Mabel Warren knew better. 'I'll see you again?' the man asked, and she replied, 'If you want me, you'll know where to find me.'

Mabel Warren said to Janet, 'I'll see you later. There are things I must do,' and she followed the girl out of the car over the rocking bridge between the coaches, stumbling and grasping for support, but with the ache in her head quite gone in the warmth and illumination of her idea. For when she said there were things to do, 'things' meant nothing vague, but a throned triumphant concept for which her brain was the lit hall and a murmuring and approving multitude. Everything fitted, that she felt above all things, and she began to calculate what space they were likely to allow her in London; she had never led the paper before. There was the Disarmament Conference and the arrest of a peer for embezzlement and a baronet had married a Ziegfeld girl. None of these stories was exclusive; she had read them on the News Agency tape, before she went to the station. They will put the Disarmament Conference and the Ziegfeld girl on the back page, she thought. There's no doubt, short of a European war or the King's death, that my story will lead the paper, and with her eyes on the girl in front, she considered the image of Dr Czinner, tired and shabby and old-fashioned in the high collar and the little tight tie, sitting in the corner of his compartment with his hands gripped on his knee, while she told him a lot of lies about Belgrade. 'Dr Czinner Alive,' she thought, working at the headlines, but that would not do at the top, for five years had passed and not many people would remember his name. 'Mystery Man's Return. How Dr Czinner Escaped Death. Exclusive Story.'

'My dear,' she gasped, holding to the rail, apparently daunted by the second bridge, the shaking metal and the sound of the linked coaches straining. Her voice did not carry, and she had to repeat her exclamation in a shout, which fitted ill with the part she was assuming—an elderly woman struggling for breath. The girl turned and came back to her, her unschooled face white and miserable, with nothing hidden from any stranger. 'What's the matter? Are you ill?'

Miss Warren did not move, thinking intensely on the other side of the overlapping plates of steel. 'Oh, my dear, how glad I am that you are English. I feel so sick. I can't cross. I'm a silly old thing, I know.' Bitterly but of necessity she played upon her age. 'If you would give me your hand.' She thought: for this game I ought to have long hair, it would be more womanly. I wish my fingers weren't yellow. Thank God I don't still smell of drink. The girl came back. 'Of course. You needn't be afraid. Take my arm,' Miss Warren gripped it with strong fingers as she might have gripped the neck of a fighting dog.

When they reached the next corridor she spoke again. The noise of the train was softened, and she was able to subdue her voice to a husky whisper. 'If only there was a doctor on the train, my dear. I feel so ill.'

'But there is one. His name's Dr John. I came over faint last night and he helped me. Let me find him.'

'I'm so frightened of doctors, dear,' said Miss Warren with a glint of triumph; it was extraordinarily lucky that the girl knew Czinner. 'Talk to me a little first till I'm calmer. What's your name, my dear?'

'Coral Musker.'

'You must call me Mabel, Mabel Warren. I have a niece just like you. I work on a newspaper at Cologne. You must come and see me one day. The darlingest little flat. Are you on a holiday?'

'I dance. I'm off to Constantinople. A girl's ill in an English show there.' For a moment with the girl's hand in hers Mabel Warren felt flustered with a longing to be generous in an absurd obvious way. Why not give up the hope of keeping Janet Pardoe and invite the girl to break her contract and take Janet's place as her paid companion? 'You are so pretty,' she said aloud.

'Pretty,' said Coral Musker. No smile softened her incredulity. 'You're pulling my leg.'

'My dear, you are so kind and good.'

'You bet I am.' She spoke with a touch of vulgarity that spoiled for a moment Mabel Warren's vision. Coral Musker said with longing, 'Leave out the goodness. Say that again about my being pretty.' Mabel Warren acquiesced with complete conviction, 'My dear, you are lovely.' The astonished avidity with which the girl watched her was touching; the word 'virginity' passed through the urban darkness of Mabel Warren's mind. 'Has no one said that to you?' Eager and unbelieving Mabel Warren implored her: 'Not your young friend in the restaurant-car?'

'I hardly know him.'

'I think you are wise, my dear. Jews are not to be trusted.'

Coral Musker said slowly, 'Do you think he thought that? That I didn't like him because he was a Jew?'

'They are used to it, dear.'

'Then I shall go and tell him that I like him, that I've always liked Jews.' Mabel Warren began to swear with a bitter obscene venom beneath her breath.

'What did you say?'

'You won't leave me like this until you've found the doctor? Look. My compartment's at the end of the corridor with my niece. I'll go there if you'll fetch him.' She watched Coral Musker out of sight and slipped into the lavatory. The train came to a sharp halt and then began to move backwards. Miss Warren recognized through the window the spires of Würzburg, the bridge over the Main; the train was shedding its third-class coaches, shunting backwards and forwards between the signal boxes and the sidings. Miss Warren left the door a little open, so that she could see the corridor. When

Coral Musker and Dr Czinner appeared she closed the door and waited for the sound of their footsteps to pass. They had quite a long walk to the end of the corridor; now, if she hurried, she would have time enough. She slipped out. Before she could close the door the train started with a lurch and the door slammed, but neither Coral Musker nor Dr Czinner looked back.

She ran awkwardly, flung from one side to the other of the corridor by the motion of the train, bruising a wrist and a knee. Passengers returning from breakfast flattened themselves against the windows to let her by, and some of them complained of her in German, knowing her to be English, and imagining that she could not understand them. She grinned at them maliciously, uncovering her great front teeth, and ran on. The right compartment was easy to find, for she recognised the mackintosh hanging in a corner, the soft stained hat. On the seat lay a morning paper that Czinner must have bought a minute or two before Würzburg station. In the brief pursuit of Coral Musker along the corridor she had thought out every move; the stranger who shared the compartment was at breakfast, Dr Czinner, seeking her at the other end of the train, would be away for at least three minutes. In that time she must learn enough to make him speak.

First there was the mackintosh. There was nothing in the pockets but a box of matches and a packet of Gold Flake. She picked up the hat and felt along the band and inside the lining; she had sometimes found quite valuable information concealed in hats, but the doctor's was empty. Now she reached the dangerous moments of her search, for the examination of a hat, even of the mackintosh pockets, could be disguised, but to drag the suitcase from the rack, to lever the lock open with her pocket-knife and lift the lid, laid her too obviously open to the charge of theft. And one blade of her knife broke while she still laboured at the lock. Her purpose was patent to anyone who passed the compartment, and she sweated a little on the forehead, growing frenzied in her haste. If I am found it means the sack, she thought: the cheapest rag in England could not stand for this; and if I'm sacked, I lose Janet, I lose the chance of Coral. But if I succeed, she thought, prying, pushing, scraping, there's nothing they won't do for me in return for such a story; another four pounds a week wouldn't be too much to demand. I'll be able to take a larger flat; when Janet knows of it, she'll return, she'll never leave me. It is happiness, security, she thought, I'll be getting in return for this, and the lock gave and the lid lifted and her fingers were on the secrets of Dr Czinner. A woollen stomach-belt was the first of them.

She lifted it with care and found his passport. It gave his name as Richard John and his profession as teaching. His age was fifty-six. That proves nothing, she thought, these shady foreign politicians know where to buy a passport. She put it back where she had found it and began to slip her fingers between his suits, half-way down in the centre of the suitcase, the spot the customs officers always miss when they turn up the contents of a bag at the bottom and at the sides. She hoped to find a pamphlet or a letter, but there was only an old Baedeker published in 1914: *Konstantinopel und Kleinasien, Balkanstaaten, Archipel, Cypern,* slipped inside a pair of trousers. But Mabel Warren was thorough: she calculated that she had about one minute of safety left, and as there was nothing else to examine she opened the Baedeker, for it was curious to find it so carefully packed away. She looked at the fly-leaf and read with disappointment the name of

Richard John written in a small fussy hand with a scratching nib, but under it was an address, The School House, Great Birchington-on-Sea, which was worth remembering; the *Clarion* could send a man down to interview the headmaster. A good story might be hidden there.

The guide-book seemed to have been bought second-hand, the cover was very worn and there was the label of a bookseller in Charing Cross Road on the fly-leaf. She turned to Belgrade. There was a one-page map, which had worked loose, but it was unmarked; she examined every page dealing with Belgrade and then every page dealing with Serbia, every page on any of the states which were now part of Yugo-Slavia. There was not so much as a smudge of ink. She would have given up the search if it were not for the position in which she had found the book. Obstinately and against the evidence of her eyes she believed that it had been hidden there and that therefore there must be something to hide. She skimmed the pages against her thumb, they ran unevenly because of the many folded maps, but on one of the early pages she found some lines and circles and triangles drawn in ink over the text. But the text dealt only with an obscure town in Asia Minor and the drawings might have been a child's scribble with ruler and compasses. Certainly, if the lines belonged to a code only an expert could decipher them. He's defeated me, she thought, with hatred, smoothing the surface of the suitcase, there's nothing here; but she felt unwilling to put back the Baedeker. He had hidden it, there must be something to find. She had risked so much already that it was easy to risk a little more. She closed the suitcase and put it back on the rack, but the Baedeker she slipped down her shirt and so under her armpit, where she could hold it with one arm pressed to her side.

But it was no use going back to her own seat, for she would meet Dr Czinner returning. It was then that she remembered Mr Quin Savory, whom she had come to the station to interview. His face was well known to her from photographs in the *Tatler,* cartoons in the *New Yorker,* pencil drawings in the *Mercury.* She looked cautiously down the corridor, her eyes blinking a little in a short-sighted manner, and then walked rapidly away. Mr Quin Savory was not to be found in the first-class carriages, but she ran him to earth in a second-class sleeper. With his chin buried in his overcoat, one hand round the bowl of a pipe, he watched with small glittering eyes the people who passed in the corridor. A clergyman dozed in the opposite corner.

Miss Warren opened the door and stepped inside. Her manner was masterful; she sat down without waiting for an invitation. She felt that she was offering this man something he wanted, publicity, and she was gaining nothing commensurate in return. There was no need to speak softly to him, to lure him into disclosures, as she had tried to lure Dr Czinner; she could insult him with impunity, for the Press had power to sell his books. 'You Mr Quin Savory?' she asked, and saw out of the corner of her eye how the clergyman's attitude changed to one of respectful attention; poor mutt, she thought, to be impressed by a 100,000 sale, we sell two million, twenty times as many people will have heard of Dr Czinner tomorrow. 'I represent the *Clarion.* Want an interview.'

'I'm a bit taken aback,' said Mr Savory, raising his chin, pulling at his overcoat.

'No need to be nervous,' said Miss Warren mechanically. She fetched her notebook from her bag and flipped it open. 'Just a few words for the English public. Travelling incognito?'

'Oh, no, no,' Mr Savory protested. 'I'm not royalty.'

Miss Warren began to write. 'Where are you going?'

'Why, first of all,' said Mr Savory brightly, as if pleased by Miss Warren's interest, which had already returned to the Baedeker and the scrawl of geometrical figures, 'to Constantinople. Then I may go to Ankara, the Far East. Baghdad. China.'

'Writing a travel book?'

'Oh, no, no, no. My public wants a novel. It'll be called *Going Abroad*. An adventure of the Cockney spirit. These countries, civilisations,' he made a circle in the air with his hand, 'Germany, Turkey, Arabia, they'll all take second pew to the chief character, a London tobacconist. D'you see?'

'Quite,' said Miss Warren, writing rapidly. ' "Dr Richard Czinner, one of the greatest revolutionary figures of the immediate post-war period, is on his way home to Belgrade. For five years the world has thought him dead, but during that time he has been living as a schoolmaster in England, biding his time." ' But for what? Miss Warren wondered. 'Your opinion of modern literature?' she asked. 'Joyce, Lawrence, all that?'

'It will pass,' Mr Savory said promptly with the effect of an epigram.

'You believe in Shakespeare, Chaucer, Charles Reade, that sort of thing?'

'They will live,' Mr Savory declared with a touch of solemnity.

'Bohemianism? You don't believe in that? Fitzroy Tavern?' ('A warrant for his arrest has been issued,' she wrote, 'but it could not be served till the trial was over. When the trial was over Dr Czinner had disappeared. Every station had been watched by the police, every car stopped. It was little wonder that the rumour of his murder by government agents spread rapidly.') 'You don't believe it's necessary to dress oddly, big black hat, velvet jacket and what not?'

'I think it's fatal,' Mr Savory said. He was now quite at his ease and watched the clergyman covertly while he talked. 'I'm not a poet. A poet's an individualist. He can dress as he likes; he depends only on himself. A novelist depends on other men; he's an average man with the power of expression. 'E's a spy,' Mr Savory added with confusing drama, dropping aitches right and left. ' 'E 'as to see everything and pass unnoticed. If people recognized 'im they wouldn't talk, they'd pose before 'im; 'e wouldn't find things out.' Miss Warren's pencil raced. Now that she had got him started, she could think quickly: no need to press him with questions. Her pencil made meaningless symbols, which looked sufficiently like shorthand to convince Mr Savory that his remarks were being taken down in full, but behind the deceiving screen of squiggles and lines, circles and squares, Miss Warren thought. She thought of every possible aspect of the Baedeker. It had been published in 1914, but was in excellent condition; it had never been much used, except for the section dealing with Belgrade; the map of the city had been so often handled that it was loose.

'You do follow these views?' Mr Savory asked anxiously. 'They're important. They seem to me the touchstone of lit'ry integrity. One can 'ave that, you know, and yet sell one hundred thousand copies.' Miss Warren, annoyed at the interruption, only just prevented herself retorting, 'Do you think we should sell two million copies if we told the truth?' 'Very interesting,' she said. 'The public will be interested. Now what do you consider your contribution to English literature?' She grinned at him encouragingly and poised her pencil.

'Surely that's for somebody else to state,' said Mr Savory. 'But one 'opes, one 'opes, that it's something of this sort, to bring back cheerfulness and 'ealth to modern fiction. There's been too much of this introspection, too much gloom. After all, the world is a fine adventurous place.' The bony hand which held the pipe beat helplessly against his knee. 'To bring back the spirit of Chaucer,' he said. A woman passed along the corridor, and for a moment all Mr Savory's attention was visibly caught up to sail in her wake, bobbing, bobbing, bobbing, like his hand. 'Chaucer,' he said, 'Chaucer,' and suddenly, before Miss Warren's eyes he gave up the struggle, his pipe fell to the floor, and stooping to find it, he exclaimed irritably, 'Damn it all. Damn.' He was a man overworked, harassed by a personality which was not his own, by curiosities and lusts, a man on the edge of a nervous breakdown. Miss Warren gloated over him. It was not that she hated him, but that she hated any overpowering success, whether it meant the sale of a hundred thousand copies or the attainment of three hundred miles an hour, which made her an interviewer and a man the condescending interviewed. Failure of the same overwhelming kind was another matter, for then she was the avenging world, penetrating into prison cells, into hotel lounges, into mean back parlours. Then with a man at her mercy between the potted palms and the piano, when he was backed against the wedding photograph and the marble clock, she could almost love her victim, asking him little intimate questions, hardly listening to the answers. Well, not so great a gulf lay, she thought with satisfaction, between Mr Quin Savory, author of *The Great Gay Round,* and such a failure.

She harped on his phrase. 'Health,' she said. 'That's your mission? None of this "adults only" stuff. They give you as school prizes.'

Her irony had been a little too obvious. 'I'm proud of it,' he said. 'The younger generation's being brought up on 'ealthy traditions.' She noticed his dry lips, the squint towards the corridor. I'll put that in about healthy traditions, she thought, the public will like it, James Douglas will like it, and they will like it still better when he's a Hyde Park case, for that's what he'll be in a few years. I'll be alive to remind them. She was proud of her power of prophecy, though she had not yet lived to see any of her prophecies fulfilled. Take an expression in the present, a line of ill-health, a tone of voice, a gesture, no more illuminating to the average unobservant person than the lines and circles in the Baedeker, and fit them to what one knew of the man's surroundings, his friends and furniture, the house he lived in, and one saw the future, his shabby waiting fate. 'My God!' said Miss Warren, 'I've got it.'

Mr Savory jumped. 'What have you got?' he asked. 'Toothache?'

'No, no,' said Miss Warren. She felt grateful to him for the illumination which now flooded her mind with light, leaving no dark corners left in which Dr Czinner might hide from her. 'Such an excellent interview, I meant. I see the way to present you.'

'Do I see a proof?'

'Ah, we are not a weekly paper. Our public can't wait. Hungry, you know, for its lion's steak. No time for proofs. People in London will be reading the interview while they eat their breakfast tomorrow.' She left him with this assurance of the public interest, when she would far rather have sown in his overworked mind, grappling already with the problem of another half million popular words, the suggestion of how people forget, how they buy one day what they laugh at the next. But she could not afford the time; bigger game called, for she believed that she had guessed the secret of the Baedeker. It had been the consideration of her own prophecies which had given her the clue. The map was loose, the paper in a Baedeker she remembered was thin and insufficiently opaque; if one fitted the map against the pen drawings on the earlier page, the lines would show through.

My God, she thought, it's not everyone who would think of that. It deserves a drink. I'll find an empty compartment and call the steward. She did not even want Janet Pardoe to share this triumph; she would rather be alone with a glass of Courvoisier where she could think undisturbed and plan her next move. But when she had found the empty compartment she still acted with circumspection; she did not pull the Baedeker from under her shirt until the steward had fetched her the brandy. And not at once even then. She held the glass to her nostrils, allowing the fumes to reach that point at the back of her nose where brain and nose seemed one. The spirit she had drunk the night before was not all dissipated. It stirred like ground vapour on a wet hot day. Swimmy, she thought, I feel quite swimmy. Through the glass and the brandy she saw the outer world, so flat and regular that it never seemed to alter, neat fields and trees and small farms. Her eyes, short-sighted and flushed already with the mere fume of the brandy, could not catch the changing details, but she noticed the sky, grey and cloudless, and the pale sun. I shouldn't be surprised at snow, she thought, and looked to see whether the heating wheel was fully turned. Then she took the Baedeker from under her shirt. It would not be long before the train reached Nuremberg, and she wanted everything settled before fresh passengers came on board.

She had guessed right, that at least was certain. When she held the map and the marked page to the light the lines ran along the course of streets, the circles enclosed public buildings: the post office, the railway station, the courts of justice, the prison. But what did it all mean? She had assumed that Dr Czinner was returning to make some kind of personal demonstration, perhaps to stand his trial for perjury. The map in that context had no meaning. She examined it again. The streets were not marked haphazardly, there was a pattern, a nest of squares balanced on another square and the balancing square was the slum quarter. The next square was made on one side by the railway station, on another by the post office, on a third by the courts of justice. Inside this the squares became rapidly smaller, until they enclosed only the prison.

A bank mounted steeply on either side of the train and the sunlight was shut off; sparks, red in the overcast sky, struck the windows like hail, and darkness swept the carriages as the long train roared into a tunnel. Revolution, she thought, it means nothing less, with the map still raised to catch the first light returning.

The roar diminished and light came suddenly back. Dr Czinner was standing in the doorway, a newspaper under his arm. He was wearing the mackintosh again, and she regarded with contempt the glasses, the grey hair and shabby moustache, the small tight tie. She laid down the map and grinned at him. 'Well?'

Dr Czinner came in and shut the door. He sat down opposite her without a sign of hostility. He knows I've got him fixed, she thought; he's going to be reasonable? He asked her suddenly, 'Would your paper approve?'

'Of course not,' she said. 'I'd be sacked tomorrow. But when they get my story, that'll be a different matter.' She added with calculated insolence, 'I reckon that you are worth four pounds a week to me.'

Dr Czinner said thoughtfully, without anger, 'I don't intend to tell you anything.' She waved her hand at him. 'You've told me a lot already. There's this.' She tapped the Baedeker. 'You were a foreign master at Great Birchington-on-Sea. We'll get the story from your headmaster.' His head dropped. 'And then,' she said, 'there's this map. And these scrawls. I've put two and two together.' She had expected some protests of fear or indignation, but he was still brooding over her first guess. His attitude puzzled her and for an anguished moment she wondered, Am I missing the best story? Is the best story not here at all, but at a south-coast school among the red-brick buildings and the pitch-pine desks and ink-stands and cracked bells and the smell of boys' clothes? The doubt made her less certain of herself and she spoke gently, more gently than she had intended, for it was difficult to modulate her husky voice. 'We'll get together,' she growled in a winning way. 'I'm not here to let you down. I don't want to interfere with you. Why, if you succeed, my story's all the more valuable. I'll promise not to release anything at all until you give the word.' She said plaintively, as if she were an artist accused of deprecating paint, 'I wouldn't spoil your revolution. Why, it'll be a grand story.'

Age was advancing rapidly on Dr Czinner. It was as if he had warded off with temporary success five years of pitch-pine smells and the whine of chalk on blackboards, only to sit now in a railway carriage and allow the baulked years to come upon him, together and not one by one. For the moment he was an old man nodding into sleep, his face as grey as the snow sky over Nuremberg. 'Now first,' said Miss Warren, 'what are your plans? I can see you depend a good deal on the slums.'

He shook his head. 'I depend on no one.'

'You are keeping absolute control?'

'Least of all myself."

Miss Warren struck her knee sharply. 'I want plain answers,' but she got the same reply, 'I shall tell you nothing.' He looks more like seventy than fifty-six, she thought; he's getting deaf, he doesn't understand what I've been saying. She was very forbearing; she felt certain that this was not success she faced, it resembled failure too closely, and failure she could love; she could be tender and soft-syllabled towards failure, wooing it with little whinnying words, as long as in the end it spoke. A weak man had sometimes gone away with the impression that Miss Warren was his best friend. She leant forward and tapped on Dr Czinner's knee, putting all the amiability of which she was capable into her grin. 'We are in this together, doctor. Don't you understand that? Why, we can even help you. Public opinion's just another name for the *Clarion*. I know you are afraid we'll be indiscreet, that we'll publish your story tomorrow and the government will be warned. But I tell you we won't breathe so much as a paragraph on the book page until you begin your show. Then I want to be able to put right across the middle page, "Dr Czinner's Own Story. Exclusive to the *Clarion*." Now, that's not unreasonable.'

'There's nothing I wish to say.'

Miss Warren withdrew her hand. Did the poor fool, she wondered, think that he would stand between her

and another four pounds a week, between her and
Janet Pardoe? He became, old and stupid and stubborn on the opposite seat, the image of all the men
who threatened her happiness, who were closing round
Janet with money and little toys and laughter at a
woman's devotion to a woman. But the image was in
her power; she could break the image. It was not a
useless act of mischief on Cromwell's part to shatter
statues. Some of the power of the Virgin lay in the
Virgin's statue, and when the head was off and a limb
gone and the seven swords broken, fewer candles were
lit and the prayers said at her altar were not so many.
One man like Dr Czinner ruined by a woman, and
fewer stupid girls like Coral Musker would believe all
strength and cunning to reside in a man. But she gave
him, because of his age, and because he reeked to her
nose of failure, one more chance. 'Nothing?'

'Nothing.'

She laughed at him angrily. 'You've said a mouthful
already.' He was unimpressed and she explained slowly
as if to a mental defective, 'We reach Vienna at eight-
forty tonight. By nine I shall be telephoning to the
Cologne office. They'll get my story through to London
by ten o'clock. The paper doesn't go to press for the
first London edition till eleven. Even if the message is
delayed, it's possible to alter the bill page for the last
edition up to three o'clock in the morning. My story
will be read at breakfast tomorrow. Every paper in
London will have a reporter round at the Yugo-Slavian
Ministry by nine o'clock in the morning. Before lunch
tomorrow the whole story will be known in Belgrade,
and the train's not due there till six in the evening. And
there won't be much left to the imagination either.
Think what I shall be able to say. Dr Richard Czinner,
the famous Socialist agitator, who disappeared from

Belgrade five years ago at the time of the Kamnetz trial, is on his way home. He joined the Orient express at Ostend on Monday and his train is due at Belgrade this evening. It is believed that his arrival will coincide with a Socialist outbreak based on the slum quarters, where Doctor Czinner's name has never been forgotten, and an attempt will probably be made to seize the station, the post office and the prison.' Miss Warren paused. 'That's the story I shall telegraph. But if you'll say more I'll tell them to hold until you give the word. I'm offering you a straightforward bargain.'

'I tell you that I am leaving the train at Vienna.'

'I don't believe you.'

Dr Czinner sucked in his breath, staring through the window at the grey luminous sky, a group of factory chimneys, and a great black metal drum. The compartment filled with the smell of gas. Cabbages were growing in the allotments through the bad air, gross bouquets sprinkled with frost. He said so softly that she had to lean forward to catch the words, 'I have no reason to fear you.' He was subdued, he was certain, and his calmness touched her nerves. She protested uneasily and with anger, as if the criminal in the dock, the weeping man beside the potted fern, had been endowed suddenly with a mysterious reserve of strength, 'I can play hell with you.'

Dr Czinner said slowly, 'There's going to be snow.' The train was creeping into Nuremberg, and the great engines that ranged themselves on either side reflected the wet steel aspect of the sky. 'No,' he said, 'there's nothing you can do which will harm me.' She tapped the Baedeker and he remarked with a flash of humour: 'Keep it as a souvenir of our meeting.' She was certain then that her fear was justified; he was escaping her, and she stared at him with rage. If I could do him an injury, she thought, watching in the mirror behind him success, in the likeness of Janet Pardoe, wandering away, lovely and undeserving and vacant, down long streets and through the lounges of expensive hotels, if I could do him an injury.

It angered her the more to find herself speechless and Dr Czinner in control. He handed her the paper and asked her, 'Do you read German? Then read this.' All the while that the train stood in Nuremberg station, a long twenty minutes, she stared at it. The message it contained infuriated her. She had been prepared for news of some extraordinary success, of a king's abdication, a government's overthrow, a popular demand for Doctor Czinner's return, which would have raised him into the position of the condescending interviewed. What she read was more extraordinary, a failure which put him completely out of her power. She had been many times bullied by the successful, never before by one who had failed.

'Communist outbreak in Belgrade,' she read. 'An attempt was made late last night by a band of armed Communist agitators to seize the station and the prison at Belgrade. The police were taken by surprise and for nearly three hours the revolutionaries were in undisturbed possession of the general post office and the goods-yards. All telegraphic communication with Belgrade was interrupted until early this morning. At two o'clock, however, our representative at Vienna spoke to Colonel Hartep, the Chief of Police, by telephone and learned that order had been restored. The revolutionaries were few in number and lacked a proper leader; their attack on the prison was repulsed by the warders, and for some hours afterwards they stayed inactive in the post office, apparently in the hope that the inhabitants of the poorer quarters of the capital would come to their help. Meanwhile the government was able to muster police reinforcements, and with the help of a platoon of soldiers and a couple of field-guns, the police recaptured the post office after a siege lasting little more than three-quarters of an hour.' This summary was printed in large type; underneath in small type was a more detailed account of the outbreak. Miss Warren sat and stared at it; she frowned a little and was conscious of the dryness of her mouth. Her brain felt clear and empty. Dr Czinner explained, 'They were three days too early.'

Miss Warren snapped at him, 'What more could you have done?'

'The people would have followed me.'

'They've forgotten you. Five years is the hell of a time. The young men were children when you ran away.'

Five years, she thought, seeing them fall on her inevitably through future days, like the endless rain of a wet winter, watching in mind Janet Pardoe's face as it worried over the first wrinkle, the first greyness, or else the smooth tight lifted skin and dark dyed hair every three weeks whitening at the roots.

'What are you going to do now?' she asked, and the promptitude and plainness of his answer, 'I've told you. I'm getting out at Vienna,' filled her with suspicion. 'That's nice,' she said, 'we'll be together. We can talk. You'll have no objection to an interview now. If you are short of money, our Vienna office will advance you some.' She was aware that he was watching her more closely then ever before. 'Yes,' he said slowly, 'perhaps we can talk,' and she was certain this time that he was lying. He's going to double, she thought, but it was difficult to see his motive. He had no choice but to get out at Vienna or at Buda-Pesth;

it would be unsafe to travel farther. Then she remembered him at the Kamnetz trial, fully aware that no jury would convict and yet giving his dangerous useless evidence while Hartep waited with the warrant. He's fool enough to do anything, she thought, and wondered for a moment whether, behind the quietness, he was already standing in the dock with his companions, uttering his defence with an eye to the packed gallery. If he goes on, she thought, I'll go, I'll stick to him, I'll have his story, but she felt curiously weak and undecided, for she had no threat left. He was beaten, leaning back in his corner old and hopeless, with the newspaper gathering dust on the floor between them, and he was triumphant, watching her leave the carriage, the Baedeker forgotten on the seat, with nothing but silence for her exclamation: 'I'll see you again at Vienna.'

When Miss Warren had gone, Dr Czinner stooped for the paper. His sleeve caught an empty glass and it fell and shattered on the floor. His hand rested on the paper and he stared at the glass, unable to concentrate his thought, unable to decide what it was he had to do, pick up the paper or gather the dangerous sharp scraps. Presently he laid the paper carefully folded across his knees and closed his eyes. He was haunted in his personal darkness by the details of the story that Miss Warren had read; he knew every turn in the stairs in the post office, he could see the exact spot where the barricade had been built. The muddling fools, he thought, and tried to feel hate for the men who had destroyed his hopes. They had ruined him with them. They had left him in an empty house which could not find a tenant because old ghosts were sometimes vocal in the rooms, and Dr Czinner himself now was not even the latest ghost.

If a face peered from a window or a voice was heard

upstairs or a carpet whispered, it might have been Dr Czinner seeking to return to a sentient life after five years of burial, working his way round the corners of desks, exposing his transparency before the blackboard and the insubordinate children, crouched in chapel at a service in which the living man had never believed, asking God with the breathing discordant multitude to dismiss him with His blessing.

And sometimes it seemed as if a ghost might return to life, for he had learned that as a ghost he could suffer pain. The ghost had memories; it could remember the Doctor Czinner who had been so loved that it was worth while for a hired murderer to fire a revolver at his head. That was the proudest memory of all, of how Dr Czinner sat in the beer-house at the poor corner of the park and heard the shot shatter the mirror behind him and knew it for the final proof of how dearly the poor loved him. But the ghost of Czinner, huddled in a shelter while the east wind swept the front and the grey sea tossed the pebbles, had learned to weep at the memory before returning to the red-brick building and tea and to the children who fashioned subtle barbs of pain. But after the final service and the customary hymns and handshakes the ghost of Czinner found itself again touching the body of Czinner; a touch was all the satisfaction it could get. Now there was nothing left but to leave the train at Vienna and return. In ten days the voices would be singing: 'Lord receive us with Thy blessing, Once again assembled here.'

Dr Czinner turned a page of the paper and read a little. The nearest he could attain to hate of these muddled men was envy; he could not hate when he remembered details no newspaper correspondent thought it worth while to give, that the man who, after firing his last shot, was bayoneted outside the sorting-room had been left-handed and a lover of Delius's music, the melancholy idealistic music of a man without a faith in anything but death. And that another, who leapt from the third-floor window of the telephone exchange, had a wife scarred and blinded in a factory accident, whom he loved and to whom he was sadly and unwillingly faithless.

But what is left for me to do? Dr Czinner put down the paper and began to walk the compartment, three steps one way to the door, three steps the other way to the window, up and down. A few flakes of snow were falling, but the wind blew the smoke of the engine back across the window, and if the flakes touched the glass at all, they were already grey like scraps of paper. But six hundred feet up, on the hills which came down to the line at Neumarkt, the snow began to lie like beds of white flowers. If they had waited, if they had waited, thought Dr Czinner, and as his mind turned from the dead to the men who lived to be tried, the impossibility of his own easy escape presented itself with such force that he exclaimed in a whisper, 'I must go to them.' But what was the use? He sat down again and began to argue with himself that the gesture would have practical value. If I give myself up and stand my trial with them, the world will listen to my defence as it would never listen to me, safe in England. The strengthening of his resolution encouraged him; he grew more hopeful; the people he thought, will rise to save me, though they did not rise for the others. Again the ghost of Czinner felt close to life, and warmth touched its frozen transparency.

But there were many things to be considered. First he had to avoid the reporter. He must give her the slip at Vienna; it ought not to be difficult, for the train did not arrive till nearly nine, and by that hour of the even-

ing, surely, he thought, she will be drunk. He shivered a
little with the cold and the idea of any further contact
with that hoarse dangerous woman. Well, he thought,
picking up the Baedeker and letting the newspaper drop
to the floor, her sting is drawn. She seemed to hate me;
I wonder why; some strange pride of profession, I suppose. I may as well go back to my compartment. But
when he reached it, he walked on, hands behind back
and Baedeker under arm, absorbed by the idea that
the ghostly years were over. I am alive again, he
thought, because I am conscious of death as a future
possibility, almost a certainty, for they will hardly let
me escape again, even if I defend myself and others
with the tongue of an angel. Faces which were familiar
to him looked up as he passed, but they failed to
break his absorption. I am afraid, he told himself with
triumph, I am afraid.

[2]

'Not *the* Quin Savory?' asked Janet Pardoe.

'Well,' said Mr Savory, 'I don't know of another.'
'The Great Gay Whirl?'

'Round,' Mr Savory corrected her sharply. *'Great
Gay Round.'* He put his hand on her elbow and began
to propel her down the corridor. 'Time for a sherry.
Fancy your being related to the woman who's been
interviewing me. Daughter? Niece?'

'Well, not exactly related,' said Janet Pardoe. 'I'm
her companion.'

'Better not.' Mr Savory's fingers closed more firmly on her arm. 'Get another job. You are too young. It's not 'ealthy.'

'How right you are,' said Janet Pardoe, stopping for a moment in the corridor and turning to him eyes luminous with admiration.

Miss Warren was writing a letter, but she saw them go by. She had laid her writing-pad upon her knee, and her fountain-pen spluttered across the paper, splashing ink and biting deep holes. *Dear Cousin Con,* she wrote, *I'm writing to you because I've nothing better to do. This is the Orient Express, but I'm not going on to Constantinople. I'm getting out at Vienna. But that's another story. Could you get me five yards of ring velvet? Pink. I'm having my flat done up again, while Janet's away. She's on the same train, but I'm leaving her at Vienna. A job of work really, chasing a hateful old man half across Europe.* The Great Gay Round *is on board, but of course you don't read books. And a rather charming little dancer called Coral, whom I think I shall take as my companion. I can't make up my mind whether to have my flat redecorated. Janet says she'll only be away a week. You mustn't on any account pay more than eight-and-eleven a yard. Blue, I think, would suit me, but of course, not navy. This man I was telling you about,* wrote Miss Warren, following Janet Pardoe with her eyes, digging the pen into the paper, *thinks himself too clever for me, but you know as well as I do, don't you, Con, that I can play hell with anyone who thinks that. Janet is a bitch. I'm thinking of getting a new companion. There's a little actress on this train who would suit me. You should see her, the loveliest figure, Con. You'd admire her as much as I do. Not very pretty, but with lovely legs. I really think I must get my flat done up. Which reminds me. You can go up to ten-and-eleven with that ring velvet. I may be going to Belgrade, so wait till you hear from me again. Janet seems to be getting a pash for this Savory man. But I can play hell with him too if I want to. Good-bye. Look after yourself. Give my love to Elsie. I hope she looks after you better than Janet does me. You've always been luckier, but wait till you see Coral. For God's sake don't forget that ring velvet. Much love. Mabel. P.S. Did you hear that Uncle John died suddenly the other day almost on my doorstep?*

Miss Warren's pen ended the letter in a large pool of ink. She enclosed it in a thick line and wrote *Sorry*. Then she wiped the pen on her skirt and rang the bell for a steward. Her mouth was terribly dry.

Coral Musker stood for a little while in the corridor, watching Myatt, wondering whether what Mabel Warren had suggested was true. He sat with head bent over a pile of papers, running a pencil up and down a row of figures, always returning it to the same numeral. Presently he laid down the pencil and put his head in his hands. Pity for a moment touched her, as well as gratitude. With the knowing eyes hidden he might have been a schoolboy, despairingly engaged on homework which would not come right. She could see that he had taken off his gloves the better to grip the pencil and his fingers were blue with cold; even the ostentation of his fur coat was pathetic to her, for it was hopelessly inadequate. It could not solve his sums or keep his fingers warm.

Coral opened the door and came in. He raised his face and smiled, but his work absorbed him. She wanted to take the work away from him and show him the solution and tell him not to let his master know that he had been helped. Who by? she wondered. Mother? Sister? Nothing so distant as a cousin, she thought, sitting down in the easy silence which was the measure of their familiarity.

Because she grew tired of watching through the window the gathering snow she spoke to him: 'You said that I could come in when I wanted to.'

'Of course.'

'I couldn't help feeling a beast,' she said, 'going away so suddenly and never thanking you properly. You were good to me last night.'

'I didn't like the idea of your staying in the compartment with that man when you were ill,' he said impatiently, tapping with his pencil. 'You needed proper sleep.'

'But why were you interested in me' She received the fatal inevitable answer: 'I seemed to know you quite well.' He would have gone back to his calculations if it had not been for the unhappy quality of her silence. She could see how he was worried and surprised and a little harassed; he thinks I want him to make love to me, she thought, and wondered, do I? Do I? It would complete the resemblance to other men she had known if he rumpled her hair a bit and pulled her dress open in getting his lips against her breast. I owe him that, she thought, and the accumulated experience of other women told her again that she owed him a good deal more. But how can I pay, she asked herself, if he doesn't press for payment? And the mere thought of performing that strange act when she was not drunk as she supposed some women were, or passionate, but only grateful, chilled her more than the falling snow. She was not even certain how one went about it, whether it would be necessary to spend a whole night with him, to undress completely in the cold carriage. But she began to comfort herself with the thought that he was like other men she had known and was satisfied with very little; the only difference was that he was more generous.

'Last night,' he said, watching her closely while he spoke, and his attitude of attention and his misunderstanding of her silence told her that after all they did not know everything of each other, 'last night I dreamed about you.' He laughed nervously. 'I dreamed that I picked you up and took you for a ride and presently you were going to . . .' He paused and evaded the issue. 'I felt excited by you.'

She became frightened, as if a moneylender were leaning across his desk and approaching very gently and inexorably to the subject of repayment. 'In your dream,' she said. But he took no notice of her. 'Then the guard came along and woke me up. The dream was very vivid. I was so excited that I bought your ticket.'

'You mean that you thought—that you wanted—'

The moneylender raised his shoulders, the moneylender sat back behind his desk, and the moneylender rang the bell for a servant to show her out to the street and strangers and the freedom of being unknown. 'I just told you this,' he said, 'so that you needn't feel you owe me anything. It was the effect of a dream, and when I'd bought the ticket, I thought you might as well use it,' and he picked up his pencil and turned back to his papers. He added formally, without thought, 'It was brash of me to think that for ten pounds—'

Those words did not at first reach her. She was too confused by her relief, even by the shame of being desirable only in a dream, above all by her gratitude. And then pursuing her out of the silence came the final words with their hint of humility—this was unfamiliar. She faced her terror of the bargain, putting out her hand and touching Myatt's face with a gratitude which had borrowed its gesture from an unknown love. 'If you want me to,' she said. 'I thought that you were bored with me. Shall I come tonight?' She laid her fingers across the papers on his knee, small square hands with powder lying thick in the hollow of the knuckles, nails reddened at the tip, hiding the rows of numerals, Mr Eckman's calculations and subterfuges and cunning concealments, offering herself with an engaging and pathetic dubiety. He said slowly, half his mind still following Mr Eckman in and out of hidden rooms, 'I thought that you disliked me'; he lifted her hands from his papers and said absentmindedly: 'Perhaps because I was Jewish.'

'You're tired.'

'There's something here I can't get straight.'

'Leave it,' she said, 'until tomorrow.'

'I haven't the time. I've got to get this done. We are not sitting still.' But in fact all sense of motion had been rapt from them by the snow. It fell so heavily that the telegraph-poles were hidden. She took her hands away and asked him with resentment, 'Then you don't want me to come?' The calmness and familiarity with which he met her proposal chilled her gratitude.

'Yes,' he said, 'come. Come tonight.' He touched her hands. 'Don't think me cold. It's because we seem to know each other so well.' He appealed to her, 'Be a little strange.'

But before she could gather her wits for a pretence, she had admitted to him, 'Yes, I feel that too,' so that there was nothing else to say, and they sat on in silence like old friends, thinking without excitement of the night before them. Her brief passion of gratitude was over, for now it seemed as unnecessary as it was unwanted. You were not grateful to an acquaintance of so long standing; you took favours and gave favours and talked a little of the weather, not indignant at a caress or embittered by an indifference; and if you saw him in the stalls, you smiled once or twice as you danced, because something had to be done with your face which was a plain one, and a man liked to be recognised from the stage.

'The snow's getting worse.'

'Yes. It'll be cold tonight.' And you smiled in case a joke was intended and said as enticingly as possible to so old a friend, 'We'll be warm,' unable to forget that night was coming, remembering all that friends had said and advised and warned, puzzled and repelled that a man should feel indifference and lust at the same time. All that morning and all through lunch the snow continued to fall, lying deep at Passau on the roof of the customs-shed, melted on the line by the steam from the engine into grey icy streams, and the Austrian officials picked their way in gum-boots and swore a little, searching the luggage perfunctorily.

PART THREE
Vienna

[1]

Josef Grünlich moved to the sheltered side of the chimney, while the snow piled itself all round him on the roof. Below the central station burned like a bonfire in the dark. A whistle screamed and a long line of lights came into view, moving slowly; he looked at his watch as a clock struck nine. That's the Istanbul Express, he thought, twenty minutes late; it may have been held up by snow. He adjusted his flat silver watch and replaced it in his waistcoat pocket, smoothing the creases over the curve of his belly. Well, he considered, it is lucky to be fat on a night like this. Before buttoning his overcoat he ran his hands between pants and trousers and adjusted the revolver which hung between his legs by a piece of string twisted around a button. Trust Josef for three things, he reminded himself comfortably, for a woman, a meal and a fat crib. He emerged from the shelter of the chimney.

It was very slippery on the roof and there was some danger. The snow beat against his eyes and caked into ice on the heels of his shoes. Once he slipped and saw for a moment rising like a fish through dark water to meet him the lit awning of a café. He whispered, 'Hail Mary, full of grace,' digging his heels into the snow, clutching with his fingers. Saved by the rim of a gutter, he rose to his feet and laughed softly; it was no good being angry with nature. A little later he found the iron arms of the fire-escape.

The climb that followed he considered the most dangerous part of the whole business, for although the escape ran down the back of the flats, out of sight of the street, it faced the goods-yard, and the yard was the limit of a policeman's beat. He appeared every three minutes, the dim lamp at the corner of a shed gleaming on his black polished gaiters, his leather belt, his pistol holster. The deep snow quietened the sound of feet, and Josef could expect no warning of his approach, but the ticking of his watch kept him in mind of danger. He waited at the head of the ladder, crouched low, uneasily conscious of his white background, until the policeman had come and gone again. Then he began his climb. He had only to pass one unoccupied storey, but as he reached the top window a light flashed on him and a whistle blew. I can't be caught, he thought incredulously, I've never been caught, it doesn't happen to me, and waited with his back to the yard for a word or a bullet, while his brain began to move like the little well-oiled wheels of a watch, one thought fitting into another and setting a third in motion. When nothing happened he turned his face from the ladder and the blank wall; the yard was empty, the light glowed from a lamp someone had carried into the loft of the goods-shed, and the whistle had been one of the many noises of the station. His mistake had wasted precious seconds, and he continued his descent with a reckless disregard of his icy shoes, two steps at a time.

When he came to the next window he tapped. There was no reply, and he murmured a mild imprecation, keeping his head turned to the corner of the yard where the policeman would very soon appear. He tapped again and this time heard the shuffle of loose slippers. The lock of the window was lifted, and a woman's voice said, 'Anton. Is that you?' 'Yes,' said Josef, 'this is Anton. Let me in quickly.' The curtain was drawn back and a thin hand pulled and pulled at the top pane. 'The bottom,' Josef whispered, 'not the top. You think me an acrobat.' When the window was raised he showed great agility for a man so fat in stepping from the escape to the sill, but he found it difficult to squeeze into the room. 'Can't you raise it another inch?' An engine hooted three times and his brain automatically noted the meaning of the signal: a heavy goods train on the down line. Then he was in the room, the woman had closed the window and the noise of the station faded.

Josef brushed the snow off his coat and his moustache and looked at his watch; nine-five; the train to Passau would not leave for another forty minutes, and he had his ticket ready. With his back to the window and the woman he took in the room casually, but every detail marched to its ordered place in his memory, the ewer and basin on the liver-coloured washstand, the chipped gilt mirror, the iron bedstead, the chamber-pot, the holy picture. He said, 'Better leave the window open. In case your master returns.'

A thin shocked voice said, 'I couldn't. Oh, I couldn't.' He turned to her with amiable mockery, 'Modest Anna,' and watched her with sharp knowledgeable eyes. She shared his age, but not his experience, standing lean and flustered and excited by the window; her black skirt lay across the bed, but she still wore her black blouse, her white domestic collar, and she held a towel before her legs to hide them.

He regarded her quizzically, 'Pretty Anna.' Her mouth fell open and she stared back at him, silent and fascinated. Josef noted with distaste her uneven and discoloured teeth: whatever else I have to do, he thought, I will not kiss her, but it was evident that she expected an embrace; her modesty was transformed into a horrible middle-aged coquetry, to which he was forced to respond. He began to talk to her in baby language, sitting down on the edge of her bed, and keeping its width between them. 'What had the pretty Anna got now then? A great big man? Oh, how he will rumple you.' He wagged a finger at her playfully, 'You and I, Anna. We'll have a good time by and by. Eh?' He squinted sideways at the door and saw with relief that it was unlocked; it would have been just like the old bitch to have locked him in and hidden the key, but no reflection of his anxiety or his distaste ruffled the plump pink face. 'Eh?'

She smiled and let out a long whistling breath. 'Oh, Anton.' He jumped to his feet, and she dropped the towel and came towards him, with the thin tread of a bird, in her black cotton stockings. 'One moment,' he said, 'one moment,' raising his hand defensively, aghast at the antique lust he had aroused. Neither of us are beauties, he thought, and the presence of a pink-and-white Madonna gave the whole situation a kind of conscious blasphemy. He stopped her by his urgent whisper, 'Are you sure there's no one in the flat?' Her face reddened as if he had made a crude advance. 'No, Anton, we are quite alone.' His brain began to work again with precision; it was only personal relationships that confused him; when there was danger, or the need of action, his mind had the reliability of a tested machine. 'Have you the bag I gave you?'

'Yes, Anton, here under the bed.' She drew out a small black doctor's bag, and he chucked her under the chin and told her that she had pretty eyes. 'Get undressed,' he said, 'and into bed. I'll be with you again in a moment.' Before she could argue or ask him to explain, he had skipped gaily through the door on his toes and closed it behind him. Immediately he looked round for a chair and wedged it under the handle, so that the door could not be opened from inside.

He was familiar from a previous visit with the room he was in. It was a cross between an office and an old-fashioned drawing-room. There was a desk, a red velvet sofa, a swivel-chair, several occasional tables, a few large nineteenth-century engravings of children playing with dogs and ladies bending over garden walls. One wall was almost covered by a large roller map of the central station, with its platforms and goods-sheds, points and signal-boxes marked in primary colours. The shapes of furniture were dimly visible now in the half-dark, shadows falling like dust-sheets over the chairs from the street lights reflected on the ceiling and the glow of a reading-lamp on the desk. Josef struck his shin against an occasional table and nearly overturned a palm. He swore mildly, and

Anna's voice called out from the bedroom, 'What is it, Anton? What are you doing?'

'Nothing,' he said, 'nothing. I'll be with you in a moment. Your master's left a light on. Are you sure he won't be back?'

She began to cough, but between the paroxysms she let him know, 'He's on duty till midnight. Anton, you won't be long?' He made a grimace. 'Just taking off a few things, Anna darling.' Through the open window the sounds of the road beat up into the room; there was a constant blowing of horns. Josef leant out and examined the street. Taxis sped up and down with luggage and passengers, but he ignored them and the flicker of sky signs, and the clinking café immediately below, questing down the pavements; few people were passing, for it was the hour of dinner, theatre, or cinema. There was no policeman to be seen.

'Anton.'

He snapped, 'Be quiet,' and drew the blinds lest he should be seen from one of the buildings opposite. He knew exactly where the safe was built into the wall; only a meal, a cinema, and a few drinks had been required to get the information from Anna. But he had feared to ask her for the combination; she might have realised that her charm was insufficient to bring him in the dark across an icy roof to her bedroom. From a small book-case behind the desk he drew six heavy volumes of *Railway Working and Railway Management,* which hid a small steel door. Josef Grünlich's mind was now clear and concentrated; he moved without hurry or hesitation. Before he set to work he noted the time, nine-ten, and calculated that he need not leave for half an hour. Ample time, he thought, and pressed a wet thumb on the safe door, the steel is not half an inch thick. He laid the black bag on the desk and unpacked his tools. His chisels were in beautiful condition, highly polished, with a sharp edge; he took a pride in the neatness of his tools as well as in the speed of his work. He might have broken the thin steel with a jemmy, but Anna would hear the blows and he could not trust her to keep silent. He therefore lit his smallest blow-pipe, first putting on smoked glasses to shield his eyes from the glare. The details of the room started out of the shadows at the first fierce jab of flame, the heat scorched his face, and the steel door began to sizzle like melting butter.

'Anton.' The woman shook the handle of the bedroom door. 'Anton. What are you doing? Why have you shut me in?' Through the low roar of the flame, he cried to her, 'Be quiet.' He heard her feeling at the lock and twisting the handle. Then she spoke again urgently, 'Anton, let me out.' Every time he removed his lips from the pipe to answer her, the flame shrank. Trusting to her timorous stupidity, he addressed her ferociously, 'Be quiet, or I'll twist your neck.' For a moment there was silence, the flame waxed, the steel door turned from a red to a white heat, then Anna called quite loudly, 'I know what you are doing, Anton.' Josef pressed his lips to the pipe and paid her no attention, but Anna's next cry startled him: 'You are at the safe, Anton.' She began to rattle the handle again, until he was forced to let the flame sink and shout at her, 'Be quiet. I meant what I said. I'll twist your ugly neck for you, you old bitch.' Her voice sank, but he could hear her quite distinctly; her lips must have been pressed to the key-hole. 'Don't, don't say that, Anton. Listen. Let me out. I've got something to tell you, to warn you.' He did not answer her, blowing the flame and the steel back to a white heat. 'I lied to you, Anton. Let me out. Herr Kolber is coming back.' He lowered the pipe and sprang round. 'What's that? What do you mean?'

'I thought you wouldn't come if you knew. There would have been time to love each other. Half an hour. And if he came in earlier, we could have lain quiet.' Josef's brain worked quickly, he wasted no time in cursing the woman, but blew out the pipe and packed it back in his bag with the chisels and the jemmy and the skeleton-key and the pot of pepper. He surrendered without a second thought one of the easiest hauls of his career, but it was his pride that he took no avoidable risks. He had never been caught. Sometimes he had worked with partners and the partners had been caught, but they bore no malice. They recognised the extraordinary nature of Josef's record and went to prison with pride that he had escaped, and afterwards to their friends they would point him out: 'That's Josef. Five years now and never jugged.'

He closed his bag and jumped a little at a strange sound outside like the twanging of a bow. 'What's that?'

Anna whispered through the door, 'The lift. Someone has rung it down.' He picked up a volume of *Railway Management,* but the safe glowed red with heat and he put it back on the desk. From below came the clang of a gate closing, the high hum of the lift. Josef stepped towards the curtain and drew the string on which the revolver dangled a couple of inches higher. He wondered whether it would be possible to escape through the window, but he remembered that there was a straight drop of thirty feet to the awning of the café. Then the gates opened and closed. Anna whispered through the key-hole: 'The floor below.'

That's all right, then, Josef thought, I can take my time. Back into Anna bedroom and then over the roof.

I shall have to wait twenty minutes for the Passau train. The chair under the handle was tightly wedged. He had to put down his bag and use both hands. The chair slid along the hardwood floor and crashed over. At the same moment the light went on.

'Stay where you are,' said Herr Kolber, 'and put your hands up.'

Josef Grünlich obeyed at once. He turned round very slowly, and during those seconds formed his plan. 'I'm not armed,' he said gently, scanning Herr Kolber with mild reproachful eyes. Herr Kolber wore the blue uniform and the round peaked cap of an assistant stationmaster; he was small and thin with a brown crinkled face, and the hand holding the revolver shook a little with excitement and age and fury. For a moment Josef's mild eyes were narrowed and focused on the revolver, calculating the angle at which it would be fired, wondering whether the bullet would go astray. No, he thought, he will aim at my legs and hit my stomach. Herr Kolber had his back to the safe and could not yet have seen the disarranged books. 'You don't understand,' Josef said.

'What are you doing at that door?'

Josef's face was still red from the glow of the flame. 'Me and Anna,' he said.

Herr Kolber shouted at him, 'Speak up, you scoundrel.'

'Me and Anna are friends. I'm very sorry, Herr Superintendent, to be found like this. Anna invited me in.'

'Anna?' Herr Kolber said incredulously. 'Why?'

Josef's hips wriggled with embarrassment. 'Well, Herr Kolber, you see how it is. Me and Anna are friends.'

'Anna, come here.' The door opened slowly, and

Anna came out. She had put on her skirt and tidied her hair. 'It's true, Herr Kolber.' She gazed with horror past him at the exposed safe. 'What's the matter with you? What are you staring at now? This is a fine kettle of fish. A woman of your age.'

'Yes, Herr Kolber, but—' She hesitated and Josef interrupted her before she could defend herself, or accuse him. 'I'm very fond of Anna.' She accepted his words with a pitiable gratitude. 'Yes, he told me that.'

Herr Kolber stamped his foot. 'You were a fool, Anna. Turn out his pockets. He's probably stolen your money.' It still did not occur to him to examine his safe, and Josef played up to the part assigned to him of an inferior thief. He knew the type to the last bluster and the last whine. He had worked with them, employed them, and seen them depart to gaol without regret. Pickpennies, he called them, and he meant by the term that they were men without ambition or resource. 'I haven't stolen her money,' he whined. 'I wouldn't do such a thing. I'm fond of Anna.'

'Turn out his pockets.' Anna obeyed, but her hands moved in his clothes like a caress. 'Now his hip pocket.'

'I don't carry a gun,' Josef said.

'His hip pocket,' Herr Kolber repeated, and Anna turned out the lining. When he saw that that pocket too was empty, Herr Kolber lowered his revolver, but he still quivered with elderly rage. 'Making my flat a brothel,' he said. 'What have you got to say for yourself, Anna? This is a fine kettle of fish.'

Anna, with her eyes on the floor, twisted her thin hands. 'I don't know what came over me, Herr Kolber', but even while she spoke she seemed to learn. She looked up and Josef Grünlich saw in her eyes affection turn to distaste and distaste to anger. 'He tempted me,' she said slowly. All the while Josef was conscious of his black bag on the desk behind Herr Kolber's back, of the pile of books and the exposed safe, but uneasiness did not hamper thought. Sooner or later Herr Kolber would discover what had brought him to the flat, and already he had noticed close to the station-master's hand a bell which probably rang in the porter's flat.

'Can I put my hands down, Herr Superintendent?'

'Yes, but don't move an inch.' Herr Kolber stamped his foot. 'I'm going to have the truth of this if I keep you here all night. I won't have men coming here seducing my maid.' The word 'men' took Josef for a second off his guard; the idea of the middle-aged Anna as an object of pursuit amused him, and he smiled. Anna saw the smile and guessed the reason. She said to Herr Kolber, 'Be careful. He didn't want me. He—' but Josef Grünlich took the accusation out of her mouth. 'I'll confess. It was not Anna I came for. Look, Herr Kolber,' and he waved his left hand towards the safe. Herr Kolber turned with his revolver pointing to the floor, and Josef shot him twice in the small of the back.

Anna put her hand to her throat and began to scream, looking away from the body. Herr Kolber had fallen on his knees with his forehead touching the floor; he wriggled once between the shots, and then the whole body would have fallen sideways if it had not been propped in its position by the wall. 'Shut your mouth,' said Josef, and when the woman continued to scream, he took her by the throat and shook her. 'If you don't keep quiet for ten minutes, I'll put you underground too—see?' He saw that she had fainted and threw her into a chair; then he shut and locked the window and the bedroom door, for he was afraid that if she returned to the bedroom, her scream might be heard by the policeman when his beat took him to the goods-yard. The key he pushed down the lavatory pan with the handle of a scrubbing-brush. He made a last survey of the study; but he had already decided to leave the black bag on the desk; he always wore gloves, and the bag would bear only Anna's finger-prints. It was a pity to lose such a fine set of tools, but he was prepared to sacrifice anything which might endanger him, even he thought, looking at his watch, the ticket to Passau. The train would not leave for another quarter of an hour, and he could not linger in Vienna so long. He remembered the express he had seen from the roof, the express to Istanbul, and wondered: Can I make it without buying a ticket? He was unwilling to leave the trail of his features behind him, and it even crossed his mind to blind Anna with one of the chisels so that she might not be able to identify him. It was a passing thought; unnecessary violence was abhorrent to him, not because he disliked violence, but because he liked to be precise in his methods, omitting nothing which was necessary and adding nothing which was superfluous. Now with great care to avoid the blood he searched Herr Kolber's pockets for the study key, and when he had found it, he paused for a moment before a mirror to tidy his hair and brush his hat. Then he left the room, locking the door behind him and dropping the key into an umbrella-stand in the hall: he intended to do no more roof-climbing that night.

His only hesitation was when he saw the lift waiting with open door, but he decided almost at once to use the staircase, for the noise of the lift would blaze his trail past other flats. All the way down the stairs he listened for Anna's screams, but only silence followed him.

The snow was still falling outside, quietening the wheels of cars, the tread of feet; but the silence up the stairs seemed to fall faster and more thickly and to disguise the signs he had left behind, the pile of books, the black bag, the scorched safe. He had never before killed a man, but as long as silence lasted, he could forget that he had taken the final step which raised him to the dangerous peak of his profession.

A door on the first floor was open, and as he passed he heard a petulant woman's voice, 'Such drawers, I tell you. Well, I'm not the President's daughter, and I said to her, give me something respectable. Thin! You've never seen—'

Josef Grünlich twisted his thick grey moustache and stepped boldly out into the street, glancing this way, glancing that, as if he were expecting a friend. There was no policeman in sight, and as the pavements had been swept clear of snow, he left no prints. He turned smartly to the left towards the station, his ears pricked for the sound of screams, but he heard nothing but the hoot of taxi-cabs and the rustle of the snow. At the end of the street the great arch of the station enticed him like the lit façade of a variety theatre.

But it would be dangerous, he thought, to hang about the entrance like a seller of lottery tickets, and suddenly with the sense of dropping all the tenement's height, floor by floor, from Herr Kolber's flat, with the sense renewed of his own resource, the hand pointing to the safe, the quick pull on the string, and the revolver levelled and fired in one moment, pride filled him. I have killed a man. He let his overcoat flap open to the night breeze; he smoothed his waistcoat, fingered his silver chain; to an imaginary female friend he raised his soft grey hat, made by the best maker in Vienna, but a little too small for him, because it had been lifted from a lavatory peg. I, Josef Grünlich, have killed a man. I am clever, he thought, I'll be too much for them. Why should I hurry like a sneak thief to the station, slip inconspicuously through doorways, hide in the shadow of sheds? There's time for a cup of coffee, and he chose a table on the pavement, at the edge of the awning, which he had seen rise towards him when he slipped on the roof. He glanced upwards through the falling snow, one floor, two floors, three floors, and there was the lighted window of Herr Kolber's study; four floors, and the shadow of the building vanished in the grey loaded sky. It would have been an ugly fall.

'Der kaffee mit milch,' he said. He stirred the coffee thoughtfully, Josef Grünlich, the man of destiny. There was nothing else to be done, he didn't hesitate. A shadow of discontent passed across his features when he thought: But I can tell no one of this. It would be too dangerous. Even his best friend, Anton, whose Christian name he had used, must remain in ignorance, for there might be a reward offered for information. Nevertheless, sooner or later, he assured himself, they would guess, and they will point me out: 'There's Josef. He killed Kolber at Vienna, but they never caught him. He's never been caught.'

He put down his glass and listened. Had it been a taxi or a noise from the station or a woman's scream? He looked round the tables; no one had heard anything odd, they were talking, drinking, laughing, and one man was spitting. But Josef Grünlich's thirst was a little dulled while he sat and listened. A policeman came down the street; he had probably been relieved from traffic duty and was on his way home, but Josef, lifting his glass, shielded his face and watched him covertly over the brim. Then quite certainly he heard a scream.

The policeman stopped, and Josef, glancing anxiously round for the waiter, rose and laid some coins upon the table; the revolver between his legs had rubbed a small sore.

'Guten Abend.' The policeman bought an evening paper and went down the street. Josef put his gloved fingers to his forehead and brought them down damp with sweat. This won't do, he thought, I mustn't get nervous; I must have imagined that scream, and he was about to sit down and finish his coffee when he heard it again. It was extraordinary that it should have passed unnoticed in the café. How long, he wondered, before she unlocks the window? Then they'll hear her. He left his table and out in the street heard the screams more clearly, but the taxis went hooting by, a few hotel porters staggered down the slippery pavement carrying bags; no one stopped, no one heard.

Something struck the pavement with the clink of metal, and Josef looked down. It was a copper coin. That's curious, he thought, a lucky omen, but stooping to pick it up, he saw at intervals, all the way from the café, copper and silver coins lying in the centre of the pavement. He felt in his trouser pocket and found nothing but a hole. My goodness, he thought, have I been dropping them ever since I left the flat? And he saw himself standing at the end of a clear trail that led, paving stone by paving stone, and then stair by stair, to the door of Herr Kolber's study. He began to walk rapidly back along the pavement, picking up the coins and cramming them into his overcoat pocket, but he had not reached the café when the glass of a window broke high up above his head and a woman's voice screamed over and over again: 'Zu Hülfe! Zu Hülfe!' A waiter ran out of the café and stared upwards; a taxi-driver put on his brakes and ground his machine to a halt by the kerb; two men who had been playing chess left their pieces and ran into the road. Josef Grünlich had thought it very quiet under the falling snow, but only now was he confronted by real silence, as the taxi stopped and everyone in the café ceased speaking, and the woman continued to scream: 'Zu Hülfe! Zu Hülfe!' Somebody said, 'Die Polizei,' and two policemen came running down the street with clinking holsters. Then everything became again as usual, except that a small knot of idle people gathered at the entrance to the flats. The two chess players went back to their game; the taxi-driver pressed his self-starter, and then because the cold had already touched his engine, climbed out to wind the handle. Josef Grünlich walked, not too rapidly, towards the station, and a newspaper seller began to pick up the coins he had left on the pavement. Certainly, Josef thought, I cannot wait for the Passau train. But neither, he began to think, could he risk arrest for traveling without a ticket. But I haven't the money to get another; even my small change has gone. Josef, Josef, he abjured himself, don't make difficulties. You must get more. You are not _going_ to give in now: Josef Grünlich, five years and never jugged. You've killed a man: surely for once you, the head of your profession, can do something which any pickpenny finds easy, steal a woman's handbag.

He kept his eyes alert as he went up the steps into the station. He must take no risks. If he was caught, he would have to face a life sentence, not a week in gaol. He must choose carefully. Several bags were almost thrust into his hands in the crowded hall, so carelessly were they guarded, but the owners looked too poor or too gad-about. The first would have only a few shillings; the others, as like as not, would keep in their bags not even small change, only a powder-puff, a lipstick, a mirror, perhaps some French letters.

At last he found what he wanted, something indeed better than he had hoped. A foreign woman, English probably, with short uncovered hair and red eyes, struggling with the door of a telephone-booth. Her bag had fallen at her feet while she put both hands to the handle. She was, he thought, a little drunk, and as she was foreign, she would have plenty of money in her bag. For Josef Grünlich the whole affair was child's play.

The door came open and Mabel Warren faced the black shining instrument which for ten years now had taken her best time and her best phrases. She stooped for her bag, but it was gone. Strange, she thought, I could have sworn—did I leave it in the train? She had eaten a farewell dinner on the train with Janet Pardoe. There had been a glass of sherry, the larger part of a bottle of hock, and two liqueur brandies. Afterwards she had been a little dazed. Janet had paid for the dinner and she had given Janet a cheque and taken the change; she had more than two pounds of small Autrian change in the pocket of her tweed jacket now, but in the bag were nearly eighty marks.

She had some difficulty in making the long distance exchange understand the number she wanted in Cologne, because her voice was a little muzzled. While she waited, balancing her top-heavy form on the small steel seat, she watched the barrier. Fewer and fewer passengers came from the platforms: there was no sign of Dr Czinner. And yet, when she looked into his compartment ten minutes from Vienna, he was wearing his hat and mackintosh and he had answered her, 'Yes, I am getting out.' She had not trusted him, and when the train drew up, she waited until he left his compartment, watched him fumbling on the platform for his ticket, and would not then have let him out of her sight if it had not been necessary to telephone the office. For if he was lying she was determined to follow him to Belgrade and she would have no further opportunity to telephone that night. Did I leave my bag in the train? she wondered again, and then the telephone rang.

She looked at her wrist-watch: 'I've got ten minutes. If he doesn't come out in five, I'll go back to the train. It won't pay him to lie to me. 'Hello. Is that the London *Clarion?* Edwards? Right. Get this down. No, my lad, this isn't the Savory story. I'll give you that in a moment. This is your bill-page lead, and you've got to hold it for half an hour. If I don't ring up again, shoot it off. The Communist outbreak at Belgrade, which was put down with some loss of life on Wednesday night, as reported in our later editions yesterday, was planned by the notorious agitator, Dr Richard Czinner, who disappeared during the Kamnetz trial (no Kamnetz, K for Kaiser, A for Arse, M for Mule, N for Navel, no not that kind. It doesn't matter; it's the same letter. E for Erotic, T for Tart, Z for Zebra. Got it?), Kamnetz trial. Note to sub-editor. See press cuttings, August, 1927. He was believed to have been murdered by Government agents, but although a warrant was out for his arrest, he escaped, and in an exclusive interview with our special correspondent described his life as a schoolmaster at Great Birchington-on-Sea. Note to newseditor: Can't get him to speak about this; get the dope from the headmaster. His name's John. The outbreak at Belgrade was untimely; it had been planned for Saturday night, by which time Dr Czinner, who left England on Wednesday evening, would have arrived in the capital and taken control. Dr Czinner learnt of the outbreak and its failure when the express by which he was travelling reached Würzburg and immediately decided to leave the train at Vienna. He was heart-broken and could only murmur over and over again to our special correspondent: "If only they had waited." He was confident that if he had been present in Belgrade, the whole working class of the city would have supported the rising. In broken accents he gave our correspondent the amazing tale of his escape from Belgrade in 1927 and described the plans now prematurely ruined. Got that? Now listen carefully. If you don't get the rest of the dope in half an hour cancel everything after "reaching Würzburg" and continue as follows: And after long and painful hesitation decided to continue his journey to Belgrade. He was heartbroken and could only murmur: "Those fine brave fellows. How can I desert them?" When he had a little recovered he explained to our special correspondent that he had decided to stand his trial with the survivors, thus living up to the quixotic reputation he gained for himself at the time of the Kamnetz trial. His popularity with the working classes is an open secret, and his action may prove a considerable embarrassment to the Government.'

Miss Warren took a long breath and looked at her watch. Only five minutes now before the train left. 'Hello. Don't run away. Here's the bromide about Savory. You've got to be quick in getting this down. They've asked for half a column, but I haven't the time. I'll give you a few sticks. Mr Quin Savory, author of *The Great Gay Round,* is on his way to the Far East in search of material for his new novel, *Going Abroad.* Although the book will have an eastern setting, the great novelist will not have quite deserted the London

111

he loves so well, for he will view these distant lands through the eyes of a little London tobacconist. Mr Savory, a slim bronzed figure, welcomed our correspondent on the platform at Cologne. He has a curt (don't be funny. I said curt. C.U.R.T.) manner which does not hide a warm and sympathetic heart. Asked to estimate his place in literature he said: "I take my stand with sanity as opposed to the morbid introspection of such writers as Lawrence and Joyce. Life is a fine thing for the adventurous with a healthy mind in a healthy body." Mr Savory, who dresses quietly and without eccentricity, does not believe in the Bohemianism of some literary circles. "They give up to sex" he said, amusingly adapting Burke's famous phrase, "what is meant for mankind." Our correspondent pointed out the warm admiration which had been felt by countless readers for Emmy Tod, the little char in *The Great Gay Round* (which incidentally is now in its hundredth thousand). "You have a wonderful knowledge of the female heart, Mr Savory," he said. Mr Savory, who is unmarried, climbed back into his carriage with a debonair smile. "A novelist," he laughed, "is something of a spy," and he waved his hand gaily as the train carried him off. It is an open secret, by the way, that the Hon. Carol Delaine, the daughter of Lord Garthaway, will play the part of Emmy Tod, the chargirl, in the British film production of *The Great Gay Round*. Got that? Of course it's a bromide. What else can one do with the little swine?'

Miss Warren clapped down the receiver. Dr Czinner had not appeared. She was angry, but satisfied. He had thought to leave her behind in Vienna station, and she pictured with pleasure his disappointment when he looked up from his paper to find her again in the doorway of his compartment. Closer than mud, she whispered to herself, that's what I'll be.

The official at the barrier stopped her: 'Fahrkarte, bitte.' He was not looking at her, for he was busy collecting the tickets of passengers who had just arrived in some small local train, women with babies in arms and one man clasping a live hen. Miss Warren tried to brush her way through: 'Journalist's pass.' The ticket collector turned to her suspiciously. Where was it?

'I've left my bag behind,' said Miss Warren.

He collected the last ticket, shuffled the pasteboard into an even pile, round which with deliberation he twisted an india-rubber ring. The lady, he explained with stubborn courtesy, had told him when she came from the platform that she had a pass; she had waved a piece of card at him and brushed by before he could examine it. Now he would like to see that piece of card.

'Damn,' said Miss Warren. 'Then my bag has been stolen.'

But the lady had just said it was in the train.

Miss Warren swore again. She knew that her appearance was against her; she wore no hat, her hair was rumpled, and her breath smelt of drink. 'I can't help it,' she said. 'I've got to get back on that train. Send a man with me and I'll give him the money.'

The ticket-collector shook his head. He could not leave the barrier himself, he explained, and it would be out of order to send any of the porters who were in the hall on to the platform to collect money for a ticket. Why should not the lady buy a ticket and then claim reimbursement from the company? 'Because,' said Miss Warren furiously, 'the lady hasn't enough money on her.'

'In that case,' the ticket-collector said gently, with a glance at the clock, 'the lady will have to go by a later train. The Orient Express will have gone. As for the bag, you need not worry. A telephone message can be sent to the next station.'

Somebody in the booking-hall was whistling a tune. Miss Warren had heard it before with Janet, the setting of a light voluptuous song, while hand in hand they listened in darkness, and the camera panned all the length of a studio street, picking a verse from this man's mouth as he leant from a window, from this woman who sold vegetables behind a barrow, from that youth who embraced a girl in the shadow of a wall. She put one hand to her hair. Into her thoughts and fears, into the company of Janet and Q. C. Savory, Coral and Richard Czinner, a young pink face was for a moment thrust, soft eyes beamed helpfully behind horn-rimmed glasses. 'I guess, ma'am, you're having some trouble with this man. I'd be vurra proud to interpret for you.'

Miss Warren spun round with fury. 'Go and eat corn,' she said and strode to the telephone box. The American had turned the scale between sentiment and anger, between regret and revenge. He thinks that he's safe, she thought, that he's shaken me off, that I can't do anything to him just because he's failed. But by the time the bell rang in the box she was quite calm. Janet might flirt with Savory, Coral with her Jew; Mabel Warren for the time being did not care. When there was a choice between love of a woman and hate of a man, her mind could cherish only one emotion, for her love might be a subject for laughter, but no one had ever mocked her hatred.

[2]

Coral Musker stared with bewilderment at the menu. 'Choose for me,' she said, and was glad that he ordered wine, for it will help, she thought, tonight. 'I like your ring.' The lights of Vienna fled by them into the dark, and the waiter leant across the table and pulled down the blind. Myatt said, 'It cost fifty pounds.' He was back in familiar territory, he was at home, no longer puzzled by the inconsistency of human behaviour. The wine list before him, the napkin folded on his plate, the shuffle of waiters passing his chair, all gave him confidence. He smiled and moved his hand, so that the stone glinted from different facets on the ceiling and on the wine glasses. 'It's worth nearly twice that.'

'Tell me about her,' said Mr W. C. Savory; 'she's an odd type. Drinks?' 'So devoted to me.' 'But who wouldn't be?' He leant forward crumbling bread and asked with caution: 'I've never been able to understand. What can a woman like that *do? . . .*'

'No, I won't have any more of this foreign beer. My stomach won't stand it. Ask them, haven't they got a Guinness. I'd just fancy a Guinness.'

'Of course you are having a great sports revival in Germany,' said Mr Opie. 'Splendid types of young

115

men, one sees. But still it's not the same as cricket. Take Hobbs and Sutcliffe . . .'

'Kisses. Always kisses.'

'But I don't speak the lingo, Amy.'

'Do you always say what a thing's worth? Do you know what I'm worth?' Her perplexity and fear broke into irritation. 'Of course you do. Ten pounds for a ticket.'

'I explained,' Myatt said, 'all about that.'

'If I was that girl there . . .' Myatt turned and saw the slender woman in her furs and was caught up and judged and set down again by her soft luminous eyes. 'You are prettier,' he said with open insincerity, trying again to catch the woman's gaze and learn the verdict. It's not a lie, he told himself, for Coral at her best is pretty, while with the stranger one could never use the insignificant measure of prettiness. But I should be dumb before her, he thought. I could not talk to her easily as I can to Coral; I should be conscious of my hands, of my race; and with a wave of gratitude he turned to Coral, 'You're good to me.'

He leant across the soup, the rolls and the cruet: 'You *will* be good to me,' 'Yes,' she said, 'tonight.'

'Why only tonight? When we get to Constantinople why shouldn't you, why shouldn't we . . .' He hesitated. There was something about her which puzzled him: one small unvisited grove in all the acres of their familiarity.

'Live with you there?'

'Why not?' But it was not the reasons against his proposal which thronged her mind, which so coloured her thoughts that she had to focus her eyes more clearly on reality, the swaying train, men and women as far

116

as she could see eating and drinking between the drawn blinds, the scraps of other people's talk.

"Yes, that's all. Kisses. Just kisses.'

'Hobbs and Zudgliffe?'

It was all the reasons in favour: instead of the chill return at dawn to a grimy lodging and a foreign landlady, who would not understand her when she asked for a hot-water-bottle or a cup of tea, and would offer for a tired head some alien substitute for aspirin, to go back to a smart flat with shining taps and constant hot water and a soft bed with a flowered silk coverlet, that indeed would be worth any pain, any night's discomfort. But it's too good to be true, she thought, and tonight when he finds me cold and frightened and unused to things, he won't want me any longer. 'Wait,' she said. 'You may not want me.'

'But I do.'

'Wait till breakfast. Ask me at breakfast. Or just don't ask me.'

'No, not crickett. Not crickett,' said Josef Grünlich, wiping his moustache. 'In Germany we learn to run,' and the quaintness of his phrase made Mr Opie smile. 'Have you been a runner yourself?'

'In my day,' said Josef Grünlich, 'I was a great runner. Nobody runned as well as I. Nobody could catch me.'

'Heller.'

'Don't swear, Jim.'

'I wasn't swearing, It's the beer. Try some of this. It's not gassy. What you had before they call Dunkel.'

'I'm so glad you like it.'

'That little char. I can't remember her name, she was lovely.'

'Come back and talk a little after dinner.'

'You won't be silly now, Mr Savory?'

'I shall ask you.'

'Don't promise. Don't promise anything. Talk about something else. Tell me what you are going to do in Constantinople.'

'That's only business. It's tricky. The next time you eat spotted dog, think of me. Currants. I am currants,' he added with a humorous pride.

'Then I'll call you spotted dog. I can't call you Carleton, can I? What a name.'

'Look, have a currant. I always carry a few with me. Have one of these in this division. Good, isn't it?'

'Juicy.'

'That's one of ours, Myatt, Myatt and Page. Now try one of these. What do you think of that?'

'Look through there in the first class, Amy. Can't you see her? Too good for us, that's what she is.'

'With that Jew? Well, one knows what to think.'

'I have the greatest respect of course, for the Roman Catholic Church,' said Mr Opie. 'I am not bigoted. As an example of organisation . . .'

'So?'

'I am silly now.'

'Juicy.'

'No, no, that one's not juicy.'

'Have I said the wrong thing?'

'That was one of Stein's. A cheap inferior currant. The vineyards are on the wrong side of the hills. It makes them dry. Have another. Can't you see the difference?'

'Yes, this is dry. It's quite different. But the other was juicy. You don't believe me, but it really was. You must have got them mixed.'

'No, I chose the sample myself. It's odd. It's very odd.'

All down the restaurant-cars fell the sudden concerted silence which is said to mean that an angel passes overhead. But through the human silence the tumblers tingled on the table, the wheels thudded along the iron track, the windows shook and sparks flickered like match heads through the darkness. Late for the last service Dr Czinner came down the restaurant-car in the middle of the silence, with knees a little bent as a sailor keeps firm foothold in a stormy sea. A waiter preceded him, but he was unaware of being led. Words glowed in his mind and became phrases. You say that I am a traitor to my country, but I do not recognise my country. The dark downward steps, the ordure against the unwindowed wall, the starving faces. These are not Slavs, he thought, who owe a duty to this frock-coated figure or to that: they are the poor of all the world. He faced the military tribunal sitting under the eagles and the crossed swords: It is you who are old-fashioned with your machine-guns and your gas and your talk of country. Unconsciously as he walked the aisle from table to table he touched and straightened the tightly-knotted tie and fingered the Victorian pin: I am of the present. But for a moment into his grandiloquent dream obtruded the memory of long rows of malicious adolescent faces, the hidden mockery, the nicknames, the caricatures, the notes passed in grammars, under desks, the ubiquitous whispers impossible to place and punish. He sat down and stared without comprehension at the bill of fare.

Yes, I wouldn't mind being that Jew, Mr Peters thought during the long angelic visitation, he's got a nice skirt all right, all right. Not pretty. I wouldn't say pretty, but a good figure, and that, said Mr Peters to himself, watching his wife's tall angularity, remembering her murmurous stomach, that's the most important thing.

It was odd. He had chosen the samples with particular care. It was natural of course that even Stein's currants should not all be inferior, but when so much was suspected, a further suspicion was easy. Suppose, for example, Mr Eckman had been doing a little trade on his own account, had allowed Stein some of the firm's consignment of currants, in order temporarily to raise the quality, had, on the grounds of that improved quality, indeed, induced Moults' to bid for the business. Mr Eckman must be having uneasy moments now, turning up the time-table, looking at his watch, thinking that half Myatt's journey was over. Tomorrow, he thought, I will send a telegram and put Joyce in charge; Mr Eckman shall have a month's holiday. Joyce will keep an eye on the books, and he pictured the scurryings to and fro, as in an ants' nest agitated by a man't foot, a telephone call from Eckman to Stein or from Stein to Eckman, a taxi ordered here and dismissed there, a lunch for once without wine, and then the steep office steps and at the top of them the faithful rather stupid Joyce keeping his eye upon the books. And all the time, at the modern flat, Mrs Eckman would sit on her steel sofa knitting baby clothes for the Anglican mission, and the great dingy Bible, Mr

Eckman's first deception, would gather dust on its un-turned leaf.

Q. C. Savory pushed the button of the spring blind and moonlight touched his face and his fish knife and turned the steel rails on the quiet up-line to silver. The snow had stopped falling and lay piled along the banks and between the sleepers, lightening the darkness. A few hundred yards away the Danube flickered like mercury. He could see tall trees fly backwards and telegraph-poles, which caught the moonlight on their metal arms as they passed. While silence held the carriage, he put the thought of Janet Pardoe away from him; he wondered what terms he could use to describe the night. It is all a question of choice and arrangement; I must show not all that I see but a few selected sharp points of vision. I must not mention the shadows across the snow, for their colour and shape are indefinite, but I may pick out the scarlet signal lamp shining against the white ground, the flame of the waiting-room fire in the country station, the bead of light on a barge beating back against the current.

Josef Grünlich stroked the sore on his leg where the revolver pressed and wondered: How many hours to the frontier? Would the frontier guards have received notice of the murder? But I am safe. My passport is in order. No one saw me take the bag. There's nothing to connect me with Kolber's flat. Ought I to have dropped the gun somewhere? he wondered, but he reassured himself: it might have been traced to me. They can tell miraculous things nowadays from a scratch on the bore. Crime grew more unsafe every year; he had heard rumours of a new finger-print stunt, some way by which they could detect the print even when the hand had been gloved. But they haven't caught me yet with all their science.

One thing the films had taught the eye, Savory thought, the beauty of landscape in motion, how a church tower moved behind and above the trees, how it dipped and soared with the uneven human stride, the loveliness of a chimney rising towards a cloud and sinking behind the further cowls. That sense of movement must be conveyed in prose, and the urgency of the need struck him, so that he longed for paper and pencil while the mood was on him and repented his invitation to Janet Pardoe to come back with him after dinner and talk. He wanted to work; he wanted for an hour or two to be free from any woman's intrusion. I don't want her, he thought, but as he snapped the blind down again, he felt again the prick of desire. She was well-dressed; she 'talked like a lady'; and she had read his books with admiration; these three facts conquered him, still aware of his birthplace in Balham, the fugitive Cockney intonation of his voice. After six years of accumulative success, success represented by the figures of sales, 2,000, 4,000, 10,000, 25,000, 100,000 he was still astonished to find himself in the company of well-dressed women, and not divided by a thick pane of restaurant glass or the width of a counter. One wrote, day by day, with labour and frequent unhappiness, but with some joy, a hundred thousand words; a clerk wrote as many in an office ledger, and yet the words which he, Q. C. Savory, the former shop assistant, wrote had a result that the hardest work on an office stool could not attain; and as he picked at his fish and watched Janet Pardoe covertly, he thought not of current accounts, royalties and shares, nor of readers who wept at his pathos or laughed at his Cockney humour, but the long stairs to London drawing-rooms, the opening of double doors, the announcement of his name, faces of women who turned towards him with interest and respect.

Soon in an hour or two he will be my lover; and at the thought and the touch of fear at a strange relationship the dark knowing face lost its familiarity. When she fainted in the corridor he had been kind, with hands that pulled a warm coat round her, a voice that offered her rest and luxury; gratitude pricked at her eyes, and but for the silence all down the car she would have said: 'I love you.' She kept the words on her lips, so that she might break their private silence with them when the public silence passed.

The Press will be there, Czinner thought, and saw the journalists' box as it had been at the Kamnetz trial full of men scribbling and one man who sketched the general's likeness. It will be my likeness. It will be the justification of the long cold hours on the esplanade, when I walked up and down and wondered whether I had done right to escape. I must have every word perfect, remember clearly the object of my flight, remember that it is not only the poor of Belgrade who matter, but the poor of every country. He had protested many times against the national outlook of the militant section of the Social-Democratic party. Even their great song was national, 'March, Slavs, march'; it had been adopted against his wishes. It pleased him that the passport in his pocket was English, the plan in his suitcase German. He had bought the passport at a little paper-shop near the British Museum, kept by a Pole. It was handed to him over the tea-table in the back parlour, and the thin spotty man, whose name he had already forgotten, had apologised for the price. 'The expense is very bad,' he complained, and while he helped his customer into his coat had asked mechanically and without interest: 'How is your business?' It was quite obvious that he thought Czinner a thief. Then he had to go into the shop to sell an *Almanach Gaulois* to a furtive schoolboy. 'March, Slavs, march.' The man who had written the music had been bayoneted outside the sorting-room.

'Braised chicken! Roast veal . . .' The waiters called their way along the carriage and broke the minute's silence. Everyone began talking at once.

'I find the Hungarians take to cricket quite naturally. We had six matches last season.'

'This beer's not better. I *would* just like a glass of Guinness.'

'I do believe these currants——' 'I love you.' 'Our agent—what did you say?' 'I said that I loved you.' The angel had gone, and noisily and cheerfully with the thud of wheels, the clatter of plates, voices talking and the tingle of mirrors, the express passed a long line of fir-trees and the flickering Danube. In the coach the pressure gauge rose, the driver turned the regulator open, and the speed of the train was increased by five miles an hour.

[3]

Coral Musker paused on the metal plates between the restaurant-car and the second-class coaches. She was jarred and shaken by the heave of the train, and for the moment she could not go on to fetch her bag from the compartment where Mr Peters sat with his wife Amy. Away from the rattling metal, the beating piston, she stepped in thought, wrapping a fur coat round her, up the stairs to her flat. On the drawing-room table was a basket of hot-house roses and a card 'with love from Carl', for she had decided to call him that. One could not say: 'I love you, Carleton,' but 'I adore you, Carl' was easy. She laughed aloud and clapped her hands with the sudden sense that love was a simple affair, made up of gratitude and gifts and familiar jokes, a flat, no work, and a maid.

She began to run down the corridor, buffeted from one side to the other, but caring not at all. I'll go into the theatre three days late, and I shall say: 'Is Mr Sidney Dunn to be found?' But of course the doorkeeper will be a Turk and only mutter through his whiskers, so I'll have to find my own way along the passage to the dressing-rooms, over a litter of fire-hoses, and I shall say 'Good afternoon' or 'Bong jour', and put my head into the general dressing-room and say 'Where's Sid?' He'll be rehearsing in front, so I'll pop out of the wings at him, and he'll say, 'Who the hell are you?' beating time while Dunn's Babies dance and dance and dance. 'Coral Musker.' 'You're three days late. What the hell do you mean by it?' And I'll say, 'I just looked in to give notice.' She repeated the sentence aloud to hear how it would sound: 'I just looked in to give notice,' but the roar of the train beat her bravado into a sound more like a tremulous wail.

'Excuse me,' she said to Mr Peters, who was drowsing in his corner a little greasy after his meal. His legs were stretched across the compartment and barred her entry. 'Excuse me,' she repeated, and Mr Peters woke up and apologised. 'Coming back to us? That's right.'

'No,' she said, 'I'm fetching my bag.'

Amy Peters folded along a seat with a peppermint dissolving in her mouth said with sudden venom, 'Don't speak to her, Herbert. Let her get her bag. Thinks she's too good for us.'

'I only want my bag. What's getting your goat? I never said a word——'

'Don't get fussed, Amy,' said Mr Peters. 'It's none of our business what this young lady does. Have another peppermint. It's her stomach,' he said to Coral. 'She's got indigestion.'

'Young lady, indeed. She's a tart.'

Coral had pulled her bag from beneath the seat, but now she set it down again firmly on Mr Peters' toes. She put her hands on her hips and faced the woman, feeling very old and confident and settled, because the nature of the quarrel brought to mind her mother, arms akimbo, exchanging a few words with a neighbour, who had suggested that she was 'carrying on' with the lodger. For that moment she was her mother; she had sloughed her own experiences as easily as a dress, the feigned gentility of the theatre, the careful speech. 'Who do you think you are?' She knew the answer:

shopkeepers on a spree, going out to Budapest on a
Cook's tour, because it was a little farther than Ostend,
because they could boast at home of being travellers,
and show the bright labels of a cheap hotel on their
suitcases. Once she would have been impressed herself,
but she had learnt to take things casually, never to
admit ignorance, to be knowing. 'Who do you think
you are talking to? I'm not one of your shopgirls. Not
that you have any in your back street.'

'Now, now,' said Mr Peters, touched on the raw by
her discovery, 'there's no call to get angry.'

'Oh, isn't there. Did you hear what she called me?
I suppose she saw you trying to get off with me.'

'We know he wasn't good enough for you. Easy
money's what you want. Don't think we want you in
this carriage. I know where you belong.'

'Take that stuff out of your mouth when you talk
to me.'

'Arbuckle Avenue. Catch 'em straight off the train
at Paddington.'

Coral laughed. It was her mother's histrionic laugh
to call the neighbours to come and see the fight. Her
fingers tingled upon her hips with excitement; she had
been good so long, never dropped an aitch, or talked
of a boy friend, or said 'pleased to meet you'. For years
she had been hovering indecisively between the classes
and belonged nowhere except to the theatre, with her
native commonsense lost and natural refinement impossible. Now with pleasure she reverted to type. 'I
wouldn't be a scarecrow like you, not if you paid me.
No wonder you've got a belly-ache with a face like
that. No wonder your old man wanted a change.'

'Now, now, ladies,' said Mr Peters.

'He wouldn't soil his hands with you. A dirty little
Jew, that's all you're good for.'

Coral suddenly began to cry, although her hands still flaunted battle, and she had voice enough to reply, 'Keep off him,' but Mrs Peters' words remained smudged, like the dissolving smoke of an aerial advertisement, across the fair prospect.

'Oh, we know he's your boy.'

'My dear,' said a voice behind her, 'don't let them worry you.'

'Here's another of your friends.'

'So?' Dr Czinner put his hand under Coral's elbow and insinuated her out of the compartment.

'Jews and foreigners. You ought to be ashamed.'

Dr Czinner picked up the suitcase and laid it in the corridor. When he turned back to Mrs Peters, he showed her not the harassed miserable face of the foreign master, but the recklessness and the sarcasm which the journalists had noted when he took the witness-box against Kamnetz. 'So?' Mrs Peters took the peppermint out of her mouth; Dr Czinner, thrusting both hands into the pockets of his mackintosh, swayed backwards and forwards upon his toes. He appeared the master of the situation, but he was uncertain how to speak, for his mind was still full of grandiloquent phrases, of socialist rhetoric. He was made harsh by the signs of oppression, but he lacked for the moment words with which to contest it. They existed, he was aware, somewhere in the obscurity of his mind, glowing phrases, sentences as bitter as smoke. 'So?'

Mrs Peters began to find her courage. 'What are you barging your head in about? It's a bit too much. First one Nosey Parker, than another. Herbert, you do something.'

Dr Czinner began to speak. In his thick accent the words assumed a certain ponderous force that silenced, though they did not convince, Mrs Peters. 'I am a doctor.' He told them how useless it was to expect from them the sense of shame. The girl last night had fainted; he had ordered her for her health to have a sleeper. Suspicion only dishonoured the suspicious. Then he joined Coral Musker in the corridor. They were out of sight of the compartment, but Mrs Peters' voice was clearly audible, 'Yes, but who pays? That's what I'd like to know.' Dr Czinner pressed the back of his head against the glass and whispered with hatred, 'Bourgeois.'

'Thank you,' Coral said, and added, when she saw his expression of disappointment, 'Can I do anything? Are *you* ill?'

'No, no,' he said. 'But I was useless. I have not the gift of making speeches.' He leant back against the window and smiled at her. 'You were better. You talked very well.'

'Why were they such beasts?' she asked.

'They are always the same, the bourgeois,' he said. 'The proletariat have their virtues, and the gentleman is often good, just and brave. He is paid for something useful, for governing or teaching or healing, or his money is his father's. He does not deserve it perhaps, but he has done no one harm to get it. But the bourgeois—he buys cheap and sells dear. He buys from the worker and sells back to the worker. He is useless.'

Her question had not required an answer. She stared at him, bewildered by the flood of his explanation and the strength of his conviction, without understanding a word of what he said. 'I didn't do them any harm.'

'Ah, but you've done them great harm. So have I. We have come from the same class. But we earn our living honestly, doing no harm but some good. We are an example against them, and they do not like that.'

Out of this explanation she picked the only phrase she understood. 'Aren't you a gentleman?'

'No, and I am not a bourgeois.'

She could not understand the faint boastfulness of his reply, for ever since she left her home it had been her ambition to be mistaken for a lady. She had studied to that end with as much care as an ambitious subaltern studies for the staff college: every month her course included a new number of *Woman and Beauty,* every week a *Home Notes;* she examined in their pages the photographs of younger stars and of the daughters of the obscurer peers, learning what accessories were being worn and what were the powders in favour.

He began to advise her gently, 'If you cannot take a holiday, try to keep as quiet as possible. Do not get angry for no reason——'

'They called me a tart.' She could see that the word meant nothing to him. It did not for a moment ruffle the surface of his mind. He continued to talk gently about her health, not meeting her eyes. He's thinking of something else, she thought, and stooped impatiently for her bag, intending to leave him. He forestalled her by a spate of directions about sedatives and fruit juices and warm clothes. Obscurely she realised a change in his attitude. Yesterday he had wanted solitude, now he would seize any excuse to keep her company a minute longer. "What did you mean,' she asked, 'when you said "My proper work"?'

'When did I say that?' he asked sharply.

'Yesterday when I was faint.'

'I was dreaming. I have only one work.' He said no more, and after a moment she picked up her bag and went.

Nothing in her experience would have enabled her to

realise the extent of the loneliness to which she had abandoned him. 'I have only one work.' It was a confession which frightened him, for it had not been always true. He had not lived beside and grown accustomed to the idea of a unique employment. His life had once been lit by the multitude of his duties. If he had been born with a spirit like a vast bare room, covered with the signs of a house gone down in the world, scratches and peeling paper and dust, his duties, like the separate illuminations of a great candelabra too massive to pawn, had adequately lit it. There had been his duty to his parents who had gone hungry that he might be educated. He remembered the day when he took his degree, and how they had visited him in his bed-sitting-room and sat quiet in a corner watching him with respect, even with awe, and without love, for they could not love him now that he was an educated man; once he heard his father address him as 'Sir'. Those candles had blown out early, and he had hardly noticed the loss of two lights among so many, for he had his duty to his patients, his duty to the poor of Belgrade, and the slowly growing idea of his duty to his own class in every country. His parents had starved themselves that he might be a doctor, he himself had gone hungry and endangered his health that he might be a doctor, and it was only when he had practised for several years that he realised the uselessness of his skill. He could do nothing for his own people; he could not recommend rest to the worn-out or prescribe insulin to the diabetic, because they had not the money to pay for either.

He began to walk the corridor, muttering a little to himself. Small flakes of snow were again falling; they were blown against the windows like steam.

There had been his duty to God. He corrected himself: to a god. A god who had swayed down crowded aisles under a bright moth-worn canopy, a god the size of a crown-piece enclosed in a gold framework. It was a two-faced god, a deity who comforted the poor in their distress as they raised their eyes to his coming between the pillars, and a deity who had persuaded them, for the sake of a doubtful future, to endure their pain, as they bowed their heads, while the surge of the choristers and the priests and the singing passed by. He had blown that candle out with his own breath, telling himself that God was a fiction invented by the rich to keep the poor content; he had blow it out with a gesture, with a curious old-fashioned sense of daring, and he sometimes felt an unreasoning resentment against those who nowadays were born without religious sense and were able to laugh at the seriousness of the nineteenth-century iconoclast.

And now there was only one dim candle to light the vast room. I am not a son, he thought, nor a doctor, nor a believer, I am a Socialist; the word mouthed by politicians on innumerable platforms, printed in bad type or bad paper in endless newspapers rang cracked. I have failed even there. He was alone, and his single light was guttering, and he would have welcomed the company of anyone.

When he reached his compartment and found a stranger there he was glad. The man's back was turned, but he spun quickly round on short stout legs. The first thing which Dr Czinner noticed was a silver cross on his watch-chain, the next that his suitcase was not in the same spot where he had left it. He asked sadly, 'Are you, too, a reporter?'

'Ich spreche kein Englisch,' the man replied. Dr Czinner said in German, while he barred the way into the corridor, 'A policy spy? You are too late.' His eyes were still on the silver cross, which swung backwards

and forwards with the man's movement; it might have
been lurching to the human stride, and for a moment
Dr Czinner flattened himself against the wall of a steep
street to let the armoured men, the spears and the
horses pass, and the tired tortured man. He had not
died to make the poor contented, to bind the chains
tighter; his words had been twisted.

'I am not a police spy.'

Dr Czinner paid the stranger small attention as he
faced the possibility that, if the words had been twisted,
some of the words might have been true. He argued
with himself that the doubt came only from the approach of death, because when the burden of failure
was almost too heavy to bear, a man inevitably turned
to the most baseless promise. 'I will give you rest.'
Death did not give rest, for rest could not exist without
the consciousness of rest.

'You misunderstand me, Herr——'

'Czinner.' He relinquished his name to the stranger
without hesitation; the time was past for disguises, and
in the new veracious air he had to doff not only the
masks of identity. There were words which he had not
inquired into closely, common slogans which he had
accepted because they helped his cause: 'Religion is
the rich man's friend.' He said to the stranger: 'If you
are not a police spy, who are you? What have you been
doing here?'

'My name,' and the fat man bobbed a little from the
waist, while a finger twisted the bottom button of his
waistcoat, is——' The name was tossed into the bright
snow-lit darkness, drowned by the roar of the train,
the clatter of steel piles, an echoing bridge; the Danube,
like a silver eel, slipped from one side to the other of
the line. The man had to repeat his name, 'Josef

Grünlich.' He hesitated and then continued, 'I was looking for money, Herr Czinner.'

'You've stolen——'

'You came back too soon.' He began slowly to explain. 'I have escaped from the police. Nothing disgraceful, Herr Czinner, I can assure you.' He twisted and twisted his waistcoat button, an unconvincing alien talker in the newly-lit air of Dr Czinner's brain, populated only by incontestable truths, by a starving face, a bright rag, a child in pain, a man staggering up the road to Golgotha. 'It was a political offense, Herr Czinner. An affair of a newspaper. A great injustice has been done me, and so I had to fly. It was for the sake of the cause that I opened your suitcase.' He blew out the word 'cause' with a warm intense breath, cheapening it into a shibboleth, an easy emotion. 'You will call the guard?' He fixed his knees, and his finger tightened on the button.

'What do you mean by your cause?'

'I am a Socialist.' The realisation came sharply to Dr Czinner that a movement could not be judged by its officers; socialism was not condemned by the adherence of Grünlich, but he was anxious, none the less, to forget Grünlich. 'I will let you have some money.' He took out his pocket-book and handed the man five English pounds. 'Good night.'

It was easy to dismiss Grünlich and it had cost him little, for money would be of no value to him in Belgrade. He did not need a lawyer to defend him: his defence was his own tongue. But it was less easy to evade the thought which Grünlich had left behind, that a movement was not condemned by the dishonesty of its officers. He himself was not without dishonesty, and the truth of his belief was not altered because he was guilty of vanity, of several meannesses; once he had got a girl with child. Even his motives in travelling first class were not unmixed; it was easier to evade the frontier police, but it was also more comfortable, more fitted to his vanity as a leader. He found himself praying: 'God forgive me.' But he was shut off from any assurance of forgiveness, if there existed any power which forgave.

The guard came and looked at his ticket. 'Snowing again,' he said. 'It is worse up the line. It will be lucky if we get through without delay.' He showed an inclination to stay and talk. Three winters ago, he said, they had had a bad time. They had been snowed up for forty-eight hours on one of the worst patches of the line, one of the bare Balkan patches; no food to be got, and the fuel had to be saved.

'Shall we reach Belgrade to time?'

'One can't tell. My experience is—snow this side of Buda, twice as much snow before Belgrade. It's a different case before we reach the Danube. It can be snowing in Munich and like summer at Buda. Good night, Herr Doktor. You'll be having patients in this cold.' The guard went down the corridor beating his hands together.

Doctor Czinner did not stay long in his compartment; the man who had shared it had left the train at Vienna. Soon it would be impossible to see even passing lights through the window; the snow was caked in every crevice and ice was forming on the glass. When a signal box or a station lamp went by its image was cut into wedges by the streaks of opaque ice, so that for a moment the window of the train became a kaleidoscope in which the jumbled pieces of coloured glass were shaken. Dr Czinner wrapped his hands for warmth in the loose folds of his mackintosh and began again to walk the corridor. He passed through the guard's van and came out into the third-class carriages which had been attached to the train at Vienna. Most of the compartments were in darkness except for a dim globe burning in the roof. On the wooden seats the passengers were settling themselves for the night with rolled coats under their heads; some of the compartments were so full that the men and women slept bolt upright in two rows, their faces green and impassive in the faint light. There was a smell of cheap red wine from the empty bottles under the seats, and a few scraps of sour bread lay on the floor. When he came near the lavatory he turned back, the smell was too much for him. Behind him the door blew open and shut with the shaking of the express.

I belong there, he thought without conviction; I should be travelling third class. I do not wish to be like a constitutional labour member taking his first-class ticket to cast his vote in a packed parliament. But he comforted himself with the thought of how he would have been delayed by frequent changes and how he might have been held up at the frontier. He remained aware nevertheless of the mixture of his motives; they had only begun to worry him since his knowledge of failure; all his vanities, meannesses and small sins would have been swept to darkness in the thrill and unselfishness of victory. But he wished, now that all depended on his tongue, that he could make his speech from the dock with a conscience perfectly clear. Small things in his past, which his enemies would never know, might rise in his own mind to clog his tongue. I failed utterly with those two shopkeepers; shall I succeed any better in Belgrade?

Because his future had an almost certain limit, he began to dwell, as he was not accustomed to do, on the past. There had been a time when a clear conscience could be bought at the price of a moment's shame: 'since my last confession, I have done this or that.' If, he thought with longing and a little bitterness, I could get back my purity of motive so easily, I should be a fool not to take the chance. My regret for what I have done is not less now than then, but I have no conviction of forgiveness; I have no conviction that there is anyone to forgive. He came near to sneering at his last belief: Shall I go and confess my sins to the treasurer of the Social-Democratic party, to the third-class passengers? The priest's face turned away, the raised fingers, the whisper of a dead tongue, seemed to him suddenly as beautiful, as infinitely desirable and as hopelessly lost as youth and first love in the corner of the viaduct wall.

It was then that Dr Czinner caught sight of Mr Opie alone in a second-class compartment, writing in a notebook.

He watched him with a kind of ashamed greed, for he was about to surrender to a belief which it had been his pride to subdue. But if it gives me peace, he protested, and at the still darkling associations of the word he pulled the door back and entered the compartment. The long pale face and pale eyes, the impression of inherited culture, embarrassed him; by his request he would admit the priest's superiority; and he was again for a moment the boy with grubby hands blushing in the dark of the confessional at his commonplace sins. He said in his stiff betraying English, 'Will you excuse me? Perhaps I am disturbing you. You want to sleep?'

'Not at all. I get out at Buda. I don't suppose I shall sleep,' he laughed deprecatingly, 'until I am safe ashore.

'My name is Czinner.'

'And mine is Opie.' To Mr Opie his name had

conveyed nothing; perhaps it was kept in mind only by journalists. Dr Czinner drew the door to and sat down in the opposite seat. 'You are a priest?' He tried to add 'father', but the word stuck on his tongue; it meant too much, it meant a grey starved face, affection hardening into respect, sacrifice into suspicion of a son grown like an enemy. 'Not of the Roman persuasion,' said Mr Opie. Dr Czinner was silent for several minutes, uncertain how to word his request. His lips felt dry with a literal thirst for righteousness, which was like a glass of ice-cold water on a table in another man's room. Mr Opie seemed aware of his embarrassment and remarked cheerfully, 'I am making a little anthology.' Dr Czinner repeated mechanically, 'Anthology?'

'Yes,' said Mr Opie, 'a spiritual anthology for the lay mind, something to take the place in the English church of the Roman books of contemplation.' His thin white hand stroked the black wash-leather cover of his note-book. 'But I intend to strike deeper. The Roman books are, what shall I say? too exclusively religious. I want mine to meet all the circumstances of everyday life. Are you a cricketer?'

The question took Dr Czinner by surprise; he had again in memory been kneeling in darkness, making his act of contrition. 'No,' he said, 'no.'

'Never mind. You will understand what I mean. Suppose that you are the last man in; you have put on your pads; eight wickets have fallen; fifty runs must be made; you wonder whether the responsibility will fall upon you. You will get no strength for that crisis from any of the usual books of contemplation; you may indeed be a little suspicious of religion. I aim at supplying that man's need.'

Mr Opie had spoken rapidly and with enthusiasm, and Dr Czinner found his knowledge of English failing him. He did not understand the words 'pad', 'wickets', 'runs'; he knew that they were connected with the English game of cricket; he had become familiar with the words during the last five years and they were associated in his mind with salty wind-swept turf, the supervision of insubordinate children engaged on a game which he could not master; but the religious significance of the words escaped him. He supposed that the priest was using them metaphorically: 'responsibility', 'crisis', 'man's need', these phrases he understood, and they gave him the opportunity he required to make his request.

'I wish to speak to you,' he said, 'of confession.' At the sound of the word he was momentarily young again.

'It's a difficult subject,' said Mr Opie. He examined his hands for a moment and then began to speak rapidly. 'I am not dogmatic on the point. I think there is a great deal to be said for the attitude of the Roman church. Modern psychology is working on parallel lines. There is a similarity in the relationship between the confessor and the penitent and that between the psychoanalyst and the patient. There is, of course, this difference, that one claims to forgive the sins. But the difference,' Mr Opie continued hurriedly, as Dr Czinner tried to speak, 'is not after all very great. In the one case the sins are said to be forgiven and the penitent leaves the confessional with a clear mind and the intention of making a fresh start; in the other the mere expression of the patient's vices and the bringing to light of his unconscious motives in practising them are said to remove the force of the desire. The patient leaves the psycho-analyst with the power, as well as the intention, of making a fresh start.' The door into the corridor opened, and a man entered. 'From that point of view,' said Mr Opie, 'confession to the psycho-analyst seems to be more efficacious than confession to the priest.'

'You are discussing confession?' the newcomer asked. 'May I draw a red 'erring across your argument? There's a literary aspect to be considered.'

'Let me introduce you to each other,' said Mr Opie. 'Dr Czinner—Mr Q. C. Savory. We really have here the elements of a most interesting discussion; the doctor, the clergyman, and the writer.'

Dr Czinner said slowly: 'Have you not left out the penitent?'

'I was going to introduce him,' Mr Savory said. 'In a way surely *I* am the penitent. In so far as the novel is founded on the author's experience, the novelist is making a confession to the public. This puts the public in the position of the priest and the analyst.'

Mr Opie countered him with a smile. 'But your novel is a confession only in so far as a dream is a confession. The Freudian censor intervenes. The Freudian censor,' he had to repeat in a louder voice as the train passed under a bridge. 'What does the medical man say?' Their polite bright attentive gaze confused Dr Czinner. He sat with head a little bent, unable to bring the bitter phrases from his mind to his lips; speech was failing him for a second time that evening; how could he depend on it when he reached Belgrade?

'And then,' said Mr Savory, 'there's Shakespeare.'

'Where is there not?' said Mr Opie. 'He strides this narrow world like a colossus. You mean——'

'What was his attitude to confession? He was born, of course, a Roman Catholic.'

'In *Hamlet*,' began Mr. Opie, but Dr Czinner waited no longer. He rose and made two short bows. 'Good night,' he said. He wanted to express his anger and

140

disappointment, but all he found to say was: 'So interesting.' The corridor, lit only by a chain of dim blue globes, sloped gray and vibrating towards the dark vans. Somebody turned in his sleep and said in German, 'Impossible. Impossible.'

When Coral left the doctor she began to run, as fast as was possible with a suitcase in a lurching train, so that she was out of breath and almost pretty when Myatt saw her pulling at the handle of his door. He had put away the correspondence from Mr Eckman and the list of market prices ten minutes ago, because he found that always, before the phrases or the figures could convey anything to his mind, he heard the girl's voice: 'I love you.'

What a joke, he thought, what a joke.

He looked at his watch. No stop now for seven hours and he had tipped the guard. He wondered whether they got used to this kind of affair on long-distance trains. When he was younger he used to read stories of king's messengers seduced by beautiful countesses travelling alone and wonder whether such good fortune would ever happen to him. He looked at himself in the glass and pressed back his oiled black hair. I am not bad-looking if my skin were not so sallow; but when he took off his fur coat, he could not help remembering that he was growing fat and that he was travelling in currants and not with a portfolio of sealed papers. Nor is she a beautiful Russian countess, but she likes me and she has a pretty figure.

He sat down, and then looked at his watch and got up again. He was excited. You fool, he thought, she's nothing new; pretty and kind and common, you can find her any night on the Spaniards road, and yet in spite of these persuasions he could not but feel that the adventure had in it a touch of freshness, of unfamiliarity. Perhaps it was only the situation: travelling at sixty miles an hour in a berth little more than two feet across. Perhaps it was her exclamation at dinner; the girls he had known were shy of using that phrase; they would say 'I love you' if they were asked, but their spontaneous tribute was more likely to be 'You're a nice boy'. He began to think of her as he had never thought before of any woman who was attainable: she is dear and sweet, I should like to do things for her. It did not occur to him for several moments that she had already reason for gratitude.

'Come in,' he said, 'come in.' He took the suitcase from her and pushed it under the seat and then took her hands.

'Well,' she said with a smile, 'I'm here, aren't I?' In spite of her smile he thought her frightened and wondered why. He loosed her hands in order to pull down the blinds of the corridor windows, so that they seemed suddenly to become alone in a small trembling box. He kissed her and found her mouth cool, soft, uncertainly responsive. She sat down on the seat which had become converted into a berth and asked him, 'Did you wonder whether I'd come?'

'You promised,' he reminded her.

'I might have changed my mind.'

'But why?' Myatt was becoming impatient. He did not want to sit about and talk; her legs, swinging freely without touching the floor, excited him. 'We'll have a nice time.' He took off her shoes and ran his hands up her stockings. 'You know a lot, don't you?' she said. He flushed. 'Do you mind that?'

'Oh, I'm glad,' she said, 'so glad. I couldn't bear it if you hadn't known a lot.' Her eyes large and scared, her face pale under the dim blue globe, first amused him, then attracted him. He wanted to shake her out

142

of aloofness into passion. He kissed her again and tried to slip her frock over her shoulder. Her body trembled and moved under her dress like a cat tied in a bag; suddenly she put her lips up to him and kissed his chin. 'I do love you,' she said, 'I do.'

The sense of unfamiliarity deepened round him. It was as if he had started out from home on a familiar walk, past the gas works, across the brick bridge over the Wimble, across two fields, and found himself not in the lane which ran uphill to the new road and the bungalows, but on the threshold of a strange wood, faced by a shaded path he had never taken, running God knows where. He took his hands from her shoulders and said without touching her: 'How sweet you are,' and then with astonishment: 'How dear.' He had never before felt the lust rising in him checked and increasing because of the check; he had always spilt himself into new adventures with an easy excitement.

'What shall I do? Shall I take off my clothes?' He nodded, finding it hard to speak, and saw her rise from the berth and go into a corner and begin to undress slowly and very methodically, folding each garment in turn and laying it neatly on the opposite seat. He was conscious as he watched her calm movements of the inadequacy of his body. He said, 'You are lovely,' and his words stumbled with an unfamiliar excitement. When she came across the carriage he saw that he had been deceived; her calm was like a skin tightly drawn; her face was flushed with excitement and her eyes were scared; she looked uncertain whether to laugh or cry. They came together quite simply in the narrow space between the seats. 'I wish the light would go right out,' she said. She stood close against him while he touched her with his hands, both swaying easily to the motion of the train. 'No,' he said.

'It would be more becoming,' she said and began to laugh quietly to herself. Her laughter lay, an almost imperceptible pool of sound, beneath the pounding and the clatter of the express, but when they spoke, instead of whispering, they had to utter the intimate words loudly and clearly.

The sense of strangeness survived even the customary gestures; lying in the berth she proved awkward in a mysterious innocent fashion which astonished him. Her laughter stopped, not coming gradually to an end, but vanishing so that he wondered whether he had imagined the sound or whether it had been a trick of the glancing wheels. She said suddenly and urgently, 'Be patient, I don't know much,' and then she cried out with pain. He could not have been more startled if a ghost had passed through the compartment dressed in an antique wear which antedated steam. He would have left her if she had not held him to her with her hands, while she said in a voice of which snatches only escaped the sound of the engine, 'Don't go. I'm sorry. I didn't mean . . .' Then the sudden stopping of the train lurched them apart. 'What is it?' she said. 'A station.' She protested with pain, 'Why must it now?'

Myatt opened the window a little way and leant out. The dim chain of lights lit the ground for only a few feet beside the line. Snow already lay inches thick; somewhere in the distance a red spark shone intermittently, like a revolving light between the white gusts. 'It isn't a station,' he said. 'Only a signal against us.' The stilling of the wheels made the night very quiet with one whistle of steam to break it; here and there men woke and put their heads out of windows and spoke to each other. From the third-class carriages at the rear of the train came the sound of a fiddle. The tune was bare, witty, mathematical, but in its passage through the dark and over the snow it became less determinate, until it picked from Myatt's mind a trace of perplexity and regret: 'I never knew. I never guessed.' There was such warmth in the carriage now between them that, without closing the window, he knelt beside the berth and put his hand to her face, touching her features with curious fingers. Again he was overwhelmed with the novel thought, 'How sweet, how dear.' She lay quiet, shaken a little by quick breaths of pain or excitement.

Somebody in the third-class carriages began to curse the fiddler in German, saying that he could not sleep for the noise. It seemed not to occur to him that he had slept through the racket of the train, and that it was the silence surrounding the precise slow notes which woke him. The fiddler swore back and went on fiddling, and a number of people began to talk at once, and someone laughed.

'Were you disappointed?' she asked. 'Was I awfully bad at it?'

'You were lovely,' he said. 'But I never knew. Why did you agree?'

She said in a tone as light as the fiddle's, 'A girl's got to learn some time.' He touched her face again. 'I hurt you.'

'It wasn't a picnic,' she said.

'Next time,' he began to promise, but she interrupted with a question which made him laugh by its gravity: 'There'll be another time? Did I pass all right?'

'You want another time?'

'Yes,' she said, but she was thinking not of his embrace, but of the flat in Constantinople and her own bedroom and going to bed at ten. 'How long will you stay out there?'

'Perhaps a month. Perhaps longer.' She whispered

with so much regret, 'So soon,' that he began to promise many things he knew very well he would regret in daylight. 'You can come back with me. I'll give you a flat in town.' Her silence seemed to emphasise the wildness of his promises. 'Don't you believe me?'

'Oh,' she said in a voice of absolute trust, 'it's too good to be true.'

He was touched by the complete absence of coquetry, and remembered again with sudden force that he had been her first lover. 'Listen,' he said, 'will you come again tomorrow?' She protested with real apprehension that he would tire of her before they reached Constantinople.

He ignored her objection. 'I'd give a party to celebrate.'

'Where? In Constantinople?'

'No,' he said, 'I've no one to invite there,' and for a moment the thought of Mr Eckman cast a shadow over his pleasure.

'What, in the train?' She began to laugh again, but this time in a contented and unfrightened way.

'Why not?' he became a little boastful. 'I'll invite everyone. It'll be a kind of wedding dinner.'

She teased him, 'Without the wedding,' but he became the more pleased with his idea. 'I'll invite everyone: the doctor, that person in the second class, the inquisitive fellow (do you remember him?)' He hesitated for a second. 'That girl.' 'What girl?' 'The niece of your friend.' But his grandiloquence was a little dashed by the thought that she would never accept his invitation; she is not a chorus girl, he thought with shame at his own ingratitude, she is not pretty and easy and common, she is beautiful, she is the kind of woman I should like to marry; and for a moment he contemplated with a touch of bitterness her inaccessibility.

Then he recovered his spirits. 'I'll get the fiddler,' he boasted, 'to play to us while we eat.'

'You wouldn't dare to invite them,' she said with shining eyes.

'I will. They'll never refuse the kind of dinner I'll pay for. We'll have the best wine they can give us,' he said, making rapid calculations of cost and choosing to forget that a train reduces all wine to a common mediocrity. 'It'll cost two pounds a head.'

She beat her hands together in approval. 'You'll never dare to tell them the reason.'

He smiled at her. 'I'll tell them it's to drink the health of my mistress.' For a long time then she lay quiet, dwelling on the word and its suggestion of comfort and permanence, almost of respectability. Then she shook her head, 'It's too good to be true,' but her expression of disbelief was lost in the whistle of steam and the grinding of the wheels into motion.

While the couplings between the carriages strained and the signal burning a green light lurched slowly by, Josef Grünlich was saying, 'I am the President of the Republic.' He woke as a gentleman in a tailcoat was about to present him with a golden key to open the new city safe deposits; he woke at once to a full knowledge of his surroundings and to a full memory of his dream. Leaning his hands upon his fat knees he began to laugh. President of the Republic, that's good, and why not? I can spin a yarn all right. Kolber and that doctor both deceived in one day. Five English pounds he gave me, because I was sharp and spotted what he was when he said, 'Police spy.' Quick, that's Josef Grünlich all over. 'Look over there, Herr Kolber.' Flick at the string, aim, fire, all in one second. And I've got away with it too. They can't catch Josef.

What was it the priest said? Josef began to laugh deep down in his belly. 'Do you play cricket in Germany?' And I said, 'No, they teach us to run. I was a great runner in my time.' That was quick if you like, and he never saw the joke, said something about 'Sobs and Hudglich'.

But it was a bad moment all the same, thought Josef, staring out into the falling snow, when the doctor spotted that his bag had been moved. I'd got my finger on the string. If he'd tried to call the guard I'd have shot him in the stomach before he could shout a word. Josef laughed again happily, feeling his revolver rub against the sore on the inside of his knee: I'd have spilt his guts for him.

PART FOUR
Subotica

[1]

The telegraph receiving set in the station-master's office at Subotica flickered; dots and dashes were spilt into the empty room. Through the open door Lukitch, the clerk, sat in a corner of the parcels office and cursed the importunate sounds. But he made no effort to rise. 'It can't be important at this hour,' he explained to the parcels clerk and to Ninitch, a young man in a grey uniform, one of the frontier guards. He shuffled a pack of cards and at the same time the clock struck seven. Outside an indeterminate sun was breaking over grey half-melted snow, the wet rails glinted. Ninitch sipped his glass of *rakia*; the heavy plum wine brought tears to his eyes; he was very young.

149

Lukitch went on shuffling. 'What do you think it's all about?' asked the parcels clerk. Lukitch shook his grimy tousled head. 'One can't tell of course. But I shouldn't be surprised all the same. It will serve her right.' The parcels clerk began to giggle. Ninitch raised his dark eyes, that could contain no expression save simplicity, and asked: 'Who is she?' To his imagination the telegraph began to speak in an imperious feminine way.

'Ah, you soldiers,' said the parcels clerk. 'You don't know half of what goes on.'

'That's true,' Ninitch said. 'We stand about for hours at a time with our bayonets fixed. There's not going to be another war, is there? Up to the barracks and down to the station. We don't have time to see things.' Dot, dot, dot, dash, went the telegraph. Lukitch dealt the pack into three equal piles; the cards sometimes stuck together and he licked his fingers to separate them. He ranged the three piles side by side in front of him. 'It's probably the station-master's wife,' he explained. 'When she goes away for a week she sends him telegrams at the oddest times, every day. Late in the evening or early in the morning. Full of tender expressions. In rhyme sometimes: "Your little dove sends all her love", or "I think of you faithfully and ever so tenderly".'

'Why does she do it?' asked Ninitch.

'She's afraid he may have one of the servants in bed with him. She thinks he'll repent if he gets a telegram from her just at the moment.'

The parcels clerk giggled. 'And of course the funny part is, he wouldn't look at his servants. His inclinations, if she only knew it, are all the other way.'

'Your bets, gentlemen,' said Lukitch and he watched them narrowly, while they put copper coins on two of the piles of cards. Then he dealt out each pack in turn. In the third pack, on which no money had been placed, was the knave of diamonds. He stopped dealing and pocketed the coins. 'Bank wins,' he said, and passed the cards to Ninitch. It was a very simple game.

The parcels clerk stubbed out his cigarette and lit another, while Ninitch shuffled. 'Was there any news on the train?'

'Everything quiet in Belgrade,' said Lukitch.

'Is the telephone working?'

'Worse luck.' The telegraph had stopped buzzing, and Lukitch sighed with relief. 'That's over, anyway.'

The soldier suddenly stopped shuffling and said in a puzzled voice, 'I'm glad I wasn't in Belgrade.'

'Fighting, my boy,' said the parcels clerk hilariously.

'Yes,' said Ninitch shyly, 'but they were, weren't they, our own people? It was not as if they were Bulgars.'

'Kill or be killed,' said the parcels clerk. 'Come, deal away, Ninitch, my boy.'

Ninitch began to deal; several times he lost count of the cards; it was obvious that something was on his mind. 'And then, what did they want? What did they want to get by it all?'

'They were Reds,' said Lukitch.

'Poor people? Make your bets, gentlemen,' he added mechanically. Lukitch piled all the coppers he had won on the same heap as the parcels clerk; he caught the clerk's eye and winked; and the other man increased his bet. Ninitch was too absorbed in his slow clumsy thoughts to realise that he had shown the position of the knave when he dealt. The parcels clerk could not restrain a giggle. 'After all,' said Ninitch, 'I am poor, too.'

'We've made our bets,' said Lukitch impatiently, and Ninitch dealt out the cards. His eyes opened a little wider when he saw that both bets had been successful; for a moment a faint suspicion affected his manner; then he counted out the coins and rose. 'Are you going to stop?' asked Lukitch.

'Must be getting back to the guard-room.'

The parcels clerk grinned. 'He's lost all his money. Give him some more *rakia* before he goes, Lukitch.' Lukitch poured out another glass and stood with bottle tipped. The telephone-bell was ringing. 'The devil,' he said. 'It's that woman.' He put the bottle down and went into the other room. A pale sun slanted through the window and touched the crates and trunks piled behind the counter. Ninitch raised his glass, and the parcels clerk sat with one finger on the pack of cards listening. 'Hello, hello!' bellowed Lukitch in a rude voice. 'Who do you want? The telegraph? I've heard nothing. I can't hang over it the whole time. I've got a lot to do in this station. Tell the woman to send her telegrams at a reasonable hour. What's that?' His voice suddenly changed. 'I'm very sorry, sir. I never dreamed . . .' The parcels clerk giggled. 'Of course. Immediately, sir, immediately. I'll send at once, sir. If you would not mind holding the line for two minutes, sir . . .'

Ninitch sighed and went out into the bitter air of the small platformless station. He had forgotten to put on his gloves, and before he could huddle them on, his fingers were nipped by the cold. He dragged his feet slowly through the first half-melted and then half-frozen mud and snow. No, I am glad I was not in Belgrade, he thought. It was all very puzzling; they were poor and he was poor; they had wives and children; he had a wife and a small daughter; they must

152

have expected to gain something by it, those Reds. The sun getting up above the roof of the customs-shed touched his face with the ghost of warmth; a stationary engine stood like a stray dog panting steam on the up-line. No train would be passing through to Belgrade before the Orient express was due; for half an hour there would be clamour and movement, the customs-officers would arrive and the guards be posted conspicuously outside the guard-room, then the train would steam out, and there would be only one more train, a small cross-country one to Vinkovce, that day. Ninitch buried his hands in his empty pockets: then would be the time for more *rakia* and another game of cards: but he had no money. Again a slight suspicion that he had been cheated touched his stubborn mind.

'Ninitch. Ninitch.' He looked round and saw the station-master's clerk plunging after him through the slush without overcoat or gloves. Ninitch thought: He has robbed me, his heart has been touched by God, he is going to make restitution. He stopped and smiled at Lukitch, as much as to say: Have no fear, I am not angry with you. 'You fool, I thought I should never make you hear,' said the clerk, panting at his side, small and grimy and ill-natured. 'Go at once to Major Petkovitch. He's wanted on the telephone. I can't make the guard-room answer.'

'The telephone went out of order last night,' Ninitch explained, 'while the snow fell.'

'Incompetence,' fumed the clerk.

'A man was coming from the town to see to it to-day.' He hesitated. 'The major won't come out in the snow. He has a fire in his room so high.'

'Fool. Imbecile,' said the clerk. 'It's the Chief of Police speaking from Belgrade. They were trying to send through a telegram, but you were talking so hard,

how could anyone hear? Be off.' Ninitch began to walk
on towards the guard-room, but the clerk screamed after him, 'Run, you fool, run.' Ninitch broke into a
trot, handicapped by his heavy boots. It's curious, he
thought, one's treated like a dog, but a moment later
he thought: After all, it's good of them to play cards
with me; they must earn in a day what I earn in a
week; and they get paid, too, he said to himself, considering the deductions from his own pay for mess, for
quarters, for fires. 'Is the major in?' he asked in the
guard-room and then knocked timidly on the door. He
should have passed the message through the serjeant,
but the serjeant was not in the room, and in any case
one never knew when an opportunity for special service might arise, and that might lead to promotion,
more food, a new dress for his wife.

'Come in.'

Major Petkovitch sat at his desk facing the door.
He was short, thin, sharp-featured, and wore pince-
nez. There was probably some foreign blood in his
family, for he was fair-haired. He was reading an out-
of-date German book on strategy and feeding his dog
with pieces of sausage. Ninitch stared with envy at
the roaring fire. 'Well, what is it?' the major asked
irritably, like a schoolmaster disturbed while going
through his pupils' exercises.

'The Chief of Police has rung up, sir, and wants you
on the telephone in the station-master's office.'

'Isn't our own telephone working?' the major asked,
trying, not very successfully, as he laid down the book,
to hide his curiosity and excitement; he wanted to
give the impression of being on intimate terms with
the Chief of Police.

'No, sir, the man hasn't come from the town yet.'

'How very trying. Where is the serjeant?'

'He's gone out for a moment, sir.'

Major Petkovitch plucked at his gloves and smoothed them. 'You had better come with me. I may need a messenger. Can you write?'

'A very little, sir.' Ninitch was afraid that the major would choose another messenger, but all he said was, 'Tut.' Ninitch and the dog followed at the major's heels across the guard-room and over the rails. In the station-master's office Lukitch was making a great show of work in a corner, while the parcels clerk hung round the door totting up entries on a folio sheet. 'The line is quite clear, sir,' said Lukitch and scowled at Ninitch behind the major's back; he envied his proximity to the instrument.

'Hello, hello, hello,' called Major Petkovitch acidly. The private soldier leant his head a little towards the telephone. Over the long miles between the frontier and Belgrade came the ghost of a cultured insolent voice with an intonation so clear that even Ninitch, standing two feet away from the instrument, could catch the measured syllables. They fell, like a succession of pins, into a deep silence: Lukitch and the parcels clerk held their breath in vain; the stationary engine across the track had stopped panting. 'Colonel Hartep speaking.' It is the Chief of Police, Ninitch thought, I have heard him speak: how proud my wife will be this evening: the story will go all round the barracks, trust her for that. She has not much reason to be proud of me, he considered simply, without self-depreciation, she makes the very most of what she has.

'Yes, yes, this is Major Petkovitch.'

The insolent voice was a little lowered; Ninitch caught the words only in snatches. 'On no account . . . Belgrade . . . search the train.'

'Should I take him to the barracks?'

The voice rose a little in emphasis. 'No. As few people must see him as possible. . . . On the spot.'

'But really,' Major Petkovitch protested, 'we haven't the accommodation here. What can we do with him?'

'. . . a few hours only.'

'By court-martial? It's very irregular.' The voice began to laugh gently. 'Myself . . . with you by lunch . . .'

'But in the event of an acquittal?'

'. . . myself,' said the voice indistinctly, 'you, Major, Captain Alexitch.' It fell lower still. 'Discreet . . . among friends,' and then more clearly, 'He may not be alone . . . suspects . . . any excuse . . . the customs. No fuss, mind.'

Major Petkovitch said in a tone of the deepest disapproval, 'Is there anything else, Colonel Hartep?' The voice became a little animated 'Yes, yes. About lunch. I suppose you haven't got much choice up there. . . . At the station . . . a good fire . . . something hot . . . cold things in the car and wine.' There was a pause. 'Remember, you're responsible.'

'For something so irregular,' began Major Petkovitch. 'No, no, no,' said the voice, 'I was referring, of course, to lunch.'

'Is everything quiet in Belgrade?' Major Petkovitch asked stiffly. 'Fast asleep,' the voice said.

'May I ask one more question?'

Major Petkovitch called, 'Hello. Hello. Hello,' in an irritated voice and then slammed down the receiver. 'Where's that man? Come with me,' and again followed by Ninitch and his dog he plunged into the cold, crossed the rails and the guard-room, and slammed the door of his room behind him. Then he wrote a number of notes very briefly and handed them to Ninitch for delivery: he was so hurried and irritated that he forgot to seal two of them. These, of course, Ninitch read; his wife would be proud of him that evening. There was one to the chief customs officer, but that was sealed; there was one to the captain at the barracks telling him to double the station guard immediately and to serve out twenty rounds of ammunition per man. It made Ninitch uneasy; did it mean war, that the Bulgars were coming? Or the Reds? He remembered what had happened at Belgrade and was very much disturbed. After all, he thought, they are our own people, they are poor, they have wives and children. Last of all there was a note for the cook at the barracks, containing detailed instructions for a lunch for three, to be served hot in the major's room at one-thirty; 'Remember, you're responsible,' it ended.

When Ninitch left the room, Major Petkovitch was again reading the out-of-date German book on strategy, while he fed his dog with pieces of sausage.

[2]

Coral Musker had fallen asleep long before the train reached Budapest. When Myatt drew a cramped arm from under her head, she woke to a grey morning like the swell of a leaden sea. She scrambled quickly from the berth and dressed; she was hurried and excited and she mislaid things. She began to sing light-heartedly under her breath: *I'm so happy, Happy-go-lucky me.* The motion of the train flung her against the window, but she gave the grey morning only a hurried glance. Lights came out here and there, one after the other, but there was not yet day enough to see the houses by; a lamp-lit bridge across the Danube gleamed like the buckle of a garter. *I just go my way, Singing every day.* Somewhere down by the river a white house glowed; it might have been mistaken for a tree trunk in an orchard, but for two lights in ground-floor rooms; as she watched, they were turned out. They've been celebrating late; she wondered, what's been going on there? and laughed a little, feeling herself at one with all daring, scandalous and youthful things. *Things that worry you Never worry me. Summer follows Spring. I just smile and* . . . Quite dressed now except for her shoes, she turned towards the berth and Myatt.

He was uneasily asleep and needed a shave; he lay in rumpled clothes, and she could connect him with the excitement and pain of the night only with difficulty. This man was a stranger; he would disclaim responsibility for words spoken by an intruder in the dark. So much had been promised her. But she told herself that that kind of good fortune did not come her way. The words of elderly experienced women were brought again to mind: 'They'll promise anything beforehand,' and the strange moral code of her class warned her: 'You mustn't remind them.' Nevertheless she approached him and with her hand tried gently to arrange his hair into some semblance of her lover's. As she touched his forehead he woke, and she faced with courage the glance which she feared to see momentarily blank with ignorance of who she was and what they had done together. She fortified herself with maxims: 'There's as good fish in the sea,' but to her glad amazement he said at once without any struggle to remember, 'Yes, we must have the fiddler.'

She clapped her hands together in relief: 'And don't forget the doctor.' She sat down on the edge of the berth and slipped on her shoes. *I'm so happy*. He remembers, he's going to keep his promise. She began to sing again: *Living in the sunlight, loving in the moonlight, Having a wonderful time*. The guard came down the corridor knocking on the door: 'Budapest.' The lights were clustering together; above the opposite bank of the river, apparently dropped half-way from the heavy sky, shone three stars. 'What's that? There. It's going. Quick.'

'The castle,' he said.

'Budapest.' Josef Grünlich, nodding in his corner, started awake and went to the window. He had a flashing glimpse of water between tall grey houses, of lights burning in upper rooms, cut off abruptly by the arch of the station, and then the train slid to rest in a great echoing hall. Mr Opie at once emerged, brisk and cheerful and laden, dumping two suitcases upon the ground, and then a golf bag, and a tennis racket in its case. Josef grinned and blew out his chest: the sight of Mr Opie reminded him of his crime. A man in Cook's uniform came by leading a tall crumpled woman and her husband; they stumbled at his heels, bewildered, and unhappy through the whistling steam and the calling of strange tongues. It seemed to Josef that he might leave the train. Immediately, because this was something which concerned his safety, he ceased to think either humorously or grandiloquently; the small precise wheels of his brain went round and like the auditing machine in a bank began to record with unfailing accuracy the debits and credits. In a train he was virtually imprisoned; the police could arrange his arrest at any point of his journey; therefore the sooner he was at liberty the better. As an Austrian he would pass unnoticed in Budapest. If he continued his

159

journey to Constantinople, he would run the risk of three more customs examinations. The automatic machine ran again through the figures, added, checked and passed on to the debit side. The police in Budapest were efficient. In Balkan countries they were corrupt and there was nothing to fear from the customs. He was farther from the scene of his crime. He had friends in Istanbul. Josef Grünlich decided to go on. The decision made, he again leant back in a dream of triumph; images of revolvers quickly drawn flashed through his mind, voices spoke of him: 'There's Josef. Five years now and never jugged. He killed Kolber at Vienna.'

'Budapest.' Dr Czinner ceased writing for a little more than a minute. That small pause was the tribute he paid to the city in which his father had been born. His father had left Hungary when a young man and settled in Dalmatia; in Hungary he had been a peasant, toiling on another man's land; in Split and eventually in Belgrade he had been a shoemaker working for himself; and yet the previous more servile existence, the inheritance of a Hungarian peasant's blood, represented to Dr Czinner the breath of a larger culture blowing down the dark stinking Balkan alleys. It was as if an Athenian slave, become a freed man in barbarian lands, regretted a little the statuary, the poetry, the philosophy of a culture in which he had had no share. The station began to float away from him; names slipped by in a language which his father had never taught him: 'Restoracioj', 'Pôsto', 'Informoj'. A poster flapped close to the carriage window: 'Teatnoj Kaj Amuzejoj', and mechanically he noted the unfamiliar names, the entertainments which would be just opening as the train arrived at Belgrade, the Opera, the Royal Orfeum, the Tabarin, and the Jardin de Paris. He remembered how his father had often commented, in the dark basement parlour behind his shop: 'They enjoy themselves in Buda.' His father, too, had once enjoyed himself in the city, pressing his face against the glass of restaurants, watching, without envy, the food carried to the tables, the fiddlers moving from group to group, making merry himself in a simple vicarious way. He had been angered by his father's easy satisfaction.

He wrote for ten minutes more and then folded the paper and slipped it into the pocket of his mackintosh. He wished to be prepared for any eventuality; his enemies he knew had no scruples; they would rather see him quickly murdered in a back street than alive in the dock. The strength of his position lay in their ignorance of his coming; he had to proclaim his voluntary presence in Belgrade before they knew that he was there, for then there could be no quick assassination of an unidentified stranger; they would have no choice but to put him upon his trial. He opened his suitcases and took out the Baedeker. Then he lit a match and held it to the corner of the map; the shiny paper burned slowly. The railway shot up in a little lick of flame, and he watched the post office square turn into tough black ash. Then the green of the park, the Kalimagdan, turned brown. The streets of the slum quarter were the last to burn, and he blew the flame to hasten it.

When the map was quite burned he threw the ash under the seat, put a bitter tablet on his tongue, and tried to sleep. He found it difficult. He was a man without humour or he would have smiled at the sudden lightness of his heart, as he recognised, fifty miles beyond Buda, a sudden break in the great Danube plain, a hill shaped like a thimble and shaggy with fir trees. A road made a great circle to avoid it and then shot straight towards the city. Road and hill were both white now under the snow, which hung in the trees in great lumps like the nests of rooks. He remembered the road and the hill and the wood because they were the first things he had noted with a sense of full security after escaping across the frontier five years before. His companion who drove the car had broken silence for the first time since they left Belgrade and called to him: 'We shall be in Buda in an hour and a quarter.' Dr Czinner had not realised till then that he was safe. Now his lightness of heart had opposite cause. He thought not that he was only fifty miles from Budapest, but that he was only seventy miles from the frontier. He was nearly home. Instinct for the moment was stronger in him than opinion. It was no use telling himself that he had no home and that his destination was a prison; for that one moment of light-hearted enjoyment it was to Kruger's beergarden, to the park at evening swimming in green light, to the steep streets and the bright rags that he was journeying. After all, he told himself, I shall see all this again; they'll drive me from the prison to the court. It was then that he remembered with unreasoning melancholy that the beer-garden had been turned into flats.

Across the breakfast table Coral and Myatt faced each other with immeasurable relief as strangers. At dinner they had been old friends with nothing to say to one another. All through breakfast they talked fast and continuously as if the train was consuming time, not miles, and they had to fill the hours with talk sufficient for a life together.

'And when I get to Constantinople, what shall I do? My room's been booked.'

'Never mind that. I've taken a room at an hotel. You'll come with me and we'll make it a double room.'

She accepted his solution with breathless pleasure, but there was no time for silence, for sitting back. Rocks, houses, bare pastures were receding at fifty miles an hour, and there was much to be said. 'We get in at breakfast time, don't we? What shall we do all day?'

'We'll have lunch together. In the afternoon I'll have to go to the office and see to things there. You can go shopping. I'll be back in the evening and we'll have dinner and go to the theatre.'

'Yes, and what theatre?' It was extraordinary to her, the transformation which the night had caused. His face no longer resembled that of all the Jewish boys she had known with half intimacy; even the gesture with which he gave and gave, the instinctive spreading of the hands, was different; his emphasis on how much he would spend, on what a good time he would give her, was unique because she believed him.

'We'll have the best seats at your theatre.'

'Dunn's Babies?'

'Yes, and we'll take them all out to dinner afterwards, if you like.'

'No.' She shook her head; she could not risk losing him now, and many of Dunn's Babies would be prettier than she. 'Let's go back to bed after the theatre.' They began to laugh over their coffee, spilling brown drops upon the tablecloth. There was no apprehension in her laugh; she was happy because pain was behind her. 'Do you know how long we've sat at breakfast?' she asked. 'A whole hour. It's a scandal. I've never done it before. A cup of tea in bed at ten o'clock is my breakfast. And two pieces of toast and some orange juice if I've got a nice landlady.'

'And when you haven't any work?'

She laughed. 'I leave out the orange juice. Are we near the frontier now?'

'Very near.' Myatt lit a cigarette. 'Smoke?'

'Not in the morning. I'll leave you to it.' She got up and at the same moment the train ground across a point and she was flung against him. She caught his arm to steady herself and over his shoulder saw a signal-box sway dizzily out of sight and a black shed against which the snow had drifted. She held his arm a moment till her giddiness passed. 'Darling, come soon. I'll be waiting for you.' Suddenly she wanted to say to him, 'Come now.' She felt afraid at being left alone when the train was in a station. Strangers might come in and take his seat, and she would be unable to make them understand. She would not know what the customs men said to her. But she told herself that he would soon tire if she made demands on him; it wasn't safe to trouble a man; her happiness was not so secure that she dared take the smallest risk with it. She looked back; he sat with head a little bent, caressing with his fingers a gold cigarette-case. She was glad later that she had taken that last glance, it was to serve as an emblem of fidelity, an image to carry with her, so that she might explain, 'I've never left you.'

The train stopped as she reached her seat, and she looked out of the window at a small muddy station. Subotica was printed in black letters on a couple of lamps; the station buildings were little more than a row of sheds, and there was a platform. A group of customs-officers in green uniforms came down between the lines with half a dozen soldiers; they seemed in no hurry to begin their search. They laughed and talked and went on towards the guard's van. A row of peasants stood watching the train, and one woman suckled a child. There were a good many soldiers about with nothing to do; one of them shooed the peasants off the rails, but they scrambled over them again twenty yards down the line. The passengers began to grow impatient; the train was half an hour late already, and no attempt had yet been made to search the luggage or examine the passports. Several people climbed on to the line and crossed the rails in hope of finding a refreshment-room; a tall thin German with a bullet head walked up and down, up and down. Coral Musker saw the doctor leave the train, wearing his soft hat and mackintosh and a pair of grey wool gloves. He and the German passed and repassed and passed again, but they might have been walking in different worlds for all the notice they took of each other. Once they stood side by side while an official looked at their passports, but they still belonged to different worlds, the German was fuming and impatient, and the doctor was smiling to himself.

When she came near him she could see the quality of his smile, vacuous and sentimental. It seemed out of place. 'Excuse me speaking to you,' she said humbly, a little frightened by his stiff respectful manner. He bowed and put his grey gloved hands behind him; she caught a glimpse of a hole in the thumb. 'I was wondering . . . we were wondering . . . if you would have dinner with us tonight.' The smile had been tidied away, and she saw him gathering together a forbidding weight of words. She explained, 'You have been so kind to me.' It was very cold in the open air and they both began to walk; the frozen mud crackled round the tops of her shoes and marked her stockings. 'It would have given me great pleasure,' he said, marshalling his words with terrible correctness, 'and it is my sorrow that I cannot accept. I am leaving the train tonight at Belgrade. I should have enjoyed . . .' He stopped in his stride with creased brows and seemed to forget what he was saying; he put the hand in the worn glove into his mackintosh pocket. 'I should have enjoyed . . .' Two men in uniform were walking up the line towards them.

The doctor put his hand on her arm and swung her gently round, and they began to walk back along the train. He was still frowning and he never finished his sentence. Instead, he began another, 'I wonder if you would mind—my glasses are frosted over—what do you see in front of us?'

'There are a few customs-officers coming down from the guard's van to meet us.'

'Is that all? In green uniform?'

'No, in grey.'

The doctor stopped. 'So?' He took her hand in his and she felt an envelope folded into her palm. 'Go quickly back to your carriage. Hide this. When you get to Istanbul post it. Go now quickly. But don't seem in a hurry.' She obeyed without understanding him; twenty steps brought her up to the men in grey and she saw that they were soldiers; they carried no rifles, but she guessed it by their bayonet sheaths. They barred her way, and for a moment she thought they would stop her; they were talking rapidly among themselves, but when she came within a few feet of them, one man stepped aside to let her by. She was relieved but still a little frightened, feeling the letter folded in her hand. Was she being made to smuggle something? A drug? Then one of the soldiers came after her; she heard his boots cracking the mud; she reassured herself that she was imagining things, that if he wanted her he would call, and his silence encouraged her. Nevertheless, she walked more rapidly. Her compartment was only one carriage away, and her lover would be able to explain in German to the man who she was. But Myatt was not in the compartment; he was still smoking in the restaurant. For a second she hesitated. I will go to the restaurant and tap on the window, but her second's hesitation had been too long. A hand touched her elbow, and a voice said something to her gently in a foreign tongue.

She swung round to protest, to implore, ready, if need be, to break away and run to the restaurant-car, but her fears were a little quietened by the soldier's large gentle eyes. He smiled at her and nodded his head and pointed to the station buildings. She said, 'What do you want? Can't you speak English?' He shook his head and smiled again and pointed, and she saw the doctor meet the soldiers and walk with them towards the buildings. There could be nothing wrong, he was walking in front of them, they were not using force. The soldier nodded and smiled and then with a great effort brought out three words of English. 'All quite good,' he said and pointed again to the buildings.

'Can I just tell my friend?' she asked. He nodded and smiled and took her arm, leading her gently away from the train.

The waiting-room was empty except for the doctor. A stove burnt in the middle of the floor, and the view from the windows was broken by lines of frost. She was conscious all the while of the letter in her hand. The soldier ushered her in gently and politely and then closed the door without locking it. 'What do they want?' she asked. 'I mustn't miss the train.'

'Don't be frightened,' he said. 'I'll explain to them;

they'll let you go in five minutes. You must let them search you if they want to. Have they taken the letter?'

'No.'

'Better give it to me. I don't want to get you into trouble.' She held out her hand and at the same moment the door opened. The soldier came in and smiled encouragingly and took the letter from her. Dr Czinner spoke to him, and the man talked rapidly; he had simple unhappy eyes. When he had gone again Dr Czinner said, 'He doesn't like it. He was told to look through the keyhole and see if anything passed between us.'

Coral Musker sat down on a wooden seat and stuck her feet out towards the stove. Dr Czinner noted with amazement, 'You are very calm.'

'It's no use getting shirty,' she said. 'They can't understand, anyway. My friend'll be looking for me soon.'

'That's true,' he said with relief. He hesitated for a moment. 'You must wonder why I do not apologise to you for this—discomfort. You see there's something I hold more important than any discomfort. I expect you don't understand.'

'Don't I, though,' she said, thinking with wry humour of the night. A long whistle shivered through the cold air and she sprang up apprehensively. 'That's not our train, is it? I can't miss it.' Dr Czinner was at the window. He freed the inner surface from steam with the palm of his hand and peered between the ridges of frost. 'No,' he said, 'it's an engine on the other line. I think they are changing engines. It will take them a long time. Don't be frightened.'

'Oh, I'm not scared,' she said, settling herself again on the hard seat. 'My friend'll be along soon. *They'll* be scared then. He's rich, you know.'

'So?' said Dr Czinner.

'Yes, and important too. He's the head of a firm. They do something with currants.' She began to laugh. 'He told me to think of him when I eat spotted dog.'

'So?'

'Yes. I like him. He's been sweet to me. He's quite different from other Jews. They're generally kind, but he—well, he's quiet.'

'I think that he must be a very lucky young man,' said Dr Czinner. The door was opened and two soldiers pushed a man in. Dr Czinner moved quickly forward and put his foot in the door. He spoke to them softly. One of them replied, the other thrust him back and closed and locked the door. 'I asked them,' he said, 'why they were keeping you here. I told them you must catch the train. One of them said it was quite all right. An officer wants to ask you a question or two. The train doesn't go for half an hour.'

'Thank you,' Coral said.

'And me?' said the newcomer in a furious voice. 'And me'

'I know nothing about you, Herr Grünlich.'

'The customs they came and they search me. They take my cannon. They say: "Why haven't you declared that you keep a cannon in possession?" I say: "No one would travel in your country without a cannon."' Coral Musker began to laugh: Josef Grünlich glared at her wickedly, then he smoothed his rumpled waistcoat, glanced at his watch, and sat down. With his hands on his flat knees he stared straight in front of him, considering.

He must have finished his cigarette by now, Coral thought. He'll have gone back to the compartment and found I'm not there. Perhaps he'll wait ten minutes before he asks one of the men at the station whether they've seen me. In twelve minutes he'll have found me. Her heart leapt when a key turned in the lock, wondering at the speed with which he had traced her, but it was not Myatt who entered, but a fair fussed officer. He snapped an order over his shoulder and two soldiers came in behind him and stood against the door.

'But what's it all about?' Coral asked Dr Czinner. 'Do they think we've smuggled something?' She could not understand what the foreigners said to each other, and suddenly she felt lost and afraid, knowing that however much these men might wish to help her, they could not understand what she said or what she wanted. She implored Dr Czinner, 'Tell them I must catch this train. Ask them to tell my friend.' He took no notice, but stood stiffly by the stove with his hands in his pockets answering questions. She turned to the German in the corner, staring at the toes of his shoes. 'Tell them that I've done nothing, please.' He raised his eyes for a moment and looked at her with hatred.

At last Dr Czinner said, 'I have tried to explain that you know nothing of the note I passed you. But he says he must keep you a little longer until the Chief of Police has questioned you.'

'But the train?' she implored, 'the train?'

'I think it will be all right. It will be here for another half an hour. I have asked him to let your friend know and he says that he will see what can be done.' She went to the officer and touched his arm. 'I must go by this train,' she said, 'I must. Do understand me, please.' He shook his arm free, and rebuked her in a sharp precise tone, his pince-nez nodding, but what the terms of the rebuke were she could not tell. Then he left the waiting-room.

Coral pressed her face to the window. Between two fronds of frost the German passed, walking up and down the track; she tried to see as far as the restaurant-car. 'Is he in sight?' Dr Czinner asked.

'It's going to snow again,' she said, and left the window. Suddenly she could bear her perplexity no longer. 'Why do they want me? What are they keeping me here for?'

He assured her, 'It's a mistake. They are frightened. There has been rioting in Belgrade. They want me, that's all.'

'But why? You're English, aren't you?'

'No, I'm one of them,' he said with some bitterness.

'What have you done?'

'I've tried to make things different.' He explained with an air of distaste for labels: 'I am a Communist.'

At once she exclaimed, 'Why? Why?' watching him fearfully, unable to hide that she felt her faith shaken in the only man, except Myatt, able and willing to help her. Even the kindness he had shown her on the train she now regarded with suspicion. She went to the bench and sat down as far as she could from the German.

'It would take a long time to tell you why,' he said. She took no notice, shutting her mind to the meaning of any words he uttered. She thought of him now as one of the untidy men who paraded on Saturday afternoons in Trafalgar Square bearing hideous banners: 'Workers of the World, Unite', 'Walthamstow Old Comrades', 'Balham Branch of the Juvenile Workers' League'. They were the kill-joys, who would hang the rich and close the theatres and drive her into dismal free love at a summer camp, and afterwards make her walk in procession down Oxford Street, carrying her baby behind a banner: 'British Women Workers'.

'Longer than I've got,' he said.

171

She took no notice. She was, for the moment in her thoughts, immeasurably above him. She was a rich man's mistress, and he was a workman. When she at last took notice of him it was with contempt: 'I suppose you'll go to gaol.'

'I think they'll shoot me,' he said.

She stared at him in amazement, forgetting their difference in class: 'Why?' He smiled with a touch of conceit: 'They're afraid.'

'In England,' she said, 'they let the Reds speak as much as they like. The police stand round.'

'Ah, but there's a difference. We do more than speak.'

'But there'll be a trial?'

'A sort of trial. They'll take me to Belgrade.'

Somewhere a horn was blowing, and the cold air was split by a whistle. 'They must be shunting,' Dr Czinner said to reassure her. A film of smoke was blown across the windows, darkening the waiting-room, and voices called and feet began to run along the track outside. Links between coaches groaned and pushed and strained, and then the thin walls shook to the grinding of pistons, the beat of heavy wheels. When the smoke cleared, Coral Musker sat quite still on the wooden bench. There was nothing to be said and her feet were stone cold. But after a while she began to read in Dr Czinner's silence an accusation, and she spoke with warmth, 'He'll come back for me,' she said. 'You wait and see.'

Ninitch let his rifle fall into the crook of his arm and beat his gloved hands together. 'That new engine's noisy,' he said, as he watched the train stretch like elastic round a bend and disappear. The points groaned back into place, and the signal on the passenger up-line rose. A man came down the steps from the box, crossed the line and disappeared in the direction of a cottage.

'Gone for lunch,' Ninitch's companion said enviously.

'I've never heard an engine as noisy as that,' Ninitch said, 'all the time I've been here.' Then his companion's remark reached him. 'The major's having a hot meal down from the barracks,' he said. But he did not tell his friend that the Chief of Police was coming from Belgrade; he kept the news for his wife.

'You are a lucky one,' his companion said. 'You'll be having a meal all right. I've often thought it must be good to be married when I see your wife come down of a morning.'

'It's not too bad,' said Ninitch modestly.

'Tell me, what does she bring you?'

'A loaf of bread and a piece of sausage. Sometimes a bit of butter. She's a good girl.' But his thoughts were not so temperate. I am not good enough for her; I should like to be rich and give her a dress and a necklace and take her to Belgrade to the theatre. He thought at first with envy of the foreign girl locked in the waiting-room, of her clothes which seemed to him very costly and of her green glass necklace, but in comparing her with his wife he soon forgot his envy and began to regard the foreigner, too, with affection. The beauty and fragility of women struck him with pathos, as he beat his great clumsy hands together.

'Wake up,' his friend whispered, and both men straightened and stood 'at ease' in a stiff attitude as a car plunged up the road to the station, breaking through the frozen surface and scattering water. 'Who the devil?' his friend whispered, hardly moving his lips, but Ninitch proudly knew; he knew that the tall ribboned officer was the Chief of Police, he even knew the name of the other officer who bounded out of the car like a rubber ball and held the door open for Colonel Hartep to alight.

'What a place,' said Colonel Hartep with amused distaste, looking first at the mud and then at his polished boots.

Captain Alexitch blew out his round red cheeks. 'They might have laid some boards.'

'No, no, we are the police. They don't like us. God knows what sort of a lunch they'll give us. Here, my man,' he beckoned to Ninitch, 'help the chauffeur out with these cases. Be careful to keep the wine steady and upright.'

'Major Petkovitch, sir . . .'

'Never mind Major Petkovitch.'

'Excuse me,' said a precise angry voice behind Ninitch.

'Certainly, Major,' Colonel Hartep smiled and bowed, 'but I am sure that there is no need to excuse you.'

'This man is on guard over the prisoners.'

'You have captured a number of them. I congratulate you.'

'Two men and a girl.'

'In that case I should imagine a good lock, a guard, a bayonet, a rifle, and twenty rounds of ammunition will meet the case.'

Major Petkovitch licked his lips. 'The police, of course, know best how to guard a prison. I bow to superior knowledge. Take the things out of the car,' he said to Ninitch, 'and bring them to my room.' He led the officers round the corner of the waiting-room and out of sight. Ninitch stared after them, until the chauffeur called out to him, 'I can't wait here in the car all day. Look lively. You soldiers aren't used to a spot of work.' He began to take the boxes out of the car, telling over their contents as he did so: 'A half case of champagne. A cold duck. Fruit. Two bottles of sherry. Sausage. Wine biscuits. Lettuce. Olives.'

'Well,' Ninitch's friend called out, 'is it a good meal?'

Ninitch stood and stared for a moment in silence. Then he said in a low voice, 'It's a feast.'

He had carried the sherry and champagne and the duck to the major's room when he saw his wife coming up the road bringing his own lunch wrapped in a white cloth. She was small and dark with her shawl twisted tightly round her shoulders; she had a malicious humorous face and big boots. He put down the case of fruit and went to meet her. 'I shall not be long,' he told her in a low voice, so that the chauffeur might not hear. 'Wait for me. I've something to tell you,' and very seriously he went back to his task. His wife sat down by the side of the road and watched him, but when he came back from the major's office, where the table was already spread and the officers were making headway with the wine, she was gone. She had left his lunch by the side of the road. 'Where is she?' he asked the other guard.

'She talked to the chauffeur and then she went back to the barracks. She seemed excited about something.'

Ninitch suffered a pang of disappointment. He had looked forward to telling his wife the story of Colonel Hartep's coming, and now the chauffeur had anticipated him. It was always the same. A soldier's life was a dog's life. It was the civilians who got high wages and robbed the soldiers at cards and abused them and even interfered between a soldier and his wife. But his resentment was brief. There were secrets he could yet discover for his wife, if he kept ears and eyes open. He waited for some time before he carried the last case to the major's room. The champagne was bubbling low;

all three men spoke at once, and Major Petkovitch's glasses had fallen in his lap. 'Such bobbles,' Captain Alexitch was saying, 'such thighs. I said to His Excellency if I was in your place . . .' Major Petkovitch drew lines on the tablecloth with a finger dipped in wine. 'The first maxim is, never strike at the wings. Crumple the centre.' Colonel Hartep was quite sober. He leant back in his chair smoking. 'Take just a trifle of French mustard; two sprigs of parsley,' but neither of his juniors paid him any attention. He smiled gently and filled their glasses.

The snow was falling again, and through the wind-blown drifts Dr Czinner saw the peasants of Subotica straggling across the line, thrusting their inquisitive twisted bodies towards the waiting-room. One man got close enough to the window to stare in and examine the doctor's face. They were separated by a few feet and a sheet of glass and the lines of frost and the vapour of their breath. Dr. Czinner could count his wrinkles, name the colour of his eyes and examine with brief professional interest a sore upon his cheek. But always the peasants were driven back by the two soldiers, who struck at them with the butts of their rifles. The peasants gave way and moved on to the line, but presently they swarmed back, obstinate, stupid and hopeless.

There had been silence in the waiting-room for a very long while. Dr Czinner went back to the stove. The girl sat with her thumbs joined and her head a little bent. He knew what she was doing; she was praying that her lover would come back for her soon, and from her secrecy he guessed that she was not accustomed to prayer. She was very frightened, and with a cold sympathy he was able to judge the measure of her fear. His experience told him two things, that prayers were not answered and that so casual a lover would not trouble to return.

He was sorry that he had involved her, but he regretted it only as he might have regretted a necessary lie. He had always recognised the need of sacrificing his own integrity; only a party in power could possess scruples; scruples in himself would be a confession that he doubted the overwhelming value of his cause. But the reflection for some reason made him bitter; he found himself envying virtues which he was not rich or strong enough to cherish. He would have welcomed generosity, charity, meticulous codes of honour to his breast if he could have succeeded, if the world had been shaped again to the pattern he loved and longed for. He spoke to her angrily: 'You are lucky to believe that that will do good,' but he found to his amazement that she could instinctively outbid his bitterness, which was founded on theories laboriously worked out by a fallible reason. 'I don't,' she said, 'but one must do something.'

He was shocked by the ease of her disbelief, which did not come from the painful reading of rationalist writers and nineteenth-century scientists, she had been born to disbelief as securely as he had been born to belief. He had sacrificed security in order to reach the same position, and for a moment he longed to sow in her some dry plant of doubt, a half-belief which would make her mistrust her judgment. He allowed the inclination to pass and encouraged her. 'He'll come back for you from Belgrade.'

'Perhaps he can't afford the time.'

'He'll telegraph to the British Consul.'

She said, 'Of course,' without conviction. The events of the night, the experience of Myatt's tenderness, swam back from her, like a lit pier, into darkness. She strained her memory in the effort to recover sight of him, but he soon became an indistinguishable member of a crowd gathered to say good-bye. It was not long before she began to question his difference from all the other Jews she had known. Even her body, rested now and healed, but the deep peace gone with the pain, was aware of no difference. She repeated, 'Of course,' because she was ashamed at her lack of faith, because it was no use grumbling away, because at any rate she was no worse off except for being a day late for the show. There's as good fish in the sea, she told herself, but feeling none the less strangely tied to a memory which lacked all conviction.

The German sat bolt upright in his corner, sleeping; his eyelids twitched, ready to rise at the least unfamiliar sound. He was accustomed to rest in strange places and to take advantage of any respite. When the door opened, his eyes were at once attentive.

A guard entered and waved his hand at them and shouted. Dr Czinner repeated what he said in English. 'We are to come out.' The snow blew in at the open door, making a grey tidemark on the threshold. They could see the peasants huddled on the line. Josef Grünlich stood up and smoothed his waistcoat, and pressed his elbow in Dr Czinner's side. 'If we runned now, eh, through the snow, all together?' 'They would shoot,' Dr Czinner said. The guard shouted again and waved his hand. 'But they shoot anyway, eh? What do they want outside'

Dr Czinner turned to Coral Musker. 'I don't think there's anything to fear. Are you coming?'

'Of course.' Then she implored him, 'Wait one moment for me. I've lost my handkerchief.' The tall thin form bent like a pair of grey compasses, went down on the knees and fetched it from beneath the seat. His awkwardness made her smile; she forgot her distrust and thanked him with disproportionate gratitude. Outside he walked with bent head to avoid the snow, smiling to himself. One guard led them and one walked behind with his rifle unslung and his bayonet fixed. They called to each other in a language she could not understand over the prisoner's heads, and she was being taken she did not know where. There was a scramble and splashing of feet over the rails and the mud as the peasants came nearer, hungry for a sight of them, and she was a little daunted by the olive faces and her own ignorance of what it was all about. She asked Dr. Czinner, 'Why are you smiling?' and hoped to hear that he had seen a way to release them all, to catch the express, to put back the hands of the clock. He said, 'I don't know. Was I smiling? It is perhaps because I am home again.' For a moment his mouth was serious, then it fell again into a loose smile, and his eyes as they peered this way and that through his frosted glasses seemed moist and empty of anything but a kind of stupid happiness.

[3]

Myatt, with his eye on the lengthening ash of his cigar, thought. These were the moments he cherished, when he felt alone with himself and feared no rebuff, when his body was satisfied and his emotions stilled. The night before he had tried in vain to work; the girl's face had come between him and the figures; now she was relegated to her proper place. Presently, as evening came on, he might need her and she would be there, and at the thought he felt tenderness and even gratitude, not least because her physical presence gone, she had left no importunate ghost. He could remember now without looking at his papers the figures he had been unable to arrange. He multiplied, divided, subtracted, seeing the long columns arrange themselves down the window, across which the transparent bodies of customs-officials and porters passed unnoticed. Presently somebody asked to see his passport, and then the ash fell from his cigar and he went back to his compartment to open his luggage. Coral was not there, but he supposed that she was in the lavatory. The customs-officer tapped her bag. 'And this?'

'It's unlocked,' he said. 'The lady is not here. You will find nothing.' When he was alone again he lay back in his corner and closed his eyes, the better to consider the affairs of Mr Eckman, but by the time the train drew out of Subotica he was asleep. He dreamed that he was mounting the stairs to Mr Eckman's office. Narrow, uncarpeted and unlit, they might have led to a disreputable flat off Leicester Square, instead of to the headquarters of the biggest currant importers in Europe. He did not remember passing through the door; the next moment he was sitting face to face with Mr Eckman. A great pile of papers lay between them and Mr Eckman stroked his dark moustache and tapped the desk with his fountain-pen, while a spider drew the veins of its web across a dry ink-well. The electric light was dim and the window was sooty and in the corner Mrs Eckman sat on a steel sofa knitting baby clothes.

'I admit everything,' said Mr Eckman. Suddenly his chair rose, until he sat high overhead, tapping with an auctioneer's hammer. 'Answer me these questions,' said Mr Eckman. 'You are on oath. Don't prevaricate. Say yes or no. Did you seduce the girl?'

'In a way.'

Mr Eckman drew a sheet of paper from the middle of the pile, and another and another, till the pile tottered and fell to the floor with the noise of falling bricks. 'This affair of Jervis. Slim work I call it. You had contracted with the trustees and had only delayed to sign.'

'It was legal.'

'And this £10,000 to Stavrog when you'd already had an offer of £15,000.'

'It's business.'

'And the girl on the Spaniards Road.

'And the £1,000 to Moults' clerk for information.

'What have I done that you haven't done? Answer me quick. Don't prevaricate. Say yes or no. My lord and gentlemen of the jury, the prisoner at the bar . . .'

'I want to speak. I've got something to say. I'm not guilty.'

'Under what clause? What code? Law of Equity? Law of Tithes? Admiralty Court or the King's Bench? Answer me quick. Don't prevaricate. Say yes or no. Three strokes of the hammer. Going, going. This fine flourishing business, gentlemen.'

'Wait a moment. I'll tell you. George. Cap. III. Section 4. Vic. 2504. Honour among Thieves.'

Mr Eckman, suddenly very small in the dingy office, began to weep, stretching out his hands. And all the washerwomen who paddled in the stream knee-deep lifted up their heads and wept, while a dry wind tore up the sand from the sea-beaches and flung it rattling against the leaves of the forest, and a voice which might have been Mrs Eckman's implored him over and over again, 'Come back.' Then the desert shook under his feet and he opened his eyes. The train had stopped, and the snow was caking on the glass of the window. Coral had not returned.

Presently somebody at the back of the train began to laugh and jeer, and others joined in, whistling and catcalling. Myatt looked at his watch. He had slept for more than two hours, and perhaps because he remembered the voice in his dream, he felt uneasy at Coral's absence. Smoke poured from the engine and a man in dungarees with a blackened face stood apart from it, gazing hopelessly. Several people called to him from the third class and he turned and shook his head and shrugged in a graceful bewildered way. The *chef de train* walked rapidly down the track away from the engine. Myatt stopped him. 'What has happened?'

'Nothing. Nothing at all. A little defect.'

'Are we stuck here for long?'

'Oh, a mere trifle. An hour, an hour and a half perhaps. We are telephoning for a new engine.'

Myatt closed the window and went into the corridor; there was no sign of Coral. He passed down the whole length of the train, looking into compartments, trying the doors of lavatories until he reached the third class. There he remembered the man with the violin and sought him through the hard wooden odorous compartments, until he ran him to earth, a small pinched fellow with a swollen eye.

'I am giving a dinner tonight,' Myatt said to him in German, 'and I want you to play for me. I'll give you fifty paras.'

'Seventy-five, your excellency.'

Myatt was hurried; he wanted to find Coral. 'Seventy-five, then.'

'Something dreamy, melancholy, to bring tears, your excellency?'

'Of course not. I want something light and cheerful.'

'Ah, well, of course? That is more expensive.'

'What do you mean? Why more expensive?'

His excellency, of course, was a foreigner. He did not understand. It was the custom of the country to charge more for light songs than for melancholy. Oh, an age-old custom. One and a half dinas?—Suddenly, dispelling his impatience and his anxiety, the joy of bargaining gripped Myatt. The money was nothing; there was less than half a crown at stake, but this was business; he would not give in. 'Seventy-five paras. Not a para more.'

The man grinned at him with pleasure: this was a stranger after his own heart. 'One dina thirty paras. It is my last word, your excellency. I should disgrace my profession if I accepted less.' The odour of stale bread and sour wine no longer disturbed Myatt; it was the smell of an ancestral market-place. This was the pure poetry of business: gain and loss hardly entered into a transaction fought out in paras, each of which was worth less than a farthing. He came a little way into the carriage, but he did not sit down. "Eighty paras.'

'Your excellency, one must live. One dina twenty-five. It would shame me to take less.'

Myatt offered the man a cigarette. 'A glass of *rakia,* your excellency?' Myatt nodded and took without distaste the thick chipped tumbler. 'Eighty-five paras. Take it or leave it.' Smoking and drinking together in a close understanding they grew fierce with each other. 'You insult me, your excellency. I am a musician.'

'Eight-seven paras, that is my last word.'

The three officers sat round the table, which had

been cleared of the glasses. Two soldiers stood before the door with fixed bayonets. Dr Czinner watched Colonel Hartep with curiosity; he had last seen him at the Kamnetz trial marshalling his lying witnesses with a graceful disregard of justice. That was five years ago, but the years had done little to alter his appearance. His hair was a fine silver above his ears and there were a few kindly wrinkles at the corners of his eyes. 'Major Petkovitch,' he said, 'will you read the charge against the prisoners? Let the lady have a chair.'

Dr Czinner took his hands from the pockets of his mackintosh and wiped his glasses. He could keep emotion from his voice, but not from his hands, which trembled a little. 'A charge?' he said. 'What do you mean? Is this a court?'

Major Petkovitch, paper in hand, snapped at him, 'Be quiet.'

'It's a reasonable question, Major,' said Colonel Hartep. 'The doctor has been abroad. You see,' he said, speaking gently and with great kindness, 'measures have had to be taken for your safety. Your life would not be safe in Belgrade. People are angry about the rising.'

'I still don't understand your right,' Dr Czinner said, 'to make more than a preliminary inquiry.'

Colonel Hartep explained. 'This is a court martial. Martial Law was proclaimed early yesterday morning. Now, Major Petkovitch.'

Major Petkovitch began to read a long document in a manuscript which he found often illegible. 'The prisoner, Richard Czinner . . . conspiracy against the Government . . . unserved sentence for perjury . . . false passport. The prisoner, Josef Grünlich, found in possession of arms. The prisoner, Coral Musker, conspiracy with Richard Czinner, against the Government.'

He laid the paper down and said to Colonel Hartep, 'I am uncertain of the legality of this court as it stands. The prisoners should be represented by counsel.'

'Dear, dear, this is certainly an oversight. Perhaps you, Major . . . ?'

'No. The court must consist of not less than three officers.'

Dr Czinner interrupted. 'Don't trouble yourselves. I will do without counsel. These others cannot understand a word of what you say. They won't object.'

'It's irregular,' said Major Petkovitch. The Chief of Police looked at his watch. 'I have noted your protest, Major. Now we can begin.' The fat officer hiccuped, put his hand to his mouth, and winked.

'Ninety paras.'

'One dina.'

Myatt stubbed out his cigarette. He had played the game long enough. 'One dina, then. Tonight at nine.' He walked rapidly back to his compartment, but Coral was not there. Passengers were scrambling from the train, talking and laughing and stretching their arms. The engine-driver was the centre of a small crowd to whom he was explaining the breakdown with humour. Although there was no house in sight two or three villagers had already appeared and were offering for sale bottled mineral waters and sweets on the end of sticks. The road ran parallel to the line, separated only by a ridge of snow; the driver of a motor-car honked his horn and shouted again and again. 'Quick car to Belgrade. A hundred and twenty dinas. Quick car to Belgrade.' It was an exorbitant rate and only one stout merchant paid him attention. A long wrangle began beside the road. 'Mineral waters. Mineral waters.' A German with cropped head paced up and down muttering angrily to himself. Myatt heard a voice saying behind him in English, 'There's going to be more snow.' He turned in the hope that it might be Coral, but it was the woman whom he had seen in the restaurant-car.

'It will be no fun to be stuck here,' he said. 'They may be hours bringing another engine. What about sharing a car to Belgrade?'

'Is that an invitation?'

'A Dutch one,' Myatt said hastily.

'But I haven't a sou.' She turned and waved her hand. 'Mr Savory, come and share a car. You'll pay my share, won't you?' Mr Savory elbowed his way out of the group of people round the driver. 'I can't make out what the fellow's saying. Something about a boiler,' he said. 'Share a car?' he went on more slowly. 'That'll be rather expensive, won't it?' He eyed the woman carefully and waited, as if he expected her to answer his question; he is wondering, of course, Myatt thought, what he will get out of it. Mr Savory's hesitation, the woman's waiting silence, aroused his competitive instincts. He wanted to unfurl the glory of wealth like a peacock's tail before her and dazzle her with the beauty of his possessions. 'Sixty dinas,' he said, 'for the two of you.'

'I'll just go along,' said Mr Savory, 'and see the *chef de train*. He may know how long . . .' The first snow began to fall. 'If you would be my guest,' said Myatt, 'Miss——'

'My name's Janet Pardoe,' she said, and drew her fur coat up above her ears. Her cheeks glowed where the snow touched them, and Myatt could follow through the fur the curve of her concealed body and compare it with Coral's thin nakedness. I shall have to take Coral too, he thought. 'Have you seen,' he said, 'a girl in a mackintosh, thin, shorter than you?'

'Oh yes,' Janet Pardoe said, 'she got out of the train at Subotica. I know whom you mean. You had supper with her last night.' She smiled at him. 'She's your mistress, isn't she?'

'Do you mean she got out with her bag?'

'Oh no. She had nothing with her. I saw her going across to the station with a customs man. She's a funny little thing, isn't she? A chorus girl?' she asked with polite interest, but her tone conveyed to Myatt a criticism not of the girl but of himself for spending his money to so little advantage. It angered him as much as if she had criticised the quality of his currants; it was a reflection on his discernment and his discretion. After all, he thought, I have spent on her no more than I should spend on you by taking you into Belgrade, and would you pay me back so readily in kind? But the unlikelihood woke desire and bitterness, for this girl was silver polished goods, while Coral was at the best a piece of pretty coloured glass, valued for sentimental reasons; the other had intrinsic worth. She is the kind, he thought, who needs more than money: a handsome body to meet her own lust, and wit and education. I am a Jew, and I have learned nothing except how to make money. But none the less her criticism angered him and made it easier to relinquish the unattainable.

'She must have missed the train. I'll have to go back for her.' He did not apologise for his broken promise, but went quickly while it was still easy to go.

The merchant was haggling with the driver. He had brought the price down to a hundred dinas, and his own offer had risen to ninety. Myatt was ashamed of his interruption, and of the contempt both men must feel for his hasty unbusinesslike manner. 'I'll give you a hundred and twenty dinas to take me to Subotica and back.' When he saw that the driver was ready to begin another argument he raised his offer. 'A hundred and fifty dinas if you take me there and back before this train leaves.'

The car was old, battered and very powerful. They drove into the face of the storm at sixty miles an hour along a road which had not been mended in a lifetime. The springs were broken and Myatt was flung from side to side, as the car fell into holes and climbed and heeled. It groaned and panted like a human being, driven to the edge of endurance by a merciless master. The snow fell faster; the telegraph-poles along the line seemed glimpses of dark space in the gaps of a white wall. Myatt leant over to the driver and shouted in German above the roar of the ancient engine, 'Can you see?' The car twisted and swerved across the road and the man yelled back at him that there was nothing to fear, they would meet nothing on the road; he did not say that he could see.

Presently the wind rose. The road which had before been hidden from them by a straight wall of snow now rose and fell back on them, like a wave of which the snow was the white stinging spume. Myatt shouted to the driver to go slower; if a tyre bursts now, he thought, we are dead. He saw the driver look at his watch and put his foot upon the accelerator and the ancient engine responded with a few more miles an hour, like one of those strong obstinate old men of whom others say, 'They are the last. We don't breed that kind now.' Myatt shouted again, 'Slower,' but the driver pointed to his watch and drove his car to its creaking, unsafe, and gigantic limit of strength. He was a man to whom thirty dinas, the difference between catching and losing the train, meant months of comfort; he would have risked his life and the life of his passenger for far less money. Suddenly, as the wind took the snow and blew it aside, a cart appeared in the gap ten yards away and right in front of them. Myatt had just time to see the bemused eyes of the oxen, to calculate where their horns would smash the glass of the windscreen; an elderly man screamed and dropped his goad and jumped. The driver wrenched his wheel round, the car leapt a bank, rode crazily on two wheels, while the others hummed and revolved between the wind and earth, leant farther and farther over till Myatt could see the ground rise like boiling milk, left the bank, touched two wheels to the ground, touched four, and roared down the road at sixty-five miles an hour, while the snow closed behind them, and hid the oxen and cart and the astonished terrified old man.

'Drive slower,' Myatt gasped, but the driver turned and grinned at him and waved an untrembling hand.

The officers sitting in a row at the table, the guards at the door, the doctor answering question after question after question receded. Coral Musker fell asleep. The night had tired her; she could not understand a word that was said; she did not know why she was there; she was frightened and beginning to despair. She dreamed first that she was a child and everything was very simple and very certain and everything had an explanation and a moral. And then she dreamed that she was very old and was looking back over her life and she knew everything and she knew what was right and what was wrong, and why this and that had happened and everything was very simple and had a moral. But this second dream was not like the first one, for she was nearly awake and she ruled the dream to suit herself, and always in the background the talking went on. In this dream she began to remember from the safety of age the events of the night and the day and how everything had turned out for the best and how Myatt had come back for her from Belgrade.

Dr Czinner too had been given a chair. He could tell from the fat officer's expression that the lie was nearly done with, for he had ceased to pay any attention to the questions, nodding and hiccuping and nodding again. Colonel Hartep kept up the appearance of justice from a genuine kindliness. He had no scruples, but he did not wish to give unnecessary pain. If it had been possible he would have left Dr Czinner until the end some scraps of hope. Major Petkovitch continually raised objections; he knew as well as anyone what the outcome of the trial would be, but he was determined that it should have a superficial legality, that everything should be done in the proper order according to the regulations in the 1929 handbook.

With his hands folded quietly in front of him, and his shabby soft hat on the floor at his feet, Dr Czinner fought them without hope. The only satisfaction he could expect to gain would be the admission of the hollowness of his trial; he was going to be quietly tucked away in earth at the frontier station after dark, without publicity. 'On the ground of perjury,' he said, 'I have not yet been tried. It's outside the jurisdiction of a court martial.'

'You were tried in your absence,' Colonel Hartep said, 'and sentenced to five years' imprisonment.'

'I think you will find that I must still be brought up before a civil judge for sentence.'

'He's quite right,' said Major Petkovitch. 'We have no jurisdiction there. If you look up Section 15——'

'I believe you, Major. We'll waive then the sentence for perjury. There remains the false passport.'

Dr Czinner said quickly, 'You must prove that I have not become a naturalised British subject. Where are your witnesses? Will you telegraph to the British Ambassador?'

Colonel Hartep smiled. 'It would take so long. We'll waive the false passport. You agree, Major?'

'No,' said Major Petkovitch, 'I think it would be more correct to postpone trial on the smaller charge until sentence—that is to say, a verdict—has been declared on the greater.'

'It is all the same to me,' said Colonel Hartep. 'And you, Captain?' The captain nodded and grinned and closed his eyes.

'And now,' Colonel Hartep said, 'the charge of conspiring.' Major Petkovitch interrupted, 'I have been thinging it over. I think "treason" should have been the word used in the indictment.'

'Treason, then.'

'No, no, Colonel. It is impossible to alter the indictment now. "Conspiracy" will have to stand.'

'The maximum penalty——?'

'Is the same.'

'Well then, Dr Czinner, do you wish to plead guilty or not guilty?'

Dr Czinner sat for a moment considering. Then he said, 'It makes little difference?' Colonel Hartep looked at his watch, and then touched a letter which lay on the table. 'In the opinion of the court this is sufficient to convict.' He had the air of a man who wishes politely but firmly to put an end to an interview.

'I have the right, I suppose, to demand that it should be read, to cross-examine the soldier who took it?'

'Without doubt,' said Major Petkovitch eagerly.

Dr Czinner smiled. 'I won't trouble you. I plead guilty.' But if this had been a court in Belgrade, he told himself, with the pressmen scribbling in their box, I would have fought every step. Now that he had nobody to address, his mind was flooded with eloquence, words which could stab and words which would have brought tears. He was no longer the angry tongue-tied man who had failed to impress Mrs Peters. 'The court adjourns,' Colonel Hartep said. In the short silence the wind could be heard wandering like an angry watchdog round the station buildings. It was a very brief interval, just long enough for Colonel Hartep to write a few sentences on a sheet of paper and push it across the table to his companions to sign. The two guards a little eased their position.

'The court finds all the prisoners guilty,' Colonel Hartep read. 'The prisoner, Josef Grünlich, is sentenced to a months' imprisonment, after which he will be repatriated. The prisoner, Coral Musker, is sentenced to twenty-four hours' imprisonment and will then be repatriated. The prisoner . . .'

Dr Czinner interrupted: 'Can I speak to the court before sentence is passed?'

Colonel Hartep glanced quickly at the window: it was shut; at the guards; their disciplined faces were uncomprehending and empty. 'Yes,' he said.

Major Petkovitch's face flushed. 'Impossible,' he said. 'Quite impossible. Regulation 27a. The prisoner should have spoken before the court adjourned.' The Chief of Police looked past the major's sharp profile to where Dr Czinner sat, bunched up on the chair, his hands folded together in grey woollen gloves. An engine hooted outside and ground slowly down the line. The snow whispered at the window. He was aware of the long ribbons on his coat and of the hole in Dr

Czinner's glove. 'It would be most irregular,' Major Petkovitch railed on, while with one hand he absent-mindedly felt for his dog under the table and pulled the beast's ears. 'I note your protest,' Colonel Hartep said, and then he spoke to Dr Czinner. 'You know as well as I do,' he said kindly, 'that nothing you can say will alter the verdict. But if it pleases you, if it will make you any happier to speak, you may.'

Dr Czinner had expected opposition or contempt and his words would have flown to meet them. Kindness and consideration for a moment made him dumb. He envied again the qualities which only confidence and power could give the possessor. Before Colonel Hartep's kindly waiting silence he was tongue-tied. Captain Alexitch opened his eyes and closed them again. The doctor said slowly, 'Those medals you won in the service of your country during the war. I have no medals, because I love my country too much. I won't kill men because they also love their country. What I am fighting for is not new territory but a new world.' His words halted; there was no audience to bear him up; and he became conscious of the artificiality of his words which did not bear witness to the great love and the great hate driving him on. Sad and beautiful faces, thin from bad food, old before their time, resigned to despair, passed through his mind; they were people he had known, whom he had attended and failed to save. The world was in chaos to leave so much nobility unused, while the great financiers and the soldiers prospered. He said, 'You are employed to bolster up an old world which is full of injustice and muddle. For people like Vuskovitch, who steal the small savings of the poor, and live for ten years fast, full, stupid lives, and then shoot themselves. And yet you are paid to defend the only system which would protect men like him. You put the small thief in prison, but the big thief lives in a palace.'

Major Petkovitch said, 'What the prisoner is saying has no bearing on the case. It is a political speech.'

'Let him go on.' Colonel Hartep shaded his face with his hands and closed his eyes. Dr Czinner thought that he was feigning sleep to mask his indifference, but he opened them again when Dr Czinner called out to him angrily, 'How old-fashioned you are with your frontiers and your patriotism. The aeroplane doesn't know a frontier; even your financiers don't recognise frontiers.' Then Dr Czinner saw that something saddened him and the thought that perhaps Colonel Hartep had no desire for his death made him again at a loss for words. He moved his eyes restlessly from point to point, from the map on the wall to the little shelf below the clock full of books on strategy and military history in worn jackets. At last his eyes reached the two guards; one stared past him, paying him no attention, careful to keep his eyes on one spot and his rifle at the correct angle. The other watched him with wide stupid unhappy eyes. That face joined the sad procession through his brain, and he was aware for a moment that he had a better audience than pressmen, that here was a poor man to be converted from the wrong service to the right, and words came to him, the vague and sentimental words which had once appealed to him and would appeal to the other. But he was cunning now with the guile of his class, staring away from the man at the floor and only letting his gaze flicker back once like a lizard's tail. He addressed him in the plural as 'Brothers'. He urged that there was no shame in poverty that they should seek to be rich, and that there was no crime in poverty that they should be oppressed. When all were poor, no one would be poor. The wealth of the world belonged to everyone.

If it was divided, there would be no rich men, but every man would have enough to eat, and would have no reason to feel ashamed beside his neighbour.

Colonel Hartep lost interest. Dr Czinner was losing the individuality of the grey wool gloves and the hole in the thumb; he was becoming a tub orator, no more. He looked at his watch and said, 'I think I have allowed you enough time.' Major Petkovitch muttered something under his breath and becoming suddenly irritable kicked his dog in the ribs and said, 'Be off with you. Always wanting attention.' Captain Alexitch woke up and said in a tone of great relief, 'Well, that's over,' Dr Czinner, staring at the floor five yards to the left of the guard, said slowly, 'This wasn't a trial. They had sentenced me to death before they began. Remember, I'm dying to show you the way. I don't mind dying. Life has not been so good as that. I think I shall be of more use dead.' But while he spoke his clearer mind told him that the chances were few that his death would have any effect.

'The prisoner Richard Czinner is sentenced to death,' Colonel Hartep read, 'the sentence to be carried out by the officer commanding the garrison at Subotica in three hours' time.' It will be dark by then, the doctor thought. No one will know of this.

For a moment everyone sat still as though they were at a concert and a movement had ended and they were uncertain whether to applaud. Coral Musker woke. She could not understand what was happening. The officers were speaking together, shuffling papers. Then one of them gave a command and the guards opened the door and motioned towards the wind and the snow and the white veiled buildings.

The prisoners passed out. They kept close to each other in the storm of snow which struck them. They had not gone far when Josef Grünlich seized Dr Czinner's sleeve. 'You tell me nothing. What shall happen to me? You walk along and say nothing.' He grumbled and panted.

'A month's imprisonment,' Dr Czinner said, 'and then you are to be sent home.'

'They think that, do they? They think they are damned clever.' He became silent, studying with close attention the position of the buildings. He stumbled on the edge of the line and muttered angrily to himself.

'And me?' Coral asked. 'What's to happen to me?'

'You'll be sent home tomorrow.'

'But I can't. There's my job. I shall lose it. And my friend.' She had been afraid of this journey, because she could not understand what porters said to her, because of the strange food, and the uncertainty at the end of it: there had been a moment as the purser called after her across the wet quay at Ostend when she would gladly have turned back. But 'things' had happened since then: she would be returning to the same lodgings, to the toast and orange juice for breakfast, the long wait on the agent's stairs with Ivy and Flo and Phil and Dick, all the affectionate people one kissed and called by their front names and didn't know from Adam. Intimacy with one person could do this—empty the world of friendships, give a distaste for women's kisses and their bright chatter, make the ordinary world a little unreal and very uninteresting. Even the doctor did not matter to her as he stalked along in a different world, but she remembered as they reached the door of the waiting-room to ask him, 'And you? What's happening to you?'

He said vaguely, forgetting to stand aside for her to enter, 'I'm being kept here.'

'Where will they take me?' Josef Grünlich asked as the door closed.

'And me?'

'To the barracks, I expect, for tonight. There's no train to Belgrade. They've let the stove out.' Through the window he tried to catch a view of the peasants, but apparently they had grown tired of waiting and had gone home. He said with relief, 'There's nothing to be done,' and with obscure humour, 'It's something to be at home.' He saw himself for a moment facing a desert of pitch-pine desks, row on row of malicious faces, and he remembered the times when he had felt round his heart the little cold draughts of disobedience, the secret signals and spurts of disguised laughter threatening his livelihood, for a master who could not keep order must eventually be dismissed. His enemies were offering him the one thing he had never known, security. There was no need to decide anyting. He was at peace.

Dr Czinner began to hum a tune. He said to Coral Musker, 'It's an old song. The lover says: "I cannot come in daylight, for I am poor and your father will set the dogs on me. But at night I will come to your window and ask you to let me in." And the girl says: "If the dogs bark, stay very still in the shadow of the wall and I will come down to you, and we will go together to the orchard at the bottom of the garden." ' He sang the first verse in a voice a little harsh from lack of use; Josef Grünlich, sitting in the corner, scowled at the singer, and Coral stood by the cold stove and listened with surprise and pleasure because he seemed to be younger and full of hope. 'At night I will come to your window and ask you to let me in.' He was not addressing a lover: the words had no power to bring a girl's face from his dry purposeful political years, but his parents bobbed at him their humorous wrinkled faces, no longer with awe for the educated man, for the doctor, for the almost gentleman. Then in a lower voice he sang the girl's part. His voice was less harsh and might once have been beautiful; one of the guards came to the window and looked in and Josef Grünlich began to weep in a meaningless Teutonic way, thinking of orphans in the snow and princesses with hearts of ice and not for a moment of Herr Kolber, whose body was borne now through the grey city snow followed by two officials in a car and one mourner in a taxi, an elderly bachelor, a great draughts player. 'Stay very still in the shadow of the wall and I will come down to you.' The world was chaotic; when the poor were starved and the rich were not happier for it; when the thief might be punished or rewarded with titles; when wheat was burned in Canada and coffee in Brazil, and the poor in his own country had no money for bread and froze to death in unheated rooms; the world was out of joint and he had done his best to set it right, but that was over. He was powerless now and happy. 'We will go to the orchard at the bottom of the garden.' Again it was no memory of a girl which comforted him, but the sad and beautiful faces of the poor who promised him rest. He had done all that he could do; nothing more was expected of him; they surrendered him their hopelessness, the secret of their beauty and their happiness as well as of their grief, and led him towards the leafy rustling darkness. The guard pressed his face to the window, and Dr Czinner stopped singing. 'It's your turn,' he said to Coral.

'Oh, I don't know any songs that you'd like,' she told him seriously, searching her memory at the same time for something a little old-fashioned and melancholy, something which would share the quality of a sad idyll with the song he had sung.

'We must pass the time somehow,' he said, and suddenly she began to sing in a small clear voice like the tinkle of a musical box:

> *'I was sitting in a car*
> *With Michael;*
> *I looked at a star*
> *With John;*
> *I had a glass of bitter*
> *With Peter*
> *In a bar;*
> *But the pips went wrong; they never go right.*
> *This year, next year*
> *(You may have counted wrong, count again, dear),*
> *Some day, never.*
> *I'll be a good girl for ever and ever.'*

'Is this Subotica?' Myatt shouted, as a few mud cottages plunged at them through the storm, and the driver nodded and waved his hand forward. A small child ran out into the middle of the road and the car swerved to avoid it; a chicken squawked and handfuls of grey feathers were flung up into the snow. An old woman ran out of a cottage and shouted after them. 'What's she saying?' The driver grinned over his shoulder: 'Dirty Jew.'

The arrow on the speedometer wavered and retreated: fifty miles, forty miles, thirty miles, twenty. 'Soldiers about,' the man said.

'You mean there's a speed limit?'

'No, no. These damned soldiers if they see a good car, they commandeer it. Same with the horses.' He pointed at the fields through the driving snow. 'The peasants, they are all starving. I worked here once, but I thought: no, the city for me. The country's dead, anyway.' He nodded towards the line which disappeared into the storm. 'One or two trains a day, that's all. You can't blame the Reds for making trouble.'

'Has there been trouble?'

'Trouble? You should have seen it. The goods yard all in flames; the post-office smashed to bits. The police were scared. There's marital law in Belgrade.'

'I wanted to send a telegram from there. Will it get through?' The car panted its way on second gear up a small hill and came into a street of dingy brick houses plastered with advertisements. 'If you want to send a telegram,' the driver said, 'I should send it from here. There are queues of newspaper men at Belgrade, and the post-office is smashed and they've had to commandeer old Nikola's restaurant. You know what that means; but you don't because you are a foreigner. It's not the bugs, nobody minds a few bugs, it's healthy, but the smells——'

'Have I got time to send a telegram here and catch the train?'

'That train,' the driver said, 'won't go for hours and hours. They've sent for a new engine, but nobody's going to pay any attention to them in the city. You should see the station, the mess—You had better let me drive you into Belgrade. I'll show you the sights too. I know all the best houses.'

Myatt interrupted him, I'll go to the post-office first. And then we'll try the hotels for the lady.'

'There's only one.'

'And then the station.'

The sending of the telegram took some time; first he had to write the mesage to Joyce in such a way that no action for libel could be brought by Mr Eckman.

He decided at last on: 'Eckman granted a month's holiday to start immediately. Please take charge at once. Arriving tomorrow.' That ought to convey what he wanted, but it then had to be put into the office code, and when the coded telegram was handed across the counter, the clerk refused to accept it. All telegrams were liable to censorship, and no coded messages could be transmitted. At last he got away, only to find that nothing was known of Coral at the hotel, which smelt of dried plants and insect powder. She must be still at the station, he thought. He left the car a hundred yards down the road in order to get rid of the driver who was proving too talkative and too helpful and pushed forward alone through the wind and snow.

He passed two sentries outside a building and asked them the way to the waiting-room. One of them said that there was no waiting-room now.

'Where can I make inquiries?'

The tallest of the guards suggested the station-master. 'And where is his office?' The man pointed to a second building, but added gently that the station-master was away; he was in Belgrade. Myatt checked his impatience, the man was so obviously good-natured. His companion spat to show his contempt and muttered remarks about Jews under his breath. 'Where can I go then to make inquiries?'

'There's the major,' the man said doubtfully, 'or there's the station-master's clerk.'

'You can't see the major. He's gone to the barracks,' the other guard said. Myatt absent-mindedly drew a little near to the door; he could hear low voices inside. The surly guard became suddenly angry and brutal; he struck at Myatt's legs with the butt of his rifle. 'Go away. We don't want spies round here. Go away, you Jew.' With the calm of his race Myatt drew away;

201

it was a superficial calm carried unconsciously like an inherited feature; beneath it he felt the resentment of a young man aware of his own importance. He leant towards the soldier with the intention of lodging in the flushed animal face some barb of speech, but he stopped in time, aware with amazement and horror of the presence of danger; in the small hungry eyes shone hatred and a desire to kill; it was as if all the oppressions, the pogroms, the chains, and the envy and superstition which caused them, had been herded into a dark cup of the earth and now he stared down at them from the rim. He moved back with his eyes on the soldier while the man's fingers felt round the trigger. 'I'll see the station-master's clerk,' he said, but his instinct told him to walk quickly back to his car and rejoin the train.

'That's not the way,' the friendly guard called after him. 'Over there. Across the line.' Myatt was thankful for the storm that roared along the line and blew gustily between him and the soldiers. Where he stood there was no prevailing wind, for it was trapped in the alleys between the buildings and sent swirling round the corners in contrary directions. He wondered at his own persistence in staying in the empty dangerous station; he told himself that he owed the girl nothing, and he knew that she would agree with him. 'We're quits,' she would say. 'You've given me the ticket, and I've given you a nice time.' But he was tied by her agreement, by her refusal to make any claim. Before so complete a humility one could be nothing else but generous. He picked his way across the line and pushed open a door. A tousled man sat at a desk drinking wine. His back was turned, and Myatt said in what he hoped was an intimidating authoritative tone, 'I want to make an inquiry.' He had no reason to be afraid of a civilian, but when the man turned and he saw the eyes grow cunning and insolent at the sight of him, he despaired. A mirror hung above the desk, and in it Myatt saw the reflection of himself quite clearly for a moment, short and stout and nasal in his heavy fur coat, and it occurred to him that perhaps these people hated him not only because he was a Jew but because he carried the traces of money into their resigned surroundings. 'Well?' said the clerk.

'I want to make an inquiry,' Myatt said, 'about a girl who was left behind here from the Orient express this morning.'

'What do you mean?' the clerk asked insolently. 'If anybody leaves the train, they leave it. They aren't left behind. Why, the train was waiting here this morning for more than half an hour.'

'Well, then, did a girl get out?'

'No.'

'Will you just examine your tickets and check that?'

'No. I said no one got out, didn't I? What are you waiting here for? I'm a busy man.'

Myatt knew suddenly that he would not be sorry to accept the clerk's word and end his search; he would have done all that lay in his power, and he would be free. He thought of Coral for a moment as a small alley, enticing a man's footsteps, but blind at the end with a windowless wall; there were others, and he thought for a moment of Janet Pardoe, who were like streets lined with shops full of glitter and warmth, streets which led somewhere. He was reaching an age when he wanted to marry and have children, set up his tent and increase his tribe. But his thoughts had been too precise; they roused his conscience on behalf of someone who had not shown the slightest hope of marriage but had been intent only on honest payment and her own affection. It came to him again as a strange and unexpected cry, her exclamation, 'I love you.' He returned from the doorway to the clerk's desk determined to do all that he could do, to scamp no effort; she might now be somewhere in discomfort, stranded without money, possibly afraid. 'She was seen to leave the train.'

The clerk groaned at him. 'What do you want me to do? Come out in the snow looking for her? I tell you I don't know a thing about her. I haven't seen any girl.' His voice trailed off as he watched Myatt take out his note-case. Myatt removed a five-dina note and smoothed it between his fingers. 'If you can tell me where she is, you can have two of these.' The clerk stammered a little, tears came to his eyes, and he said with poignant regret, 'If I could, if I only could. I am sure I should be glad to help.' His face lit up and he suggested hopefully, 'You ought to try the hotel.' Myatt put the case back in his pocket; he had done all that he could do; and he went out to find his car.

For the last few hours the sun had been obscured, but its presence had been shown in the glitter of the falling snow, in the whiteness of the drifts; now it was sinking and the snow was absorbing the greyness of the sky; he would not get back to the train before dark. But even the hope of catching the train became faint, for he found when he reached his car that the engine had frozen, in spite of rugs spread across the radiator.

[4]

Josef Grünlich said: 'It is all very well to sing.' Although he complained of their inanition his eyes were red with weeping, and it was with an effort that he put away from him the little match girls and the princesses with hearts of ice. 'They will not catch me so easily.' He began to walk round the walls of the waiting-room pressing a wet thumb to the woodwork. 'Never have I been imprisoned. It may surprise you, but it is true. At my time of life one cannot start something like that. And they are sending me back to Austria.'

'Are you wanted there?'

Josef Grünlich pulled down his waistcoat and set the little silver cross shaking. 'I do not mind telling you. We are all together, eh?' He twisted his neck a little in a sudden access of modesty. 'I have slaughtered a man at Vienna.'

Coral said with horror, 'Do you mean that you are a murderer?' Josef Grünlich thought: I should like to tell them. It's too good to be a secret. Quickness? Why—'Look over there, Herr Kolber,' flick of the string, aim, fire twice, wriggle, man dead, all in two seconds; but better not. He encouraged himself with the cautious motto of his profession, the poker-work injunction to keep pride in bounds—'One never knows.' He ran his finger inside his collar and said airily, 'I had to. It was an affair of honour.' His hesitation was

205

infinitesimal. 'He had—how do you say it?—made my daughter big.' With difficulty he prevented himself laughing as he thought of Herr Kolber, small and dry, and of his petulant exclamation, 'This is a pretty kettle of fish.'

'You mean you killed him,' Coral asked with amazement, 'just because he'd played around with your daughter?'

Josef Grünlich raised his hands and asked absentmindedly, his eyes straying to the window and measuring its height from the ground, 'What could I do? Her honour, my honour . . .'

'Gosh,' said Coral, 'I'm glad I haven't a father.'

Josef Grünlich said suddenly, 'A hairpin perhaps.'

'What do you mean, a hairpin?'

'Or a pocket knife?'

'I haven't got any hairpins. What would I want hairpins for?'

'I have a paper-cutter,' Dr Czinner said. As he handed it over, he said, 'My watch has stopped. Could you tell me how long we have been back here?'

'An hour,' said Josef.

'Two hours more then,' Dr Czinner remarked thoughtfully. Neither of the others heard him. Josef tiptoed to the door, paper-cutter in hand, and Coral watched him. 'Come here, Fraülein,' Josef said, and when she was beside him he whispered to her, 'Have you some grease?' She gave him a pot of cold cream from her bag and he spread the cream thickly over the lock of the door, leaving a little space clear. He began to laugh gently to himself, bent almost double, with his eye to the lock. 'Such a lock,' he whispered jubilantly, 'such a lock.'

'What do you want the cream for?'

'Quiet,' he said. 'It will make what I do quieter.'

He came back to the cold stove and waved them together. 'That lock,' he told them in an undertone, 'is nothing. If we could send one guard away we could run.'

'You'll be shot,' Dr Czinner said.

'They cannot shoot all three at once,' Grünlich said. He dropped two suggestions into their silence: 'The dark. The snow,' and then stood back, waiting for their decision. His own mind worked smoothly. He would be the first out of the door, the first away; he could run faster than an old man and a girl; the guard would fire at the nearest fugitive.

'I should advise you to stay,' Dr Czinner said to Coral. 'You aren't in any danger here.'

Grünlich opened his mouth to protest, but he said nothing. They all three watched the window and the passing of one of the guards, rifle slung across his shoulder. 'How long will it take you to open the door?' Dr Czinner asked.

'Five minutes.'

'Get to work then.' Dr Czinner tapped on the window and the other guard came. His large friendly eyes were pressed close to the glass and he stared into the waiting-room. The room was darker than the open air and he could see nothing but dim shapes moving restlessly here and there for warmth. Dr Czinner put his mouth close to the glass and spoke to him in his own tongue. 'What is your name?' Scratch, scratch, scratch went the paper knife, but when it slipped the whine was hushed by the layer of cream.

'Ninitch,' said the ghost of a voice through the glass.

'Ninitch,' Dr Czinner repeated slowly. 'Ninitch. I used to know your father, I think, in Belgrade.' Ninitch showed no doubt of the easy lie, flattening his

nose against the window, but all his view of the waiting-room was cut off by the doctor's features. 'He died
six years ago,' he said.

Dr Czinner took what was only a small risk to one
acquainted with the poor in Belgrade and of the food
they eat. 'Yes. He was ill when I knew him. Cancer
of the stomach.'

'Cancer?'

'Pains.'

'Yes, yes, in the belly. That was him. They came
on at night, and he would get very hot in the face.
My mother used to lie beside him with a cloth to dry
his skin. Fancy you knowing him, your honour. Shall
I open the window so that we can talk better?' Grünlich's knife scratched and scratched and scratched; a
screw came out and tinkled like a needle on the floor.

'No,' Dr Czinner said. 'Your companion might not
like it.'

'He's gone up to the town to the barracks to see
the major. There's a foreigner been here making inquiries. He thinks there's something wrong.'

'A foreigner?' Dr Czinner asked. His mouth had
gone dry with hope. 'Has he gone?'

'He's just gone back to his car, down the road.'
The waiting-room was full of shadows. Dr Czinner
turned for a moment from the window and asked
softly, 'How is it going? Can you be quick?'

'Two minutes more,' Grünlich said.

'There's a foreigner with a car down the road. He's
been making inquiries.'

Coral put her hands together and said softly, 'He's
come back for me. You see. You said he wouldn't.'
She began to laugh gently, and when Dr Czinner whispered to her to keep calm, she said, 'I'm not hysterical.
I'm just happy,' for it had occurred to her that this

frightening adventure had been, after all, for the best; it had shown that he was fond of her, otherwise he would never have troubled to come back. He must have missed the train, she thought, and we shall have to spend the night together in Belgrade, perhaps two nights, and she began to dream of smart hotels, and dinners and his hand on her arm.

Dr Czinner turned back to the window. 'We are very thirsty,' he said. 'Have you any wine?'

Ninitch shook his head. 'No.' He added doubtfully, 'Lukitch has a bottle of *rakia* across the way.' Dusk had already made the way longer; there was no moon to light the street of the rails and the lamp in the station-master's office might have been a hundred yards away and not a hundred feet.

'Be a good fellow and get us a drink.'

He shook his head. 'I mustn't leave the door.'

Dr Czinner did not offer him money; instead he called through the glass that he had attended Ninitch's father. 'I gave him tablets to take when the pain was too bad.'

'Little round tablets?' Ninitch asked.

'Yes. Morphia tablets.'

Ninitch with his face pressed against the glass considered. It was possible to see the thoughts moving like fish in the translucent eyes. He said, 'Fancy your giving him those tablets. He used to take one whenever the pain came, and one at night too. It made him sleep.'

'Yes.'

'What a lot I shall have to tell my wife.'

'The drink,' Dr Czinner prompted him.

Ninitch said slowly, 'If you tried to escape while I was gone, I should get into trouble.' Dr Czinner said, 'How could we escape? The door's locked and the window is too small.'

'Very well, then.'

Dr Czinner saw him go and turned with a sigh of unhappiness to the others. 'Now,' he said. His sigh was for the loss of his security. The struggle was renewed. It was his distasteful duty to escape if he could.

'One moment,' Grünlich said, scratching at the door.

'There's no one outside. The guard's the other side of the line. When you come out of the door turn to the left and turn to the left again between the buildings. The car's down the road.'

'I know all that,' said Grünlich, and another screw tinkled to the floor. 'Ready.'

'I should stay here.' Dr Czinner said to Coral.

'But I couldn't. My friend's just down the road.'

'Ready,' Grünlich said again, scowling at them. They gathered at the door. 'If they fire,' Dr Czinner said, 'run crookedly.' Grünlich pulled the door open and the snow blew in. It was not so dark outside as it had been in the room; the stationmaster's lamp across the rails lit up the figure of the guard in the window. Grünlich dived first into the storm; with head bent almost to his knees he bounced forward like a ball. The others followed. It was not easy to run. The wind and snow were enemies allied to drive them back: the wind broke their speed and the snow blinded them. Coral gasped with pain as she ran into a tall iron pillar with a trunk like an elephant's used for watering engines. Grünlich was far ahead of her; Dr Czinner was a little behind; she could hear the painful effort of his lungs. Their footsteps made no sound in the snow, and they dared not shout to the driver of the car.

Before Grünlich had reached the gap between the buildings, a door slammed, someone called, and a rifle was fired. Grünlich's first effort had exhausted him. The distance between him and Coral lessened. The guard fired twice, and Coral could hear the buzz of the bullets far overhead. She wondered whether he was deliberately aiming high. Ten seconds more and they would pass the corner out of his sight and be visible from the car. She heard a door open again, a bullet whipped up the snow beside her and she ran the faster. She was almost side by side with Grünlich when they reached the corner. Dr Czinner exclaimed behind her and she thought he was urging her to run faster, but before she turned the corner she looked back and saw that he was hugging the wall with both hands. She stopped and called out, 'Herr Grünlich,' but he paid her no attention, bundling round the building and out of sight.

'Go on,' Dr Czinner said.

The light shining from the horizon behind the thinner clouds faded. 'Take my arm,' she said. He obeyed, but his weight was too much for her, though he tried to ease it with one hand against the wall. They reached the corner. The rear lamp of the car blinked through the dusk and snow a hundred yards away, and she stopped. 'I can't do it,' she said. He made no answer, and when she took her hand away he slid down to the snow.

For a few seconds she wondered whether to leave him. She told herself with conviction that he would never have waited for her. But then she was in no great danger and he was. She stood hesitating, bent down to watch his pale old face; she noticed that there was blood on his moustache. Voices sounded round the corner, and she found she had no time to decide. Dr Czinner was sitting with his back to a wooden door which was on the latch, and she pulled him inside and closed it again, but she was afraid to shoot the bolt.

Someone ran by, an engine spluttered. Then the car roared into activity and distance took the sound and subdued it to a murmur. The shed had no windows: it was quite dark, and it was too late now for her to leave him.

She felt in Dr Czinner's pockets and found a box of matches. When she struck one the roof shot above her like a bean-stalk. Something blocked the shed at one end, stacked half-way to the roof. Another match showed her fat sacks piled more than twice the height of a man. In Dr Czinner's right-hand pocket was a folded newspaper. She tore off a page and made a spill, so that she might have enough light to drag him across the shed, for she was afraid that at any moment the guard would open the door. But his weight was too much for her. She held the spill close to his eyes to see whether he was conscious, and the stinging smoke woke him. He opened his eyes and watched her with perplexity. She whispered to him, 'I want to hide you in the sacks.' He did not seem to understand and she repeated the sentence very slowly and distinctly.

He said, 'Ich spreche kein Englisch.'

Oh, she thought, I wish I'd left him; I wish I was in the car now. He must be dying; he can't understand a word I say, and she was terrified at the idea of being left all alone in the shed with a dead man. Then the flame went out, choked in its own ash. She searched for the newspaper again on hands and knees and tore a page and folded it and made another spill. Then she found that she had mislaid the matches, and on hands and knees she felt the floor all round her. Dr Czinner began to cough, and something moved on the floor close to her hands. She nearly screamed for fear of rats, but when at last she had found the matches and lit a spill, she saw it was the doctor who had moved. He was crawling crookedly towards the end of the shed. She tried to guide him, but he seemed unaware of her. All the slow way across she wondered why no one came to look in the shed.

Dr Czinner was completely exhausted when he reached the sacks and he lay down with his face buried against them; he had been bleeding from the mouth. Again all the responsibility was hers. She wondered whether he was dying and she put her mouth close to his ear. 'Shall I get help?' She was afraid that he would answer her in German, but this time he said quite clearly, 'No, no.' After all, she thought, he's a doctor; he must know. She asked him, 'What can I do for you?' He shook his head and closed his eyes; he was no longer bleeding and she thought him better. She pulled sacks down from the pile and made a kind of cave large enough to shelter them, piling the sacks at the entrance, so that no one could see them from the door. The sacks were heavy with grain, and the work was unfinished when she heard voices. She crouched low in the hole with her fingers crossed for luck, and the door opened, a torch flashed over the sacks above her head. Then the door was shut and quiet returned. It was a long time before she had the courage to finish her work.

'We'll miss the train,' Myatt said as he watched the driver turn and turn the starting handle; the self-starter was useless.

'I will take you back quicker,' the man said. At last the engine began to wake, grumble, fall asleep and wake again. 'Now we're off,' he said. He climbed into his seat and turned on the front lamps, but while he was coaxing the engine into a steady roar, there was an explosion in the dusk behind. 'What's that?' Myatt asked thinking the car had back-fired. Then it happened again, and a little afterwards there was another sound like the popping of a cork. 'They are firing in the station,' the driver said, pushing at the self-starter. Myatt knocked his hand away. 'We'll wait.'

The man repeated, 'Wait?' He explained hurriedly, 'It's the soldiers. We had better be off.' He could not know how closely Myatt echoed his advice. Myatt was frightened; he had seen in the soldiers' attitude the spirit which made pogroms possible; but he remained obstinate; he was not quite satisfied that he had done everything he could to find the girl in Subotica.

'They are coming,' the man said. Along the road from the station someone was running. At first he eluded them in the falling snow. Then they could make out a man dodging a little this way and a little that. He was upon them with surprising speed, short and fat, clawing at the door to climb in. 'What's up?' Myatt asked him. He spluttered a little at the mouth. 'Drive off quick.' The door stuck and he bundled himself over the top and collapsed out of breath in the back seat.

'Is there anybody else?' Myatt asked. 'Are you alone?'

'Yes, yes, alone,' the man assured him. 'Drive away quick.'

Myatt leant back and tried to see his face. 'No girl?'

'No. No girl.'

There was a flash of light somewhere by the station buildings and a bullet scraped the mudguard. The driver, without waiting for an order, thrust down his foot and sent the car ricocheting from hole to hole along the road. Myatt again studied the stranger's face. 'Weren't you on the Istanbul express?' The man

nodded. 'And you haven't seen a girl at the station?'
The man became voluble. 'I will tell you all about it.'
His speech was indistinct; many phrases were taken
from his mouth by the plunging car; he said he had
been detained for not declaring a little piece of lace,
a very small little piece of lace, and had been badly
treated by the soldiers and fired on when he escaped.
'And you saw no girl?'

'No. No girl.' He met Myatt's gaze with a complete
honesty. It would have needed a long inquisition to
spy at the back of the blank eyes the spark of malice,
the little glint of cunning.

Although the wooden walls trembled with the wind,
it was warm among the sacks, in the dark, in the unwindowed shed. Dr Czinner turned to escape the pain
in his chest and turned again, but it pursued him; only
in the moment of turning did he gain a few strides;
when he was still, the pain was on him. So all through
the night he turned and turned. There were times when
he became conscious of the wind outside and mistook
the rustle of the snow for the movement of the pebbles
at the sea's edge. During those moments a memory of
his years of exile took shape in the barn, so that he
began to recite declensions and French irregular verbs.
But his resistance was weakened, and instead of showing an obstinate sarcastic front to his tormentors, he
wept.

Coral Musker laid his head in an easier position, but
he moved it again, turning it and turning it, muttering
rhythmically, tears falling down his cheeks and on to
his moustache. She gave up the attempt to help him and
tried to escape into the past from her own fear, so that
if their thoughts had been given a form visible to each
other, a strange medley would have filled the barn.

Under coloured lights which spilt out 'It's a Baby' a clergyman rumpled his gown across his arm and dived at a black-board with a piece of chalk; several children pursued another with taunts in and out of stage doors, up and down agents' stairs. In a glass shelter on a grey sea-front a woman gave a neighbour a piece of her mind, while a bell tolled for tea or chapel.

'Wasser,' Dr Czinner whispered. 'What do you want?' She bent down to him and tried to see his face. 'Wasser.'

'Shall I fetch someone?' He did not hear her.

'Do you want something to drink?' He paid her no attention, repeating 'Wasser' again and again. She knew that he was not conscious, but her nerves were worn and she was irritated by his failure to answer her. 'All right then, lie there. I've done all I can, I'm sure.' She scrambled as far away from him as she could and tried to sleep, but the trembling of the walls kept her awake, the moaning of the wind made her aware of desolation, and she crept back to Dr Czinner's side for company and comfort. 'Wasser,' he whispered again. Her hand touched his face and she was astonished at the heat and dryness of the skin. Perhaps he wants water, she thought, and was at a loss for a minute where to find it until she realised that it was falling all round her and piling itself against the walls of the shed. She was warned by a faint doubt: should somebody in a fever be given water? But remembering the dryness of his skin, she gave way to pity.

Although water was all round her, it was not easily or quickly reached. She had to light two spills and climb from the hole among the sacks without extinguishing them. She opened the door of the shed boldly, for she would have have welcomed discovery now, but the night was dark and there was no one to be seen.

She gathered a handful of snow and went back into the shed and closed the door; the draught of the closing door blew out her light.

She called to Dr Czinner, but he made no reply, and she was frightened at the thought that he might be dead. With one hand held in front of her face she walked forward and was brought up short by the wall. She waited a moment before trying again and was glad to hear a movement. She went to it and was again stopped by the wall. She thought with rising fear: it must have been a rat that moved. The snow in her hand was beginning to melt. She called out again, and this time a whisper answered. She jumped, it was so close to her, and feeling sideways her hand immediately touched the barricade of sacks. She began to laugh, but rebuked herself: Now don't be hysterical. Everything depends on you; and she tried to comfort herself with the assurance that this was her first star part. But it was difficult to play with confidence in the dark without applause.

When she had found the hole among the sacks most of the snow was melted or spilt, but she pressed what was left against the doctor's mouth. It seemed to ease him. He lay still, while the snow upon his lips melted and trickled between his teeth. He was so quiet that she lit a spill to see his face and was astonished at his shrewd conscious gaze. She spoke to him, but he was too full of thought to answer.

He was taking in his position, the force of his second failure. He knew that he was dying; he had been brought to consciousness by the touch of cold upon the tongue; and after a moment of bewilderment, remembered everything. He could tell where he had been shot from the pain; he was aware of his own fever and of the secret bleeding within. For a moment he thought it his duty to brush the snow from his lips, but then he realised that he had no more duties to anyone but himself.

When the girl lit the spill he was thinking: Grünlich has escaped. It amused him to consider how hard it would be for a Christian to reconcile the escape with his own death. He smiled a little, maliciously. But then, his Christian training took an ironical revenge, for he too began to try to reconcile the events of the last few days and to wonder in what he had erred and how it was that others had succeeded. He saw the express in which they had travelled breaking the dark sky like a rocket. They clung to it with every stratagem in their power, leaning this way and leaning that, altering the balance now in this direction, now in that. One had to be very alive, very flexible, very opportunist. The snow on the lips had all melted and its effect was passing. Before the spill had flickered to its end, his sight had dimmed, and the great shed with its cargo of sacks floated away from him into darkness. He had no sense that he was within it; he thought that he was left behind, watching it disappear. His mind became confused; and soon he was falling through endless space, breathless, with a windy vacancy in head and chest, because he had been unable to retain his foothold on what was sometimes a ship and at other times a comet, the world itself, or only a fast train from Ostend to Istanbul. His mother and father bobbed at him their seamed thin faces, followed him through the ether, past the rush of stars, telling him that they were glad and grateful, that he had done what he could, that he had been faithful. He was breathless and could not answer them, tugged downward in great pain by gravity. He wanted to say to them that he had been damned by his faithfulness, that one must lean this way and that, but he had to listen all the way to their false comfort, falling and falling in great pain.

It was impossible to tell in the barn the progress of the dark; when Coral struck a match to see her watch, she was disappointed to find how slowly time went by. After a while the store of matches became low and she did not dare to strike another. She wondered whether to leave the shed and surrender herslf, for she began to despair now of seeing Myatt again. He had done more than could have been expected of him by returning; it was unlikely that he would come back again. But she was frightened of the world outside, not of the soldiers, but of the agents, the long stairs, the landladies, the old life. As long as she lay by Dr Czinner's side, she retained something of Myatt, a memory they both possessed.

Of course, she told herself, I can write to him, but months might pass before he was again in London, and she couldn't expect either his affection or desire to last when she was away. She knew too, that she could make him see her when he returned. He would feel that it was his duty at least to give her lunch, but 'I'm not after his money', she whispered aloud in the dark barn beside the dying man. Her sense of desolation, the knowledge that for some reason, God alone knew why, she loved him, made her for a moment protestant. Why not? Why shouldn't I write him? He might like it; he might want me still, and if he doesn't, why shouldn't I put up a fight? I'm tired of being decent, of doing the right thing. Her thoughts were very close to Dr Czinner's when she exclaimed to herself that it didn't pay.

But she knew too well that it was her nature, she was born so and she must make the best of it. She would be a fumbler at the other game; relentless when she ought to be weak, forgiving when she ought to be hard. Even now she could not dwell long with envy and admiration at the thought of Grünlich driving away into the dark beside Myatt; her thoughts returned with a stupid fidelity to Myatt himself, to her last sight of him in the restaurant-car with his fingers caressing his gold cigarette case. But she was aware all the time that there was no quality in Myatt to justify her fidelity; it was just that she was like that and he had been kind. She wondered for a moment whether Dr Czinner's case was not the same; he had been too faithful to people who could have been served better by cunning. She heard his difficult breathing through the dark and thought again without bitterness or criticism, it just doesn't pay.

The fork of roads sprang towards the headlights. The driver hesitated for a fraction too long, then twisted his wheel and sent the car spinning round on two wheels. Josef Grünlich fell from one end of the seat to the other, gasping with fear. He did not dare to open his eyes again until the four wheels were on the ground. They had left the main road, and the car was bounding down the ruts of a country lane, splashing a fierce light on the budding trees and turning them to cardboard. Myatt leaned back from his seat beside the driver and explained, 'He's avoiding Subotica and is going over the line by a cattle crossing. You had better hold tight.' The trees vanished and suddenly they were roaring downhill between bare snow-draped fields. The lane had been churned by cattle into mud which had frozen. Two red lights sprang up towards them from below, and a short stretch of rail glinted with emerald drops. The lights swung backward and forward and a voice could be heard above the engine, calling.

'Shall I drive through them?' the man asked calmly,

his foot ready to fall on the accelerator. 'No, no!' Myatt exclaimed. He saw no reason why he should get into trouble for a stranger's sake. He could see the men holding the lanterns. They wore grey uniforms and carried revolvers. The car stopped between them, jumping the first rail and coming to rest tilted like a stranded boat. One of the soldiers said something which the driver translated into German. 'He wants to see our papers.'

Josef Grünlich leant back quietly against the cushions with his legs crossed. One hand played idly with his silver chain. When one of the soldiers caught his eye he smiled gently and nodded; anyone would have taken him for a rich and amiable business man, travelling with his secretary. It was Myatt who was flurried, sunk in his fur coat, remembering the woman's cry of 'Dirty Jew', the sentry's eyes, the clerk's insolence. It was in some such barren quarter of the world, among frozen fields and thin cattle, that one might expect to find old hatreds the world was outgrowing still alive. A soldier flashed his lamp in his face and repeated his demand with impatience and contempt. Myatt took out his passport, the man held it upside down and examined closely the lion and the unicorn; then he brought out his one word of German:

'Englander?'

Myatt nodded and the man threw the passport back on the seat and became absorbed in the driver's papers, which opened out into a long streamer like a child's book. Josef Grünlich leant cautiously forward and took Myatt's passport from the seat in front. He grinned when the red light was flashed on his face and flourished the passport. The guard called his friend, they stood and examined him under the light, speaking together in low voices, paying no attention to his gesture. 'What do they want?' he complained without altering his fixed fat smile. One of the men gave an order, which the driver translated. 'Stand up.'

With Myatt's passport in one hand, the other on his silver chain, he obeyed, and they moved the lights from his feet to his head. He had no overcoat and shivered with the cold. One of the men laughed and prodded him in the stomach with a finger. 'They want to see if it's real,' the driver explained.

'What's real?'

'Your roundness.'

Josef Grünlich had to feign amusement at the insult and smile and smile. His self-esteem had been pricked by two anonymous fools whom he would never see again. Someone else would have to bear the pain of his indignity, for it had been his pride, as it was now his grief, that he never forgot an injury. He did his best by pleading with the driver in German, 'Can't you run them down?' and he grinned at the men and waggled the passport, while they discussed him point by point, Then they stood back and nodded, and the driver pressed the starter. The car lifted over the rails, then slowly climbed a long rutted lane, and Josef Grünlich looking back saw the two red lamps bobbing like paper lanterns in the darkness.

'What did they want?'

'They were looking for someone,' the driver said. But that Josef knew well. Hadn't he killed Kolber in Vienna? Hadn't he escaped only an hour ago from Subotica under the eyes of a sentry? Wasn't he the cute one, the cunning fellow, who was quick and never hesitated? They had closed every road to cars and yet he slipped through. But like a small concealed draught the thought came to him that if they had been seeking him they would have found him. They were looking for someone else. They thought someone else of more importance. They had circulatd the description of the old slow doctor and not of Josef Grünlich, who had killed Kolber and whose boast it was—'five years now and never jugged.' The fear of speed left him. As they hurtled through the dark in the creaking antique car, he sat still, brooding on the injustice of it all.

Coral Musker woke with the sense of strangeness, of difference. She sat up and the sack of grain creaked under her. It was the only sound; the whisper of falling snow had stopped. She listened, and realised with fear that she was alone. Dr Czinner had gone; she could no longer hear his breathing. Somewhere from far away the sound of a car changing gear reached her through the dusk. It came to her side like a friendly dog, fawning and nuzzling.

If Dr Czinner is gone, she thought, there's nothing to keep me here. I'll go and find that car. If it's the soldiers they won't do anything to me; it may be . . . Longing kept the sentence open like the beak of a hungry bird. She put out a hand to steady herself, while she got upon her knees, and touched the doctor's face. He did not move, and though the face was warm, she could feel the blood as crisp and dry round his mouth as old skin. She screamed once and then was quiet and purposeful, feeling for the matches, lighting a spill. But her hand shook. Her nerves were bending, even though they had not given way, beneath the weight of her responsibilities. It seemed to her that every day for the past week had loaded her with something to decide, some fear which she must disguise. 'Here's this job at Constantinople. Take it or leave it. There are a dozen girls on the stairs'; Myatt pressing the ticket into her bag; her landlady advising this and that; the sudden terror of strangeness on the quay at Ostend with the purser calling after her to remember him.

In the light of the spill she was again surprised by the doctor's knowledgeable stare, but it was a frozen knowledge which never changed. She looked away and looked back and it was the same. I never knew he was as bad as that, she thought. I can't stay here. She even wondered whether they would accuse her of his death. These foreigners, whose language she could not understand, were capable of anything. But she delayed too long, while the spill burned down, because of an odd curiosity. Had he too once had a girl? The thought robbed him of impressiveness, he was no longer terrifying dead, and she examined his face more closely than she had ever dared before. Manners went out with life. She noticed for the first time that his face was curiously coarse-featured; if it had not been so thin it might have been repulsive; perhaps it was only anxiety and scant food which had lent it intelligence and a certain sensibility. Even in death, under the shaking blue light of a slip of newspaper, the face was remarkable for its lack of humour. Perhaps, unlike most men, he had never had a girl. If he had lived with somebody who laughed at him a bit, she thought, he would not now be here like this; he wouldn't have taken things so seriously; he'd have learnt not to fuss, to let things slide; it's the only way. She touched the long moustaches. They were comic; they were pathetic; they could never let him seem tragic. Then the spill went out and he might have been buried already for all she could see of him and soon for all she thought of him, her mind swept away by faint sounds of a cruising car and of footsteps. Her scream had not gone unheard.

A narrow wash of light flowed under the ill-fitting door; voices spoke; and the car came humming gently down the road outside. The footsteps moved away, a door opened, and through the thin walls of the barn she heard somebody routing among the sacks next door; a dog snuffled. It brought back the level dull Nottingham fields, on a Sunday, the little knot of miners with whom she once went ratting, a dog called Spot. In and out of barns the dog went while they all stood in a circle armed with sticks. There was an argument going on outside, but she could not recognise any of the voices. The car stopped, but the engine was left softly running.

Then the door of the shed opened and the light leaped upwards to the sacks. She raised herself on an elbow and saw, through a crack of her barricade, the pale officer in pince-nez and the soldier who had been on guard outside the waiting-room. They crossed the floor towards her and her nerves gave way; she could not bear to wait all the slow time till she was discovered. They were half turned from her and when she got to her feet and called out, 'Here I am,' the officer jumped round, pulling out his revolver. Then he saw who it was, and asked her a question, standing still in the middle of the floor with his revolver levelled. She thought she understood him and said, 'He's dead.'

The officer gave an order and the soldier advanced and began to pull away the sacks slowly. It was the same man who had stopped her on the way to the restaurant-car, and she hated him for a moment until he raised his face and smiled at her miserably and apologetically, while the officer bombarded him from behind with little barbed impatiences. Suddenly, as he pulled away the last sack at the cave mouth, their faces almost touched, and in that instant she got as much from him as from conversation with a quiet man.

Major Petkovitch, when he saw that the doctor made

no movement, crossed the shed and shone the light full on the dead face. The long moustaches paled in the glow and the open eyes cast back the light like plates. The major held out his revolver to the soldier. The good humour, the remnants of simple happiness, which had remained somewhere behind the façade of misery, collapsed. It was as if all the floors of a house fell and left the walls standing. He was horrified and inarticulate and motionless; and the revolver remained lying in the major's palm. Major Petkovitch did not lose his temper; he watched the other with curiosity and determination through his gold pince-nez. He had all the feeling of a barracks at his finger's end; beside the worn books on German strategy there stood on his shelves a little row of volumes on psychology; he knew every one of his privates with the intimacy of a confessor, how far they were brutal, how far kind, how far cunning and how far simple; he knew what their pleasures were— *rakia* and gaming and women; their ambitions, though these might be no more than an exciting or a happy story to tell a wife. He knew best of all how to adjust punishment to character, and how to break the will. He had been impatient with the soldier as he pulled so slowly at the sacks, but he was not impatient now; he let the revolver lie in his palm and repeated his command quite calmly, gazing through the gold rims.

The soldier lowered his head and wiped his nose with his hand and squinted painfully along the floor. Then he took the revolver and put it to Dr Czinner's mouth. Again he hesitated. He laid his hand on Coral's arm, and with a push sent her face downwards to the floor, and as she lay there, she heard the shot. The soldier had saved her from the sight, but he could not save her from her imagination. She got up and fled to the door, retching as she ran. She had expected the relief of darkness, and the glare of the headlamps outside came like a blow on the head. She leant against the door and tried to steady herself, feeling infinitely more alone than when she woke and found Dr Czinner dead; she wanted Myatt desperately, with pain. People were still arguing beside the car, and there was a faint smell of liquor in the air.

'What the hell?' a voice said. The knot of people was torn in two, and Miss Warren appeared between them. Her face was red and sore and triumphant. She gripped Coral's arm. 'What's happening? No, don't tell me now. You're sick. You're coming with me straight out of this.' The soldiers stood between her and the car, and the officer came from the shed and joined them. Miss Warren said rapidly in a low voice, 'Promise anything. Don't mind what you say.' She put a large square hand on the officer's sleeve and began to talk ingratiatingly. He tried to interrupt her, but his words were swept away. He took off his glasses and wiped them and was lost. Threats would have been idle, she might have protested all night, but she offered him the one bait it would have been against his nature to refuse, reason. And behind the reason she offered she allowed him to catch a glimpse of a different, a more valuable reason, a high diplomatic motive. He wiped his glasses again, nodded, and gave in. Miss Warren seized his hand and squeezed it, imprinting deep on the wincing finger the mark of her signet ring.

Coral slid to the ground. Miss Warren touched her and she tried to shake herself free. After the great noise the earth was swimming up to her in silence. Very far away a voice said, 'Your heart's bad,' and she opened her eyes again, expecting to see an old face beneath her. But she was stretched along the back seat of a car and Miss Warren was covering her with a rug. She poured out a glass of brandy and held it to Coral's mouth; the car starting shook them together and spilled the brandy over her chin; Coral smiled back at the flushed, tender, rather drunken face.

'Listen, darling,' Miss Warren said, 'I'm taking you back with me to Vienna first. I can wire the story from there. If any dirty skunk tries to get at you say nothing. Don't even open your mouth to say no.'

The words conveyed nothing to Coral. She had a pain in her breast. She saw the station lights go out as the car turned away towards Vienna and she wondered with an obstinate fidelity where Myatt was. The pain made breathing difficult, but she was determined not to speak. To speak, to describe her pain, to ask for help would be to empty her mind for a moment of his face; her ears would lose the sound of his voice whispering to her of what they would do together in Constantinople. I won't be the first to forget, she thought with obstinacy, fighting with all the other images which strove for supremacy, the scarlet blink of the car down the dusky road, Dr Czinner's stare in the light of the spill; fighting desperately at last against pain, against breathlessness, against a desire to cry out, against a darkness of the brain which was robbing her even of the images she fought.

I remember. I haven't forgotten. But she could not restrain one cry. It was so low that the humming motor drowned it. It never reached Miss Warren's ears any more than the renewed whisper which followed it: I haven't forgotten.

'Exclusive,' Miss Warren said, drumming with her fingers on the rugs. 'I want it exclusive. It's my story,' she claimed with pride, allowing somewhere at the back of her mind, behind the headlines and the leaded type, a dream to form of Coral in pyjamas pouring out coffee, Coral in pyjamas mixing a cocktail, Coral asleep in the redecorated and rejuvenated flat.

PART FIVE
Constantinople

[1]

'Hello, hello. Has Mr Carleton Myatt arrived yet?'

The small lively Armenian, with a flower in his buttonhole, answered, in an English as trim and well cut as his morning coat, 'No. I am afraid not. Is there any message?'

'Surely the train is in?'

'No. It is three hours late. I believe the engine broke down near Belgrade.'

'Tell him Mr Joyce . . .'

'And now,' said the reception clerk, leaning confidentially over the counter towards two rapt American girls, who watched him with parted lips, under beautiful plucked brows, 'what can I advise for you two ladies this afternoon? You should have a guide for the bazaars.'

'Perhaps you, Mr Kalebdjian,' they said almost in the same breath; their wide avaricious virginal eyes followed him as he swung round at the buzz of the telephone: 'Hello. Hello. Long-distance personal call? Right. Hello. No, Mr Carleton Myatt has not arrived yet. We expect him any moment. Shall I take a message? You will ring up again at six. Thank you.'

'Ah,' he said to the two Americans, 'if I could, it would be such a pleasure. But duty keeps me here. I have a second cousin though, and I will arrange that he shall meet you here tomorrow morning and take you to the bazaar. Now this afternoon I would suggest that you take a taxi to the Blue Mosque by way of the Hippodrome, and afterwards visit the Roman cisterns. Then if you took tea at the Russian restaurant in Pera, and came back here for dinner, I would recommend you to a theatre for the evening. Now if that suits you, I'll order you a taxi for the afternoon from a reliable garage.'

They both opened their mouths at once and said, 'That'll be swell, Mr Kalebdjian,' and while he was ringing up his third cousin's garage in Pera, they moved across the hall to the dusty confectionary stall and wondered whether to buy him a box of candies. The great garish hotel with its tiled floors and international staff and its restaurant in imitation of the Blue Mosque had been built before the war; now that the Government had shifted to Ankara and Constantinople was feeling the competition of the Piraeus, the hotel had sunk a little in the world. The staff had been cut, and it was possible to wander through the great empty lounge without meeting a page and the bells notoriously did not ring. But at the reception counter Mr

Kalebdjian opposed the general inertia in his well-cut coat.

'Is Mr. Carleton Myatt in, Kalebdjian?'

'No, sir, the train's late. Would you care to wait?'

'He's got a sitting-room?'

'Ah, naturally. Here, boy, show this gentleman to Mr Myatt's room.'

'Give him my card when he comes in.'

The two Americans decided not to give Mr Kalebdjian a box of Turkish delight, but he was so sweet and pretty they wanted to do something for him and they stood lost in thought, until he appeared suddenly at their elbow: 'Your taxi is here, ladies. I will give the driver full directions. You will find him most reliable.' He led them out and saw them safely away. The little stir and bustle subsided like dust, and Mr Kalebdjian went back into the silent hall. For a moment it had been almost as in the old days at the height of the season.

No one came in for a quarter of an hour; an early fly nipped by the cold died noisily against a window-pane. Mr Kalebdjian rang up the housekeeper's room to make sure that the heating was turned on in the rooms, and then he sat with his hands between his knees with nothing to think about and nothing to do.

The swing doors turned and turned, and a knot of people entered. Myatt was the first of them. Janet Pardoe and Mr Savory followed him and three porters with their luggage. Myatt was happy. This was his chosen ground; an international hotel was his familiar oasis, however bare. The nightmare of Subotica faded and lost all reality before Mr Kalebdjian advancing to meet him. He was glad that Janet Pardoe should see how he was recognised in the best hotels far away from home.

'How are you, Mr Carleton Myatt? This is a great joy.' Mr Kalebdjian shook hands, bowing from the hips, his incredibly white teeth flashing with genuine pleasure.

'Glad to see you, Kalebdjian. Manager away as usual? These are my friends, Miss Pardoe and Mr Savory. The whole of this hotel is on Kalebdjian's shoulders,' he explained to them. 'You are making us comfortable? That's right. See that there's a box of sweets in Miss Pardoe's room.'

Janet Pardoe began softly, 'My uncle's meeting me,' but Myatt swept aside her objection. 'He can wait one day. You must be my guest here tonight.' He was beginning to unfurl again his peacock tail with a confidence which he borrowed from the palms and pillars and Mr Kalebdjian's deference.

'There've been two telephone calls for you, Mr Carleton Myatt, and a gentleman is waiting to see you in your room.'

'Good. Give me his card. See to my friends. My room the usual one?' He walked rapidly to the lift, his lips pursed with exhilaration, for there had been in the last few days too much that had been uncertain and difficult to understand, and now he was back at work. It will be Mr Eckman, he thought, not troubling to look at the card, and suddenly quite certain of what he would say to him. The lift rose uneasily to the first floor and the boy led him down a dusty passage and opened a door. The sunlight poured into the room and he could hear the yapping of cars through the open window. A fair stocky man in a tweed suit got up from the sofa. 'Mr Carleton Myatt?' he asked.

Myatt was surprised. He had never seen this man before. He looked at the card in his hand and read Mr Leo Stein. 'Ah, Mr Stein.'

'Surprised to see me?' said Mr Stein. 'Hope you don't think me precipitate.' He was very bluff and cordial. Very English, Myatt thought, but the nose betrayed him, the nose which had been straightened by an operation and bore the scar. The hostility between the open Jew and the disguised Jew showed itself at once in the conjurer's smiles, the hearty handclasp, the avoidance of the eyes. 'I had expected our agent,' Myatt said.

'Ah, poor Eckman, poor Eckman,' Stein sighed, shaking his blond head.

'What do you mean?'

'My business here really. To ask you to come and see Mrs Eckman. Very worrying for her.'

'You mean he's gone?'

'Disappeared. Never went home last night. Very mysterious.'

It was cold. Myatt shut the window and with his hands in the pockets of his fur coat walked up and down the room, three paces this way and three paces that. He said slowly, 'I'm not surprised. He couldn't face me, I suppose.'

'He told me a few days ago that he felt you didn't trust him. He was hurt, very hurt.'

Myatt said slowly and carefully, 'I never trust a Jew who has turned Christian.'

'Oh come, Mr Myatt, isn't that a little dogmatic?' Stein said with a trace of discomfort.

'Perhaps. I suppose,' Myatt said, stopping in the middle of the room, with his back to Stein, but with Stein's body reflected to the knees in a gilt mirror, 'he had gone further in his negotiations than he had ever let me know.'

'Oh, the negotiations,' Stein's image in the mirror

was less comfortable than his voice, 'they, of course, were finished.'

'He had told you we wouldn't buy?'

'He'd bought.'

Myatt noddde. He was not surprised. There must have been a good deal behind Eckman's disappearance. Stein said slowly, 'I'm really worried about poor Eckman. I can't bear to think he may have killed himself.'

'I don't think you need worry. He's just retired from business, I expect. A little hurriedly.'

'You see,' Stein said, 'he had worries.'

'Worries?'

'Well, there was the feeling that you didn't trust him. And then he didn't have any children. He wanted children. He had a lot to worry him, Mr Myatt. One must be charitable.'

'But I am not a Christian, Mr Stein. I don't believe that charity is the chief virtue. Can I see the paper he signed?'

'Of course.' Mr Stein drew a long envelope folded in two from the pocket of the tweed coat. Myatt sat down, spread the pages out on a table, and read them carefully. He made no comment and his expression conveyed nothing. No one could have told how great was his happiness at being back with figures, with something that he could understand and that had no feelings. When he had finished reading, he leant back and stared at his nails; they had been manicured before he left London, but they needed attention already.

Mr Stein asked gently, 'Had a good journey? Trouble in Belgrade didn't affect you, I suppose?'

'No,' Myatt said, with an absent mind. It was true. It seemed to him that the whole unexplained incident at Subotica was unreal. Very soon he would have forgotten it because it was isolated from ordinary life and because it had no explanation. He said, 'Of course you know we could drive a coach through this agreement.'

'I don't think so,' Mr Stein said. 'Poor Eckman was your accredited agent. You left him in charge of the negotiations.'

'He never had the authority to sign this. No, Mr Stein, this is no good to you, I'm afraid.'

Mr Stein sat down on the sofa and crossed his legs. He smelt of pipe smoke and tweeds. 'Of course, Mr Myatt,' he said, 'I don't want to force anything down your throat. My motto is: Never let down a fellow business man. I'd tear that agreement up now Mr Myatt, if it was the fair thing to do. But you see, since poor Eckman signed this, Moults' have given up. They won't reopen their offer now.'

'I know just how far Moults' were interested in currants,' Myatt said.

'Well, you see, under the circumstances, and in all friendliness, Mr Myatt, if you tear that agreement up, I shall have to fight it. Mind if I smoke?'

'Have a cigar.'

'Mind if I have a pipe?' He began to stuff a pale sweet tobacco into the bowl.

'I suppose Eskman got a commission on this?'

'Ah, poor Eckman,' Mr Stein said enigmatically. 'I'd really like you to come along and see Mrs Eckman. She's very worried.'

'She has no need to worry if his commission was big enough.' Mr Stein smiled and lit his pipe. Myatt began to read the agreement over again. It was true that it could be upset, but courts of law were chancy things. A good barrister might give a lot of trouble. There were figures one would rather not see published. After all Stein's business was of value to the firm. What he disliked was the price and the directorship granted to

Stein. Even the price was not out of the question, but he could not bear the intrusion of a stranger into the famliy business. He said, 'I'll tell you what I'll do. We'll tear this up and make you a new offer.'

Mr Stein shook his head. 'Come now, that wouldn't be quite fair to me, would it, Mr Myatt?' Myatt decided what he would do. He did not want to worry his father with a lawsuit. He would accept the agreement on condition that Stein resigned the directorship. But he was not going to show his hand yet; Stein might crumple. 'Sleep on it, Mr Stein,' he advised.

'Well, that,' Mr Stein said cheerfully, 'I doubt if I shall be allowed to do. Not if I know the girls of today. I'm meeting a niece here this afternoon. She travelled out on your train from Cologne. Poor Pardoe's child.'

Myatt took out his cigar-case, and while he chose and cut a cigar, decided what he would do. He began to despise Stein. He talked too much and gave away unnecessary information. No wonder his business had not prospered. At the same time Myatt's vague attraction to Stein's niece crystallised. The knowledge that her mother had been a Jewess made him feel suddenly at home with her. She became approachable, and he was ashamed of the stiffness of his company the night before. They had dined together in the train on his return from Subotica, but all the time he had been on his best behaviour. He said slowly, 'Oh yes, I met Miss Pardoe on the train. In fact she's down below now. We came from the station together.'

It was Mr Stein's turn to weigh his words. When he spoke it was at a slight significant tangent. 'Poor girl, she's got no parents. My wife thought we ought to have her to stay. I'm her guardian, you see.' They sat side by side with the table between them. On it lay the agreement signed by Mr. Eckman. They did not mention it; business seemed laid aside, but Stein and Myatt knew that the whole discussion had been reopened. Each was aware of the thought in the other's mind, but they spoke in evasions.

'Your sister,' Myatt said, 'must have been a lovely woman.'

'She got her looks from my father,' Mr Stein said. Neither would admit that they were interested in Janet Pardoe's beauty. Even her grandparents were mentioned before her. 'Did your family come from Leipzig?' Myatt asked.

'That's right. It was my father who brought the business here.'

'You found it a mistake?'

'Oh, come now, Mr Myatt, you've seen the figures. It wasn't as bad as that. But I want to sell out and retire while I can still enjoy life.'

'How do you mean?' Myatt asked with curiosity. 'How enjoy life?'

'Well, I'm not very much interested in business,' Mr Stein said.

Myatt repeated with amazement, 'Not interested in business?'

'Golf,' said Mr Stein, 'and a little place in the country. That's what I look forward to.'

The shock passed, and Myatt again noted that Stein gave away too much information. Stein's expansive manner was his opportunity; he flashed the conversation back to the agreement: 'Why do you want this directorship then? I think perhaps I could come near to meeting you on the money question if you resigned the directorship.'

'I don't want it for myself necessarily,' said Mr Stein, puffing at his pipe between his phrases, squinting sideways at Myatt's lengthening ash, 'but I'd like—for the sake of tradition, you know—to have one of the family on the board.' He gave a long candid chuckle. 'But I have no son. Not even a nephew.'

Myatt said thoughtfully, 'You'll have to encourage your niece,' and they both laughed and walked downstairs together. Janet Pardoe was nowhere to be seen.

'Miss Pardoe gone out?' he asked Mr Kalebdjian.

'No, Mr Myatt, Miss Pardoe has just gone to the restaurant with Mr Savory.'

'Ask them to wait lunch twenty minutes, and Mr Stein and I will join them.'

There was a slight tussle to be last through the swing door; the friendship between Myatt and Mr Stein grew rapidly.

When they were in a taxi on the way to Mr. Eckman's flat, Stein spoke. 'This Savory,' he said, 'who's he?'

'Just a writer,' said Myatt.

'Is he hanging round Janet?'

'Friendly,' Myatt said. 'They met on the train.' He clasped his hands over his knees and sat silent, contemplating seriously the subject of marriage. She is very lovely, he thought, she is refined, she would make a good hostess, she is half Jawish.

'I'm her guardian,' said Mr Stein. 'Ought I perhaps to speak to him?'

'He's well off.'

'Yes, but a writer,' said Mr Stein. 'I don't like it. They are chancy. I'd like to see her married to a steady fellow in business.'

'She was introduced to him, I think, by this woman she's been living with in Cologne.'

'Oh yes,' said Mr Stein, uncomfortably, 'she's been earning her own living since her poor parents died. I didn't interfere. It's good for a girl, but my wife thought we ought to see something of her, so I invited her here. Thought perhaps we could find her a better job near us.'

They swerved round a miniature policeman standing on a box to direct traffic and climbed a hill. Below them, between a tall bare tenement and a telegraph-pole, the domes of the Blue Mosque floated up like a cluster of azure soap bubbles.

Mr Stein was still uneasy. 'It's good for a girl,' he repeated. 'And the firms been taking up all my time lately. But when this sale is through,' he added brightly, 'I'll settle something on her.'

The taxi drew into a small dark courtyard, containing a solitary dustbin, but the long stair they climbed was lighted by great windows and the whole of Stamboul seemed to flow out beneath them. They could see St Sophia and the Fir Tower and a long stretch of water up the western side of the Golden Horn towards Eyub. 'A fine situation,' said Mr Stein. 'There's not a better flat in Constantinople,' and he rang the bell, but Myatt was thinking of the cost and wondering how much the firm had contributed to Mr Eckman's view.

The door opened. Mr Stein did not trouble to give his name to the maid, but led the way down a white panelled passage which trapped the sun like a tawny beast between its windows. 'A friend of the family?' Myatt suggested. 'Oh, poor Eckman and I have been quite intimate for some time now,' said Mr Stein, flinging open a door on to a great glassy drawing-room, in which a piano and a bowl of flowers and a few steel chairs floated in primrose air. 'Well, Emma,' said Mr Stein, 'I've brought along Mr Carleton Myatt to see you.'

There were no dark corners in the room, no shelter from the flow of soft benevolent light, but Mrs Eckman had done her best to hide behind the piano which stretched like a polished floor between them. She was small and grey and fashionably dressed, but her clothes did not suit her. She reminded Myatt of an old family maid who wears her mistress's discarded frocks. She had a pile of sewing under her arm and she whispered her welcome from where she stood, not venturing any farther on to the sun-splashed floor.

'Well, Emma,' said Mr Stein, 'have you heard anything from your husband?'

'No. Not yet. No,' she said. She added with bright misery, 'He's such a bad correspondent,' and asked them to sit down. She began to hide away needles and cotton and balls of wool and pieces of flannel in a large work-bag. Mr Stein stared uncomfortably from steel chair to steel chair. 'Can't think why poor Eckman bought all this stuff,' he breathed to Myatt.

Myatt said: 'You mustn't worry, Mrs Eckman. I've no doubt you'll hear from your husband today.'

She stopped in the middle of her tidying and watched Myatt's lips.

'Yes, Emma,' said Mr Stein, 'directly poor Eckman knows how well Mr Myatt and I agree, he'll come hurrying home.'

'Oh,' Mrs Eckman whispered from her corner, away across the shining floor, 'I don't mind if he doesn't come back here. I'd go to him anywhere. This isn't *home*,' she said with a small emphatic gesture and dropped a needle and two pearl buttons.

'Well, I agree,' Mr Stein remarked and blew out his cheeks. 'I don't understand what your husband sees in all this steel stuff. Give me some good mahogany pieces and a couple of arm-chairs a man can go to sleep in.'

'Oh, but my husband has very good taste,' Mrs Eckman whispered hopelessly, her frightened eyes peering out from under her fashionable hat like a mouse lost in a wardrobe.

'Well,' Myatt said impatiently, 'I'm sure you needn't worry at all about your husband. He's been upset about business, that's all. There's no reason to think that he's—that anything has happened to him.'

Mrs Eckman emerged from behind the piano and came across the floor, twisting her hands nervously. 'I'm not afraid of that,' she said. She stopped between them and then turned round and went back quickly to her corner. Myatt was startled. 'Then what are you afraid of?' he asked.

She nodded her head at the bright steely room. 'My husband's so modern,' she said with fear and pride. Then her pride went out, and with her hands plunged in her work-basket, among the buttons and the balls of wool, she said, 'He may not want to come back for me.'

'Well, what do you think of that?' Mr Stein said as he went downstairs.

'Poor woman,' Myatt said.

'Yes, yes, poor woman,' Mr Stein repeated, blowing his nose in an honest emotional way. He felt hungry, but Myatt had more to do before lunch, and Mr Stein stuck close. He felt that with every taxi they shared, their intimacy grew, and apart altogether from their plans for Janet Pardoe, intimacy with Myatt was worth several thousand pounds a year to him. The taxi rattled down a steep cobbled street out into the cramped square by the general post office, and then down-hill again to Galata and the docks. At the top of a dingy stair they reached the small office, crammed with card indexes and dispatch-boxes, with only one window that looked out on to a high wall and the top of a steamer's funnel. Dust lay thick on the sill. It was the room which had given birth to the great glassy drawing-room, as an elderly mother may bear an artist as her last child. A grandfather clock, which with the desk filled most of the remaining space, struck two, but early as it was Joyce was there. A typist disappeared into a kind of boot cupboard at the back of the room.

'Any news of Eckman?'

'No, sir,' said Joyce. Myatt glanced at a few letters and then left him, crouched like a faithful dog over Eckman's desk and Eckman's transgressions. 'And now lunch,' he said. Mr Stein moistened his lips. 'Hungry?' Myatt asked.

'I had an early breakfast,' said Mr Stein without reproach.

But Janet Pardoe and Mr Savory had not waited for them. They were drinking coffee and liqueurs in the blue tiled restaurant when Myatt and Mr Stein exclaimed how lucky it was that his niece and Myatt had met already and were friends. Janet Pardoe said nothing, but watched him with peaceful eyes, and smiled once at Myatt. She seemed to Myatt to be saying, 'How little does he know of us,' and he smiled back before he remembered that there was nothing to know.

'So I suppose you two,' said Mr Stein, 'kept each other company all the way from Cologne.'

Mr Savory asserted himself, 'Well, I think your niece saw more of me,' but Mr Stein swept on, eliminating him. 'Got to know each other well, eh?'

Janet Pardoe opened her soft pronounced lips a little way and said softly, 'Oh, Mr Myatt had another friend he knew better than me.' Myatt turned his head to order lunch, and when he gave his attention again to them, Janet Pardoe was saying with a sweet gentle malice, 'Oh, she was his mistress, you know.'

Mr Stein laughed heartily. 'Look at this wicked fellow. He's blushing.'

'And you know she ran away from him,' said Janet Pardoe.

'Ran away from him? Did he beat her?'

'Well, if you ask him he'll try and make a mystery about it. When the train broke down he motored all the way back to the last station and looked for her. He was away ages. And the mystery he tries to make of it. He helped someone to escape from the customs.'

'But the girl?' Mr Stein asked, eyeing Myatt roguishly.

'She ran away with a doctor,' Mr Savory said.

'He'll never admit it,' Janet Pardoe said, nodding at Myatt.

'Well, really, I'm a little uneasy about it,' Myatt said. 'I shall telephone to the consul at Belgrade.'

'Telephone to your grandmother,' Mr Savory exclaimed and looked with a bright nervousness from one to the other. It was his habit when he was quite certain of his company to bring out some disarming colloquialism which drew attention to the shop counter, the apprentices' dormitory, in his past. He was still at times swept by an intoxicating happiness at being accepted, at finding himself at the best hotel, talking on equal terms to people whom he had once thought he would never know except across the bales of silk, the piles of tissue-paper. The great ladies who invited him to their literary At Homes were delighted by his expressions. What was the good of displaying a novelist who had risen from the bargain counter if he did not carry with him some faint trace of his ancestry, some remnant from the sales?

Mr Stein glared at him. 'I think you would be quite right,' he said to Myatt. Mr Savory was abashed. These people were among the minority who had never read his books, who did not know his claim to attention. They thought him merely vulgar. He sank a little in his seat and said to Janet Pardoe, 'The doctor. Wasn't *your* friend interested in the doctor?' but she was aware of the others' disapproval, and did not trouble to search her mind for the long dull story Miss Warren had told her. She cut him short, 'I can't keep count of all the people Mabel's interested in. I don't remember anything about the doctor.'

It was only the vulgarity of Mr Savory's expression to which Mr Stein objected. He was very much in favour of a little honest chaff about the girl. It would seal his valuable intimacy with Myatt. When the first course was on the table, he brought the conversation round again. 'Now tell us some more of what Mr Myatt's been up to.'

'She's very pretty,' said Janet Pardoe, with audible charity. Mr Savory glanced at Myatt to see whether he was taking offence, but Myatt was too hungry; he was enjoying his late lunch. 'On the stage, isn't she?' he asked.

'Yes. Variety.'

'I said she was a chorus girl,' Janet Pardoe remarked. 'There was something just the faintest bit common. Had you met her before?'

'No, no,' Myatt said hurriedly. 'Just a chance meeting.'

'The things that go on in these long-distance trains,' Mr Stein exclaimed with relish. 'Did she cost you much?' He caught his niece's eye and winked. When she smiled back, he was pleased. It would have been tiresome if she had been one of those old-fashioned girls in front of whom one could not talk openly; there was nothing he liked better than a little bit of smut

245

in female company; so long, of course, he thought, with his eye turning with disapproval to Mr Savory, as it was quite refined.

'Ten pounds,' Myatt said, nodding to the waiter.

'My dear, how expensive,' said Janet Pardoe, and she watched him with respect.

'I'm joking,' Myatt said. 'I didn't give her any money. I got her a ticket. Besides, it was just a friendship. She's a good creature.'

'Ah, ha,' said Mr Stein. Myatt drained his glass. Across the blue tiles a waiter came, pushing a trolley. 'The food's very good here,' said Mr Savory. Myatt expanded in the air of home, faintly aromatic with cooking; in one of the public rooms a Rachmaninoff Concerto was being played. One might have been in London. At the sound of the music a memory swam up into his mind and broke in scarlet light; people stuck their heads out of windows, laughing, talking, jeering at the fiddler. He said slowly to himself, 'She was in love with me.' He had never meant the words to drop audibly into the bare blue restaurant; he was embarrassed and a little shocked to hear them; they sounded boastful, and he had not meant to boast; there was nothing to boast about in being loved by a chorus girl. He blushed when they all laughed at him.

'Ah, these girls,' Mr Stein said, shaking his head, 'they know how to get round a man. It's the glamour of the stage. I remember when I was a young fellow how I'd wait outside the stage door for hours just to see some little hussy from the front row. Chocolates. Suppers.' He was stopped for a moment by the sight of a duck's grey breast on his plate. 'The lights of London,' he said.

'Talking of theatres, Janet,' Myatt said, 'will you do

a show with me tonight?' He used her Christian name, feeling quite at ease now that he knew that her mother was Jewish and that her uncle was in his pocket.

'I should love to, but I've promised Mr Savory to have dinner with him.'

'We could go along to a late cabaret.' But he had no intention of allowing her to dine with Mr Savory. All the afternoon he was too busy to see her; there were hours he had to spend at the office, straightening out all the affairs which Mr Eckman had so ingeniously tangled; he had visits to pay. At half-past three driving through the Hippodrome he saw Mr Savory taking photographs in the middle of a group of children; he worked rapidly; three times he squeezed his bulb while the taxi went by, and each time the children laughed at him. It was half-past six when Myatt returned to the hotel.

'Is Miss Pardoe about, Kalebdjian?' Mr Kalebdjian knew everything that went on in the hotel. Only his his restlessness explained the minuteness of his information; he would make sudden dives from the deserted hall, rattle upstairs and down again, penetrate into distant lounges, and then be back at his desk with his hands between his knees, doing nothing. 'Miss Pardoe is changing for dinner, Mr Carleton Myatt.' Once when a member of the Government was staying in the hotel, Mr Kalebdjian had startled a meticulous caller from the British Embassy: 'His Excellency is in the lavatory. But he will not be more than another three minutes.' Trotting down corridors, listening at bathroom doors, back again with nothing to do but turn over in his mind a little sheaf of information, that was Mr Kalebdjian's life.

Myatt tapped on Janet Pardoe's door. 'Who's that?'
'May I come it?'

247

'The door's not locked.'

Janet Pardoe had nearly finished dressing. Her frock lay across the bed and she sat before her dressing-table powdering her arms. 'Are you really going to have dinner with Savory?' Myatt asked.

'Well, I promised to,' Janet said.

'We could have had dinner at the Pera Palace, and then gone to the Petits Champs.'

'It would have been lovely, wouldn't it,' Janet Pardoe said. She began to brush her eyelashes.

'Who's that?' Myatt pointed at a large photograph in a folding frame of a woman's square face. The hair was bobbed and the photographer had tried to dissolve in mist the rocky outline of the jaw.

'That's Mabel. She came with me on the train as far as Vienna.'

'I don't remember seeing her.'

'Her hair's cut short now. That's an old photograph. She doesn't like being taken.'

'She looks grim.'

'I put it up there in case I began to feel naughty. She writes poetry. There's some on the back. It's very bad, I think. I don't know anything about poetry.'

'Can I read it?'

'Of course. I expect you think it very funny that anyone should write me poetry.' Janet Pardoe stared into the mirror.

Myatt turned the photograph round and read.

> 'Naiad, slim, water-cool,
> Borne for a river,
> Running to the sea:
> Endure a year longer
> Salt, rocky, narrow pool'

'It doesn't rhyme. Or does it?' Myatt asked. 'What does it mean, anyway?'

'I think it's meant as a compliment,' Janet Pardoe said, polishing her nails.

Myatt sat down on the edge of the bed and watched her. What would she do, he wondered, if I tried to seduce her? He knew the answer: she would laugh. Laughter was the perfect defence of chastity. He said, 'You aren't going to have dinner with Savory. I wouldn't be seen dead with a man like that. A counter-jumper.'

'My dear,' Janet Pardoe said, 'I promised. Besides he's a genius.'

'You are going to come downstairs with me, jump into a taxi, and have dinner at the Pera Palace.'

'Poor man, he'll never forgive me. It would be fun.'

And that's that. Myatt thought, pulling at his black tie, everything is easy now that I know her mother was Jewish. It was easy to talk hard all through dinner and to put his arm round her as they walked from the Pera Palace to the Petits Champs near the British Embassy. The night was warm, for the wind had dropped, and the tables in the garden were crowded. Subotica became the more unreal when he remembered the snow driven against his face. On the stage, a Frenchwoman in a dinner-jacket pranced up and down with a cane under her arm, singing a song about 'Ma Tante', which Spinelli had made popular in Paris more than five years before. The Turkish gentlemen, drinking coffee, laughed and chattered and shook their small dark feathery heads like noisy domestic birds, but their wives, so lately freed from the veil, sat silent and stared at the singer, their faces pasty and expressionless. Myatt and Janet Pardoe walked along the garden's edge, looking for a table, while the Frenchwoman screeched and laughed and pranced, flinging her desperate indecencies towards the inattentive and the unamused. Pera fell steeply away below them, the lights of fishing boats in the Golden Horn flashed like pocket torches, and the waiters went round serving coffee. 'I don't believe there's a table. We shall have to go into the theatre.' A fat man waved his hand and grinned. 'Do you know him?' Myatt thought for a moment, walking on. 'Yes, I think. . . . A man called Grünlich.' He had seen him clearly only twice, once when he had climbed into the car and once when he had climbed out into the light of the waiting train. His memory therefore was dim, as of someone he had known better a long while ago in another country. When they had passed the table, he forgot him.

'There's an empty one.' Under the table their legs touched. The Frenchwoman disappeared, swinging her hips, and a man flung cartwheels on to the stage from the wings. He got to his feet, took off his hat, and said something in Turkish which made everyone laugh.

'What did he say?'

'I couldn't hear,' Myatt said. The man threw his hat into the air, caught it, leant forward until he was bent double, and called out a single word. All the Turkish gentlemen laughed again, and even the pasty faces smiled. 'What did he say?'

'It must have been dialect. I couldn't understand it.'

'I'd like something sentimental,' Janet Pardoe said. 'I drank too much at dinner. I'm feeling sentimental.'

'They give you a good dinner, don't they?' Myatt said with pride.

'Why don't you stay there? People say that it's the best hotel.'

'Oh well, you know, ours is pretty good, and I like Kalebdjian. He always makes me comfortable.'

'Still the best people—'

A troupe of girls in shorts danced on the stage. They wore guards' caps and they had hung whistles round their necks, but the significance was lost on the Turkish audience, which was not used to guards dressed in shorts. 'I believe they are English girls,' Myatt said, and he suddenly leant forward.

'Do you know one of them?'

'I thought—I hoped,' but he was not sure that it had not been fear he felt at the appearance of Dunn's Babies. Coral had not told him she was going to dance at the Petits Champs, but very likely she had not known. He remembered her staring with brave bewilderment into the noisy dark.

'I like the Pera Palace.'

'Well, I did stay there once,' Myatt said, 'but something embarrassing happened. That's why I never went again.'

'Tell me. But don't be silly, you must. Do tell me.'

'Well, I had a friend with me. She seemed quite a nice young thing.'

'A chorus girl?'

Dunn's Babies began to sing:

> 'If you want to express
> That feeling you've got,
> When you're sometimes cold,
>   sometimes hot.'

'No, no. She was the secretary of a friend of mine. Shipping.'

'Come up here,' Dunn's Babies sang. 'Come up here,' and some English sailors sitting at the back of the garden clapped and shouted: 'Wait for us. We're coming.' One sailor began to push his way between the tables towards the stage.

> *'If you want to express*
> *That kind of gloom*
> *You feel alone in a double*
>   *room . . .'*

The man fell on his back and everyone laughed. He was very drunk.

Myatt said, 'It was terrible. She suddenly went mad at about two o'clock in the morning. Shouting and breaking things. The night porter came upstairs, and everybody stood about in the passage. They thought I was doing something to her.'

'And were you?'

'No. I'd been fast asleep. It was terrible. I've never spent a night there since.'

'Come up here. Come up here.'

'What was she like?'

'I can't remember a thing about her.'

Jane Pardoe said softly, 'You can't think how tired I am of living with a woman.' Accidentally their hands touched on the table and then stayed side by side. The fairy lights hanging in the bushes gleamed back at him from her necklace, and at the very end of the garden, over her shoulder Myatt saw Mr Stein pressing his way between the tables, pipe in hand. It was a mass attack. He knew that he only had to lean forward now to ask her to marry him and he would have arranged far more than his domestic future; he would have bought Mr Stein's business at Mr Stein's figure, and Mr Stein would have a nephew on the board and be satisfied. Mr Stein came nearer and waved his pipe; he had to make a detour to avoid the drunk man on the ground, and during that moment's grace Myatt summoned to his assistance any thoughts likely to combat the smooth and settled future. He remembered Coral and the sudden strangeness of their meeting, when he had thought that all was as familiar as cigarette smoke, but her face eluded him, perhaps because the train at that moment had been almost in darkness. She was fair, she was thin, but he could not remember her features. I have done all I can for her, he told himself; we should have said good-bye in any case in a few weeks. It's about time I settled down.

Mr Stein waved his pipe again, and Dunn's Babies stamped their feet and blew their whistles.

> *Waiting at the station*
> *For a near relation,*
> *Puff, puff, puff, puff—'*

Myatt said, 'Don't go back to her. Stay with me.'

> *'Puff, puff, puff, puff,*
> *The Istanbul train.'*

She nodded and their hands moved together. He wondered whether Mr Stein had the contract in his pocket.

About the Author

Graham Greene was born in 1904 and educated at Berkhamsted School, where his father was the headmaster. On coming down from Balliol College, Oxford, where he published a book of verse, he worked for four years as a sub-editor on *The Times*. He established his reputation with his fourth novel *Stamboul Train*, which he classed as an "entertainment" in order to distinguish it from more serious work. In 1935 he made a journey across Liberia, described in *Journey Without Maps*, and on his return was appointed film critic of the *Spectator*. In 1926 he had been received into the Roman Catholic Church and was commissioned to visit Mexico in 1938 and report on the religious persecution there. As a result he wrote *The Lawless Roads* and, later, *The Power and the Glory*.

Brighton Rock was published in 1938 and in 1940 he became literary editor of the *Spectator*. The next year he undertook work for the Foreign Office and was sent out to Sierra Leone in 1941—43. One of his major postwar novels, *The Heart of the Matter*, is set in West Africa and is considered by many to be his finest book. This was followed by *The End of the Affair, The Quiet American*, a story set in Vietnam, *Our Man in Havana*, and *A Burnt-Out Case*. His most recent novels are *The Comedians, Travels with My Aunt*, and *The Honorary Consul*. In 1967 he published a collection of short stories under the title: *May We Borrow Your Hus-*

band? His autobiography, *A Sort of Life,* was published in 1971.

In all, Graham Greene has written some thirty novels, "entertainments," plays, children's books, travel books, and collections of essays and short stories. He was made a Companion of Honour in 1966.